The Thaw

Susan Slater

Books by Susan Slater
THE BEN PECOS MYSTERY SERIES

The Pumpkin Seed Massacre
Yellow Lies
Thunderbird
Firedancer
Under a Mulberry Moon
The Thaw
A Way to the Manger (a Christmas novella)

THE DAN MAHONEY MYSTERY SERIES

Flash Flood
Rollover
Hair of the Dog
Epiphany

STANDALONE NOVELS

0-60
Five O'Clock Shadow

The Thaw

Ben Pecos Mysteries, Book 6

Susan Slater

Secret Staircase Books

The Thaw
Published by Secret Staircase Books, an imprint of
Columbine Publishing Group LLC
PO Box 416, Angel Fire, NM 87710

Book layout and design by Secret Staircase Books
Cover illustrations © Aliaksandr Narouski, Arak
Rattanawijittakorn, and Artyom Yefimov

First trade paperback edition: May, 2020
First e-book editions: May, 2020
+ + +

Publisher's Cataloging-in-Publication Data

Slater, Susan
The Thaw / by Susan Slater
p. cm.
ISBN 978-1649140005 (paperback)
ISBN 978-1649140012 (e-book)

1. Pecos, Ben (Fictitious character)—Fiction. 2. Native
American—Fiction. 3. Alaska—Fiction. I. Title

Ben Pecos Mystery Series : Book 6
Slater, Susan, Ben Pecos mysteries.

BISAC : FICTION / Mystery & Detective.
813/.54

+ + +

This is the most unusual dedication I've ever made. I dedicate *The Thaw* to a part of who I am, to a grandmother and grandfather shrouded in secrecy until my mother died at 94 in 2006. Only then did I find her actual birth certificate and the names of her parents: Anna Laura Freude and William Stephens.

My mother was born at The Willows, an unwed mothers' home in Kansas City, MO, in 1913 and given up for adoption at the age of five days. Anna Laura, age 19, named her baby, Leah, and went on to marry the baby's father, William Stephens, age 25, the following year. They had five more children—full sisters and brothers that my mother never knew about.

Most of the Stephens' clan lived in Alaska. My daughter currently lives in Sitka. It seems fitting that this book is dedicated to all my Alaskan relatives—some I know but most I'll never meet.

+ + +

Prologue

It was a nose that poked up through the ice first. Just a nose—pinkish gray, hard as a rock. Frozen solid. No hint of it being attached to anything, a face, or a body. Just this one periscoping gesture of defiance—this 'you can't bury me, I'll come back' attitude that captured his imagination. But who? Young? Old? Male? Female? One of them or an outsider?

No one in the village was missing. No radio message beaten out on tundra drums to alert anyone within listening range to be on the lookout for maybe an elder who had wandered off. And it was too early in the year for the tundra to give up its secrets. Still winter, only February, too cold to excavate.

He visited every day. When blowing snow obscured it, he wiped it clean, meticulously dusting away the offending powder and carefully returned it to being that strange beacon in an all-white landscape. Yet, all the time sensing this was his nemesis, his Moriarty.

He knew better, but he didn't tell anyone about the nose. If it didn't belong to anyone from his community, then it belonged to an outsider. Possibly someone who had no good reason to be there. It was best to keep it as his secret until he knew differently.

But more than that, it had become a friend—had a reason for being there. Something he could relate to. Unmoving, frozen in time ... a metaphor for his life? Thirty-eight years old and still looking for answers. Trying to relate to a birthplace that probably wouldn't even exist for his grandchildren.

In a place so desolate and forbidding it had never seen a tourist, well, at least not on a steady basis. But it was home. Who said, "Home is something you somehow haven't to deserve." Frost, he was pretty sure it was Robert Frost. "Home is the place, where when you have to go there, they have to take you in." Fitting. He could relate to that. He was an outside insider. Welcome, but not really. Something different always caused suspicion.

He'd been away to school ... in the lower forty-eight. And he had stayed long enough to get ahead, buy the car of his dreams, go in with friends on a restaurant. So, why had he come back? Friends told him he was wasting his talent. There wasn't a place for him on the tundra. A lawyer in a village that was slowly sinking into the waters that had sustained it for a few thousand years. Where was the sense in that?

He'd been in the lower forty-eight when Katrina hit. Young, in grad school at Tulane. The Ninth Ward, the devastation, the Superdome packed with humanity and the feces and rot that went with overcrowding of the desperate. But it was the decimation of the above-ground cemetery that he'd never forget—the bobbing of wooden boxes broken open to reveal the past. Sometimes open to reveal surprises. Grandma buried with a fetus. Who knew she was pregnant? Or maybe the straw boss— arms around a young girl dressed in the rags of servitude, someone from the plantation's work force. Where was the body of his wife? Was she in one of the surprise double-occupancy boxes? Perhaps laid to rest beside her lover? The skull that had a single bullet hole in its forehead? Life and lives lived spilled out in muddy waters, secrets no more.

Is this what his village had to look forward to? Life spilled not in blood but in water? An ocean once friendly, the provider of food and livelihood, now turned villain? Where was the manpower to stop it? The knowledge and money to save a people from themselves ... their very own way of life? Where were those who could foresee the future? Those who cared. But maybe there was no one left to care. It was no secret that young people left in droves to establish their lives elsewhere. Hadn't he? Had caring what happened to his village been a part of his life? No. Not for a very long time.

Same for his nose in the ice. Was there someone who cared for this nose? At least, *had* cared for it? Or was this bit of humanity just another casualty of hardships on the tundra? Or maybe man's inhumanity to man? Not the elements but flesh and blood getting even, plotting and executing revenge?

But wasn't that what he was planning? A revenge, of sorts? Get even with an old friend who wouldn't even see it coming. Yet, in his not knowing, deserved it. Neglect, self-serving, pompous even—go on with your life never minding the toll that it might take on the innocent. The ones you cast aside. Would he have the nerve to lure his friend into facing his wrong? Making restitution even?

First, he'd have to get him here. And he thought he had just the plan—if he could talk others into supporting it. But he'd know fairly quickly. The town hall was tonight.

Chapter 1

The meeting in the gym at the town's community center started at six-thirty with a potluck. There would be some of his favorites—food provided by the best village cooks, lots of it and dishes that he remembered from his childhood like Akutaq, Eskimo ice cream. In the old days whale blubber was whipped from a gelatinous mass to a fluffy, aerated bowl of a frosting-like substance. Whipped together with sugar and tundra snow, blueberries were added to the blubber mixture to make his favorite dessert. Some people used seal oil or moose tallow. But in the interest of saving time, and with blubber and other animal tallows scarce or nonexistent, Crisco was used today— whipped with copious amounts of sugar and blueberries then chilled with tundra snow. The cold, sweet-tart, concoction always made him ignore his high cholesterol and reach for seconds.

He pushed through the first set of suction-sealed, double doors and opened the ones to the gym floor. The small chamber off the large room connecting it with the outside, steps up from the street, acted as an airlock. Warm air was precious and not to be wasted, leaked to a sub-zero exterior. He scanned the room looking for familiar faces.

"E.J., over here. Sit with Mama."

The gymnasium—that all-purpose room that doubled as an entertainment center for aspiring basketball enthusiasts on a Friday night, men and boys; then, with podium added and a dais with four chairs for town leadership, also became the seat of local government like tonight.

His mother and auntie had gotten there before him. Both wore heavy, designer rip-off, Muk Luk boots, a present from a cousin in Seattle. Neither one had ever visited that city but a sample of what some shoe-maker thought an Alaskan native might wear gave them an edge. Some slight advantage in a popularity contest among the older people in the village. A real 'look at me; I'm with it' appearance.

Yet, he knew that the cold would seep upward through the polyurethane soles and faux fur calf coverings of the boots and would be considered only appropriate for early summer wear. Both women dressed in their Sunday best tonight and that called for the designer boots. One could suffer for fashion when showing off. His mother, Ahnah, and her sister, Uki, were matriarchs within their respective families. Local business owners of some renown, they were women to be reckoned with and listened to.

The folding chairs were set up theater style—twelve to a row, five rows. Sixty would be a crowd but expected tonight given the topics that demanded attention. Some would say that the agenda items were long overdue—if they were just being addressed now, wasn't it too much, too late? He guessed time would tell. His mother would say, 'better late than never' and that's probably where the village was in its belief, too.

Village leadership had had its collective head in the sand for years. Now, they were fighting the inevitable—watching the ice melt, seeing the ocean rise coming ever closer to the front porches of over half of thirty-one villages in the state. Or worse—communities losing entire structures with schools, churches, and even clinics literally falling into the water. Watching animals displaced from their century-old homes and their once invincible food chain simply disappear. What could dull this ongoing challenge? Take the reality out of everyday living. Drugs? Some would say they go hand in hand. Catastrophe without a clear solution was easier overlooked, ignored even for years until it tapped you on the shoulder—came so close it destroyed your food source, and now marched on your shelter. Another needle in a vein, a snort off the pipe—life-style threats didn't happen in euphoria.

He nodded recognition. Of course, the two women were sitting in the front row, plates of food balanced precariously on ample laps. He knew he'd be introduced by the panel and he'd have his chance to talk, but he preferred to sit in the back and observe. Though tonight he'd probably be tapped to sit on the dais. This wasn't a family night for him; he was working. As counsel hired by the state, he needed to listen to the ideas of his elders. And, offer advice. He was the one who was being paid to present possible solutions—ways to curb the inevitable and

maintain a centuries old way of life. A gargantuan task—
maybe one not attainable. At least not revisited in the same
manner that his grandfathers would have recognized.

Once having had the attention of Washington DC,
the village would soon be without federal help in either
manpower or money. This plan—whatever the village
decided—would be the swan song, map out the intended
expenditure for the remaining allocated monies, turn
resulting plans over to the state and hire someone to
oversee and do the mandatory final reporting—the
tedious endgame bookkeeping that the federal program
demanded— and hope for the best. Elliot James Takanni
had been loaned to his village by the state agency that
currently controlled his paycheck and was investing heavily
in researching a relocation schedule.

It would take time; so, he was probably loaned on a semi-
permanent basis. But how much say in the final outcome
would he have? Moving a village by building a new one
and providing not just brick and mortar support but the
usually overlooked empathetic, personal, understanding of
people faced with the obliteration of the way of life they
once knew—right down to the very houses where they had
been born. He had some good ideas, not just band-aids,
but answers. He'd find out tonight if anyone valued his
problem-solving skills.

"How's my baby doing? Aren't you hungry? I'll save
a seat; you go get a plate before it's all picked over. Aunt
Uki's ice cream is going fast but first you taste my Muktuk.
It's breaded and fried just like you like. The soy sauce is on
the counter behind the food table."

He nodded and resigned himself to sitting in the front
row. He'd get a plate of food and join them. It was true he

liked fried whale blubber. Anymore, it was a treat. Even if he hadn't been chosen to speak, he probably would have come for the food anyway. And he wasn't the only one with an appetite. A regular chow-line was forming on each side of the two six-foot folding tables that had been pushed together. If the topics for discussion weren't going to be met with enthusiasm, the food certainly was. Plates were being piled high. And food made from age-old recipes was disappearing first. The nutritionist, who would be speaking before he did, would be challenged but wasn't her topic about returning to native foods? Restricting intake might be a stumbling block, but not food origin.

The meeting wouldn't start until the village council was seated. And even though the village had only five miles of paved road within its parameters and no one could leave by car, four of the six leaders owned vehicles. Tonight, he hadn't seen one car he recognized in the parking lot.

There were to be three guest speakers—the nutritionist from the State offices, a fiscal officer for the twenty-eight Alaskan villages on or close to the coast, and him. They had already set up audio-visual equipment, and two high school boys were busy plugging in and testing overhead projectors and positioning flip charts.

He chose the old-fashioned way of imparting knowledge—a handout. He took twenty more out of his briefcase and handed them to the young man who was placing a copy on each chair seat. He knew paper branded him as low-tech, but he also understood that the Elders would need something to take back to offices and homes—facts to ruminate over, have at their fingertips if called upon to quote the statistics that he would give them. If the village was going to support him, they would need the ammunition when asking for additional federal money and not appear to just have their hands out. And these were not people used to taking notes from material flashed on a screen over their heads. This group screamed hands-on only.

It would take a solid plan to get their vote, not some pie-in-the-sky speculation. People were skeptical; they had been promised solutions before. The state agency was wise to place one of their own back in their midst. LJ counted on people listening to him, trusting him. And this time he thought he had the plan and the personnel that would give him a "yes" vote from the community. He felt that "blip" of excitement, realizing he'd know soon.

In addition to the building—design and placement of structures which would be left to the architects and engineers—he was going to propose a clinic devoted to treating drug addiction, the number one problem faced by the village. But not just treatment, the complete picture—good health, jobs, education—all monitored by experts. Heal the community, not just move them. If the village addressed this one area that cried out for attention and solutions, trust would be restored in its leaders. And he had just the psychologist to head it up—Ben Pecos. A man devoted to preserving the indigenous man's way of life. Someone from both worlds—Indian and Anglo—and successful in each.

He made himself believe that was his primary goal—the betterment of the native Alaskan. But a part of him knew he wanted to shake up his friend's world. Teach him a lesson in responsibility, in caring. And possibly save a life, offer an opportunity, at least, for a better life and a future of promise to someone whose tomorrow looked bleak at best. Ben Pecos was in for a surprise. It was going to be interesting to see how he would accept the challenge.

The trick would be getting Ben to Alaska. The full village council might be able to sway Indian Health Service to place him on loan. And it wouldn't have to be full time or even long term—something temporary, staff the outreach services, make certain funding was available for an entire agenda, design and develop programs, coordinate with the local clinic—that would be enough for starters. Impressive even, and a plan which possibly could be completed in six months. His initial feelers into a loan of personnel had been met positively. He had been all but assured that a loan would be made, that the powers who be in the Indian Health Service were only waiting on the village vote to go ahead. He wondered if IHS had already alerted Ben.

"Elliot James Takanni—am I seeing a ghost?" The tweed pants suit, red fox fur collar and high heeled boots gave her away as an outsider. Almost. The chin tattoo proclaimed her a Native—she wasn't from his village but one farther north, closer to Nome. He knew the four striated lines running from bottom lip to underneath her chin were a tribal statement repeatedly seen among millennial Alaskan women.

"Wendy. I didn't see you come in. I see the State is sending its big guns to our modest, little meeting out here in the sticks."

A dismissive laugh, "Big guns? You must believe all the bullshit you read in the papers."

"Come on, 'fess up. Founder of Alaskan Edibles, a Fairbanks startup that just went public. And which grossed over two million its first year, now employs over one hundred locals—"

"I can't believe you've paid attention to what I'm doing."

"Just curious about an old friend," he said.

"I'm flattered. And Raven? I'm a happy customer of your sister's tat parlor in Anchorage, but I haven't seen her in a couple years."

"Yeah, not sure that's what my family had in mind when they bankrolled her degree in graphic arts. But she's doing well—even comes home every once in a while."

"I'd love to see her."

"I thought she might come for the meeting but looks like I'm wrong. So, are you the headliner, or am I?"

"If I remember correctly, it's the oceanographer/land management specialist, then me, and you bring up the rear. I like your idea of an opioid clinic."

"Sounds like someone leaked my bright idea."

"The mayor is my uncle—probably explains my being here. He shared the agenda. He thought Alaskan Edibles would be a good fit—encourage people to move if that's the land management suggestion. There's land available fairly close by the proposed site that would sustain more than one berry crop—it could be lucrative for any number of families."

"Old habits change slowly—if at all. Not sure you can convince a bunch of fishermen to till soil."

"One of the reasons for tonight's meeting is to put the fear of God in everyone—impress upon them the need to act, right? And certainly, some who fish for a living would need to continue, just maybe not everyone. But even if fishing was set up on a rotating basis with farming to fall back on, I don't see the idea as popular. I think the village will be much more receptive to having a clinic dedicated to rehabbing drug users. That's tearing families apart. It's tangible, happening now—not some maybe-if-or-when scenario."

"I hope you're right but as a village, we need to address all concerns."

A voice from the front of the room silenced any further conversation. "Everybody find a seat. Let's welcome our speakers." The man at the edge of the dais motioned for E.J. and Wendy to join him and the village council on the makeshift stage. "We'll take a break in an hour. Don't worry. There will still be food. We're holding some good stuff in reserve."

E.J. got his mother's attention and pointed to the stage. She nodded and waved to Wendy. Small towns. Everybody knew everybody—or in the case of Moose Flats, everybody was related. A village of six hundred and ninety-one inhabitants—and two women were pregnant. Not the numbers that would get the world's attention; yet, perfect size for a test group. So, any innovative plan to save a village from disappearing into the ocean, giving its inhabitants alternatives to their life style by taking drugs out of the picture and offering proven paths to improving each family's income had to have some kind of world importance, however small.

He was just looking over his notes when the door to the auditorium opened and a strikingly beautiful woman stepped inside. The hood of her beaded, light parka fell away from her head releasing a cascading tumble of jet-black hair that spilled over her shoulders, framing her face in layered sections without a part. She brushed hair away from her face with a heavily tattooed hand. Just one tiny part of the ink that covered her body. He knew from contests that, stripped to a bikini, she had little to no undecorated skin left.

Even from across the room, E.J. could see his sister's smoky-shadowed eyes search the audience before meeting his in recognition. A slight nod and Raven moved toward their mother in the front row. As always people made room for her. She simply had that aura—her beauty, her assertiveness?

E.J. was never certain where her seeming magic came from. But once again he watched as her smile seemed to coax a man to give her his seat in the row behind their mother. That enigmatic smile could cast a spell as quickly and easily as it could stoically freeze in place making it impossible to decipher her feelings. Was she appreciative of favors bestowed? Who knew?

She was accustomed to favors—in all, but one thing. And that had colored her life forever. He loved his sister and would see this wrong righted. It was only a matter of time now. At some level he prayed that he could count on Ben.

He turned back to the people beside him. A swarthy, plump man in a checkered plaid shirt stood and walked to the mic. "You all know me. And you voted me village leader because I promised a way out of our problems. Well, I'm delivering on that promise tonight. Listen and take notes; be prepared to give us your opinion when the speakers finish. Our first speaker will be Dr. Wade Francis, University of Alaska's own specialist in land management. He's given his attention the last few years to the world's glaciers and the changes reported worldwide. Moose Flats has not been exempt. Several Alaskan villages are being threatened with extinction, not just ours. Kivalina, Newtok,

Shishmaref, and Shaktoolik are all in perilous positions.

"We've been chosen to apply for federal relief aid—which we can match, but more of that later. We need to show the state a viable plan to save our way of life—no, I'm not being melodramatic—actually, our very homes and livelihood are at risk. At the end of the meeting we'll break up into discussion groups, focus groups actually. Later you'll be asked to vote on the proposals presented. I don't have to tell you how critical this is. We need your support, but we need to hear your concerns, too. Dr. Francis? Let's get this meeting started."

The man in black-rimmed glasses chose not to use the mic but stepped off the dais and moved closer to his audience which now had grown to some eighty or ninety villagers. The gymnasium's custodial help was hurriedly handing out folding chairs from a rack at the back.

"If it's any consolation, Moose Flats and Miami have the same concerns. I've been working on those concerns for some twenty-five years now. And never in that time have the consequences been more eminent or the results more dire. Think about it. Thirty-one communities in Alaska are in a position to be lost—structures, burial grounds, sustaining food sources—all in danger by rising water, be it rivers or ocean, or melting ice which greatly impacts life as you know it. Another two hundred and thirty villages are currently affected by sea rise and need a plan for the upcoming years—not in immediate danger, but will be very shortly."

His first slide depicted the amount of shoreline Moose Flats lost each year in the last five—seventy feet. Not only were structures in danger of toppling into the ocean, but the shoreline was so radically redrawn and shallow that fuel ships could no longer easily navigate a mooring. Ice pack was disappearing close to the village, negating any exchange of goods by dogsled. He clicked to a slide showing mushers commanding dogs pulling wheeled trikes.

The village had become self-sustaining in its isolation but only with air-drops of supplies when the weather permitted. Still, this new life was fragile, not something that could continue indefinitely but an eco-system in danger of collapse—not a matter of if, but when. Dwindling wildlife threatened to disrupt the food chain. Fish spawned elsewhere, taking their predators with them. This meant that seal and bear no longer could thrive nearby. Land for any cultivation of foodstuffs had disappeared. A move was necessary to preserve life itself.

The lecture was compelling. E.J. noted several of the older men in the audience nodding affirmatively—some taking notes. There was no whispering; Professor Francis had everyone's attention as he continued. "Relocation is the life preserver. It will cost approximately one hundred and eighty million dollars to uproot Moose Flats and establish it a mere two miles across the river to the east. Some estimate the cost to move approximately seven hundred people will be well over two hundred million.

"And it very well might be. Think about the scope of our task. We will be moving everything. We propose that we move structures, graves, and preserve anything that might be useful in relocating and rebuilding. For example, brick, concrete block, pipe fittings, and wood—all reusable building materials will be salvaged. Our proposed start date is June 1. Some basics are already there—stubbed-in electrical, for example, along with trenches and piping for sewer connections. Our proposed completion date is September 30. Yes, I know, the timeline is short—ridiculously so. The offer from private industry to match any federal and state funds to build permanent housing in the new location before the move commences was accepted last fall. A good start has been made. You will literally have walk-in ready shelter complete with generators and eco-friendly solar energy by this date.

"I know solar energy might not make sense at first, but think about it. Even though Arctic tundra summers are short, maybe fifty to sixty days total, around the solstice the sun shines nearly twenty-four hours each day. This roughly equates to the total amount of solar exposure that some tropical areas receive. I don't know about you, but I'd take solar energy over fossil fuel anytime. Let's save our tundra from fracking and drilling and use our heads instead of our billfolds. Let's make the new Moose Flats a model for all of Alaska to follow."

A burst of applause and several people in the audience rose to speak—would the local superintendent of schools have a say in the design and application of a K-12 facility? Could they have a bigger gymnasium? Would those businesses that wished to relocate have access to prime locations equal to what they currently had? Would there be a village manifesto? If so, who would draw it up? How beholden to Washington would they be? Or to the state? Would there be any new agencies? In health care, for example, or would they still be expected to travel long distances to be seen at a hospital?

Mayor Arthur KooToo again stood and took the mic from Dr. Francis. "What did I tell you? This is exciting stuff. And what a perfect segue into what our next speaker wants to share. My niece, Wendy KooToo, you're up."

Wendy walked to the lectern, paused, and sorted through her notes before speaking. "I want to talk about food. I'm a nutritionist by training. First, I want to compliment those who contributed so many native dishes for tonight's potluck. Can you imagine those tables without one Alaskan staple? In support of Dr. Francis, if the ice layer is treacherously thin—too thin for a man to walk on, what happens to your hunting—your supplying your family with meat, tallow for food and lamps, furs for clothing? Two years ago the largest settlement close to Moose Flats caught over six hundred walruses. Does anyone want to guess how many were caught this year?"

No hands were raised.

"Exactly thirty-six. We are suffering 'food-insecurity'. We don't know how long our food chain will last. Not only are the breeding and birthing grounds of walruses disappearing, there's fast becoming no sea ice to support the butchering of any thousand-pound animal. So, is the answer continuing to pay thirty bucks for a pizza? A frozen sub with manufactured cheese? Fifteen dollars for a gallon of milk? Saving recipes of something our grandmother made but will never be made the same way again—has this become our way of life, not ever to return to the way it was? I cannot over emphasize the severity of the problems we face.

"You may be wondering why I'm going to take thirty minutes of your time tonight to talk about native food when it would appear that my esteemed colleagues are the ones addressing truly pressing and frightening problems. Yet, I ask you to consider that all three of us are talking about the same thing—survival. Think about it. Can something as simple as food—something we've always taken for granted threaten our very lives? Of course, it can. I ask you, what is more integral, more center to our very existence than what we eat? As farfetched as it may sound, I can make a case for many life-threatening health issues being a direct result of a dwindling *native* food supply.

"Some of you know depression. Often this is the result of life-style changes. Despair at not being able to provide even the basics for your families. More communicable diseases follow a warming climate—for example, deer ticks are finding their way farther and farther north. And with those ticks comes serious illness. Our children are making decisions out of desperation—leaving after high school to seek employment or further training far from home. That is, *if* they graduate from high school at all. Many, impacted by the dire existence of their families, drop out hoping to aid in the hunt for food. Fewer than half of all eligible seniors graduate. Let me repeat, fewer than half."

Wendy paused and looked at her notes before glancing out at the audience. "This next topic is one we shy away from. Domestic violence is a reality often swept under the table. But it's epidemic in scope. Alaska rates first in this crime. Time and again the everyday triggers include men idled by lack of, or a greatly reduced, livelihood. Inactivity has led to drug use. Again, Alaska has the dubious honor of leading all states in the number of drug and opioid induced deaths. I think E.J. has some information to share on that topic in a few minutes.

"But what kind of message are we giving our children? We must become prosperous again. The plan I'm going to show you involves raising our own food—not just relying on nature's bounty or lack thereof."

"I fish. I ain't no farmer." A man in the back yelled out.

"Fish can be farmed. Very successfully, I might add. There are dozens of examples from salmon to tilapia." Wendy quickly followed up. "But tonight I'm going to talk about raising berries. Our native blueberries to be exact. In addition, raspberries and low-bush cranberries would also be lucrative crops. There is land available in the interior on a co-op basis that would put food on your tables and money in your pockets."

E.J. watched as Wendy clicked through a series of slides depicting farms with native Alaskan workers. She had the crowd's attention, he had to give her that. And, maybe most importantly, she made sense. It remained to be seen if she could sell this life-saving idea—in spite of it being a *life-changing* one. More women in the audience seemed to be nodding affirmatively than men. But that didn't surprise him. Family protection was as strong in the home as on the outside. After a few questions concerning annual return on investments, Wendy smiled and extended the mic.

Finally, it was his turn at the podium. E.J. recognized the mayor and the three councilmen sitting with him on the dias but also waved away the mic and stepped off the dais to be closer to the audience. "Most of you know me. I grew up in this village. I've spent some time in the lower forty-eight before coming back." He stopped and good-naturedly acknowledged the boos. "Give me a break, guys. I'm here, now. I've seen the error in my ways."

"That mean you'll find a nice girl and I'll get some grandchildren?"

"C'mon, Mom. No promises on that score—you know that." Again, he paused until the laughter subsided. Even Raven leaned forward and patted their mother on the shoulder, seeming to enjoy the banter. "I can say I'm

here—came back to my home— to invest my time and
energy in promoting a healthier way of life. For starters,
I wholeheartedly agree with the proposal to relocate our
community. We've heard some pretty compelling reasons
tonight as to why we have to do it. In the meantime, we
need to offer state-of-the-art support services. In particular,
I agree that we need to upgrade our clinic facilities. What
I'm about to propose can be started immediately. It doesn't
need four walls to be effective—and frankly, it can't wait.

"I want us to sign onto a plan already in motion under
the auspices of the Denali Commission. Before the agency
is dismantled, they are accepting last minute proposals—I
think we have a chance at some support. Because our
purpose will be to stem the ever-growing number of opioid
and drug-related deaths in the village, we automatically
move to the top five areas singled out for immediate need.
The Alaska Native Tribal Health Consortium is eager to
establish programs in outlying areas. I don't think anyone's
going to dispute that we qualify based on that criteria.

"My position as a lawyer representing Moose Flats
is to take care of the paperwork. I can talk legalese and
make certain that we meet all deadlines. And I can make
certain we get our fair share of the monies divided up
among applicants. In addition, I'd like to put forth a name
for Director of a new, expanded clinic. We'll be ahead
of the game and be more likely to get attention if we
show proactive planning. We're going to need someone
with knowledge of native programs—best, even, if that
individual is native himself. Dr. Benson Pecos is a Pueblo
man. From New Mexico. His degrees are in psychology
and his work experience has been on reservations. As an
employee of Indian Health Services, he's available to us for

most of the upcoming year—at least until the end of the summer and possibly through October."

Suddenly the sound of chairs being scooted back abruptly erupted as Raven stood and pushed to the end of the row. Not turning to even look at him, she didn't stop until she had reached the back of the gymnasium and swung the heavy steel-framed door of the inner entrance to one side—pulling it closed behind her as she left.

Chapter 2

E.J. paused. Had he expected anything different? Should he have shared his plans with his sister first? No, the first order of business was still to establish a clinic. Get the support of the community. Unfinished business with Raven was secondary, even as important as it was to his family.

The rest of his presentation was uneventful. He pointed out that the drug problem was not just behavioral and shouldn't be pushed off onto law enforcement as a police concern. He believed, as did others, that what the village was experiencing was a medical problem—one that needed to be treated as such—diagnosed with an opportunity for a cure. There needed to be hope.

And there was more and more support to view it as the result of greed—big pharma and doctors looking to benefit off of a family's pain. That needed to be recognized, the culprits weeded out and replaced with competent and caring individuals aware of the damage already done, but committed to changing that in the future. E.J. knew Ben was the man who could do it. He had no ties to the village. He would not be blinded by money or position. He would be impartial and fair in all dealings. E.J. was right in believing it had to be someone from the outside—the village was incapable of cleaning up its own act.

There were thoughtful questions from the audience. Would there be a cost to them above what IHS might contribute? How soon would the clinic start up? What would be prerequisite for getting into the program? Would there be an age limit? He fielded almost every concern and finally sat down, feeling that his proposal was supported by the village. After a brief break, the next step was small group discussion with a leader for every group of ten to twelve participants. Then they would reconvene and vote.

+ + +

He didn't hurry but stayed to help put chairs away after the meeting. He knew his sister would be waiting for him at his mother's house. He didn't think she'd see the logic to what he was doing—the necessity of it. There would be screaming and tears and threats. He was ready but he knew Ben in his ignorance, wasn't.

He was right, of course. The euphoria gained by having the entire village vote one hundred percent to adopt his plan quickly evaporated when he saw her, arms crossed, standing on the porch, in front of their mother's front door.

"When were you going to tell me?"

"I should have before this."

"Somehow letting me hear it in front of a gathering of the village elders and our neighbors was safer, wasn't it? Plan already in place, pretty much assured of an affirmative vote—no chance I could derail it."

"I wasn't thinking that way."

"Do you think I'm so incompetent that you have to speak for me? Take over my life? Dictate how I live?"

"I'm through watching you do nothing."

"Do NOTHING? For ten years I've been doing nothing?"

"Yeah. You certainly don't have what's yours—what's owed you."

"What would you know about owing? Can you say you don't owe your mother something? You were never one to help. When the going gets rough, off you go, scholarships and a paid for, full ride to schools of your choice. Family be damned, only E.J. counts."

The front door opened. "Children, children, there's no need to share our family grievances with the neighbors." Their mother stood in the doorway, "Finish talking inside."

"I'm finished. I need to think. Tonight has been too upsetting. I don't even want to be in the same house as E.J. I'll be back in time to feed the dogs in the morning. No, Mama, don't worry, I'm sure you want to talk with E.J. now." Raven pulled away as her mother tried to put a hand on her arm and didn't turn back as she stepped off the porch and began walking up the gravel-packed street.

He watched as the darkness enveloped Raven finally obscuring her image all together. So where would she spend the night? On Aunty Uki's couch probably, but she'd try to find Brant first. He didn't feel good about chasing her away from their mother's house, from Raven's own room. The blame was his—for a lot of things. A moonless night without streetlights was a kind of definition of black. It fit his mood. What if he was wrong? Wrong in the way he was treating Raven and very wrong in what he was about to do to Ben. He wished he could just walk off into oblivion. Instead, he followed his mother into the house.

Chapter 3

The letter had been terse. Obviously, the board had already made its decision—Dr. Ben Pecos would be loaned, once again. Even though he'd spent the last six months in the Sunshine State with the promise of furthering his career with IHS in the Everglades, Florida might remain as just a great place for a honeymoon and never really materialize as 'home'. He reread the part introducing him to his new territory. Alaska. And not Fairbanks or Anchorage or even something cushy like Sitka or Juneau. No, he was being assigned to the sticks— Moose Flats. Like who had ever heard of Moose Flats, even though it vaguely jogged his memory. But he couldn't bring up the association.

What might be more of a problem was Julie—and not being able to have her with him. Specifically, her new

position at the *Miami Herald* as editor-in-chief of the
paper's leisure magazine—the monthly insert that recapped
what the area had to offer year-round citizens and visitors
alike and involved overseeing twelve editors, writers, and
photographers—not to mention the daily update of the
online version. It was a once-in-a-lifetime opportunity.
This wasn't a position one could leave to follow a husband
half-way around the world for a six-month assignment on
the snow-packed tundra. His clinical duties as originally
outlined in his IHS contract that would have put him just
outside Miami would be shelved for the time being—not
scrapped, he hoped. He'd have to make certain the new
clinic in Sawgrass country would only be put on hold.

Even if he could get by all that, it was the starting date
that rankled—be there Monday. Today was Wednesday.
Four and a half days to prepare—he might as well have
joined the military. But, yes, he understood the severity of
the situation and the moving deadline the village was under.
He appreciated and was flattered at being tasked with the
responsibility of establishing a concentrated approach to
what was not just one village's challenge but could work as
a blueprint for others. He could see the logic in setting up
this one first, learn from any mistakes, then do it right—
there, in the Everglades.

He'd even gotten a call from an old friend, E.J. Takanni.
A roommate from a graduate workshop at Tulane. Ben
had been twenty-four that summer. Ten years ago? Could
it have been that long? Almost. After staying in touch for
a while, they'd finally drifted apart. What was it everyone
called E.J.? Yeah, wolfman. Takanni meant wolf in his native
language and not because he had any excess body hair or
howled at the moon. But if Ben were being truthful, didn't

he let the friendship die because of E.J.'s sister? After he'd met Julie, it just seemed the right thing to do. Let Raven go and establish his own life.

Ben had dated Raven for one summer. There was a place on her body—or used to be—that professed their love—initials in a heart, beneath a bear and a wolf. But it became time for him to move on. She wanted more than he could give her. They were kids or, at least, she was. Twenty-four and eighteen. Too much lay ahead of them. Graduate school for him—four more years, maybe more, to a Ph.D. Then it was payback time to the government. No student loans, just commitment. Uncle Sam became Big Brother.

For Raven? He wasn't sure what she wanted. She'd talked about college but then he'd heard that she'd moved back to Alaska to be with her mother. Would it be awkward to meet again after all this time? Maybe. They hadn't exactly parted on good terms. Lots of demands, lots of yelling. That part he remembered all too well. And there was Julie now. He hoped he wasn't going to be put in a position to have to explain Raven.

He dragged out a couple suitcases, but would still have to ship some things. He had a down parka from ski trips to New Mexico and would still need it for another month or so up there, but it was bulky enough to take up one suitcase by itself. He didn't look forward to the cold and the dark. But would he really notice with the amount of work facing him? He'd be pretty much tied to a desk planning, then overseeing several programs. Education would be a big part of his approach. He'd already put in several calls this morning to the University of Alaska, Anchorage, for some backup help. Internships wouldn't be out of the question and might be the least disruptive way to go. There was time to design and implement a Master's level summer program and get it in the school's catalog. Some of the prep work could, of course, be done online.

Aside from disrupting his life, he was pretty excited about the opportunity to make an impact on current problems of native peoples. He was getting a little ahead of himself but it was not out of the question to envision a book, possibly a lecture series, maybe even petitioning Congress to act on his guidelines. The Ben Pecos approach to health crises involving the unauthorized use of opioids by native people in isolated areas without direct clinical access. Or something along those lines. He could make a name for himself. He was a green Ph.D. ripe for this kind of assignment. He only hoped Julie could see it that way.

Chapter 4

Decisions. Huge, life-altering, frighteningly permanent ones. Could she face the answers? Not knowing the reaction? The outcome? That would be permanent, too. E.J. simply didn't understand what he'd done. He should know she would never give up what was hers. To say she'd done nothing the last ten years was cruel, but maybe understandable from a man's point of view—get what's yours now, ask questions later. How would the new, sometimes, boyfriend react? Would Brant understand? Or feel left out, lied to, tossed aside even. Think their life had been a sham—her professed love meaningless because she was putting another first in her feelings.

Brant had supported her coming back. He made her promise not to mourn losing her shop in Anchorage in order to move because he would help her to start over.

And she wanted him to come with her, to move back to the village so that he could help his father and grandfather fish. The very way of life that was now in jeopardy.

Actually, he was coming back to his roots in order to get clean. Leave the temptations behind. This move was as much for him as it was for her. He was only still with her because of two doses of Narcan. He was fragile. The simplest of obstacles and his old coping skills blocked rational thought. Drugs were not far away and never out of mind.

She could think of nothing worse than Ben Pecos showing up on her doorstep—but maybe what could be worse, he would be in charge of the clinic. The one lifeline that Brant would need to stay alive. Brant would not be forgiving of old baggage. Definitely not the handsome, well-educated former love of her life. The one she'd never mentioned.

Brant. Did she love him? Feel sorry for him? Was she only using him? Taking advantage of what he obviously felt for her? She had certainly been in the right place at the right time for him to come into her life. Yet, she knew if she squinted hard in the mirror, she could still see the puffy flesh along her jawline. The bruise was almost gone now, but the hurt was there and the fear. What would she accidentally say to make it happen again?

She'd made a hundred excuses for him—she'd provoked him, he was high, he didn't know what he was doing … he hadn't meant to hurt her. How much longer could she shield him? Lie to those around her, knowing that at some level they knew but cared enough for her to perpetuate the charade and not embarrass her?

She was getting cold. Had it been stupid to walk away

from her mother's house and her own warm bedroom? She wouldn't even look for Brant. She'd spend the night with her aunt and return to her mother's house in the morning. Brant was out with friends—partying in a Carton Condo at the edge of the village. There probably wasn't even room for one more person to crash in the four shipping crates cobbled together, a make-shift roof, one window, and one door. The area was full of the huge crates, makeshift homes, the tundra condos. Originally the crates were filled with appliances, furniture, even an ATV or two. And each spring the thaw, sometime late May, would bring the first barge up the Kuskokwim river loaded with crates filled with these household necessities ordered by communities along the way.

The rail-car sized containers were stacked on the dock, unloaded with the help of the excited purchasers of goods. Finally, empty and resting on solid ground, they could then be purchased for building purposes. With land and building materials at a premium in the state, after the addition of a roof and a door, these sturdy units only required insulation, and inside walls—this finished partitioning provided a warm, protected refuge against the environment. And the arrival of the barges was always an excuse for a village-wide celebration—a particularly special Alaskan holiday.

Everyone always came out on the dock to cheer the barge's landing. Actually, she looked forward to what was usually breakfast that turned into brunch with celebrating that often carried over into the afternoon. She just made certain that her Mimosas were virgin. Liquor in the morning wasn't her thing, but she enjoyed the camaraderie of her village. The hugs and slaps on the back were a sign of congratulations, of relief that the giver of these acts of friendship had survived yet another winter. Survival was to be commended and celebrated. This is what made her home special ... why, perhaps, she couldn't leave it and why it had been so important to come back. Yes, it was different. Rustic was, perhaps, too kind of a word. Would her friends in the lower forty-eight understand living in a rail car? It was cheap housing by Alaskan standards, but even then you needed an extra ten to twelve thousand to complete the living unit. Everything was so expensive. Thirty dollars last week on two gallons of milk. It was difficult to provide simple necessities for a family.

Still, this was home. What used to be a safe place to raise children. Would it survive being relocated? Its men pushed into new and often overwhelming jobs—jobs they were not suited for, not trained to adapt to the new required skills that expected each to be computer savvy. Even planting and harvesting berries required bookkeeping, online record-keeping—especially if government money was involved. Could anyone put down his fishing nets, sell his boat, and till the ground or punch a clock?

Sometimes a little time away made her appreciate her life here more. Yet, as she turned up the short front walk of her Aunt's house, she could hear the sound of music and laughter coming from the house next door. Another party. The drugs and booze would be free and flowing. How much would a pill be tonight? Forty dollars? Sixty? Those were lower forty-eight prices. She'd seen oxy go for a hundred just last week. She took a deep breath, stamped the powdery snow from her boots and reached for the doorknob. Then withdrew her hand and just stood there listening to the revelry.

She had decisions to make. A part of those decisions

involved putting an end to enabling. She wasn't a part of the pill-popping, drugged-out group of losers next door. Yes, she'd call her friends losers. Did that include Brant? She thought it probably did.

She could only do so much. She just needed to admit the obstacles to their relationship. Involuntarily her fingertips lightly touched her cheekbone—last month's head-pivoting slap across the face. She still had to cover the fading greenish purple bruise with makeup. Yes, he had hit her. Again. Her jaw still ached when she tried to chew anything tougher than soft bread. She needed to admit that there had been a second episode. Say it out loud.

But then he'd apologized profusely—he didn't know it had happened until he helped her up off the floor. Something had kept him from stopping—the yelling, the threats, the mocking demeanor he'd used to belittle her. He was her meal-ticket and he loved and hated her for it—for dragging him back, making him face his demons.

He had the power but she was a problem-solver, a savior who could fix anything. Even him. Or so she had thought.

When the recession hit, she had to make changes. Move on, choose something else to do. She'd try to sell her business in Anchorage, Tats4Two, and invest, what could have been one hundred thousand dollars, in dogs. Sledding dogs—the best to be found, pedigrees of winners. It was going to be the start of a new life. One that took dedication and hard work but was filled with excitement and promise. There would be some who would call her foolish but she had raced with her father when she was young—mushed with him until he died by taking his own life. She had made a promise to a dead man that she would never forget their dreams; she would breed dogs, run dogs, and win in his name. She had a mission. She didn't belong with the losers next door even if she knew she should look for Brant. She couldn't risk being part of a toxic atmosphere. She had responsibilities, ones that gave her a reason for living. She turned back to the door, quietly opened it, and stepped into her aunt's living room.

Chapter 5

The dog yard was a full quarter acre. The brightly colored dog-boxes were the center of twelve-foot radius circles. Dogs who trained to run a thousand-mile race and exercised three or more times a week, running 120 miles, didn't need unlimited space to roam. They had to keep their tie-ups free from entanglement with their neighbors and get exercise as they wanted but no long-distance romps. An owner saw to it that each dog would not encroach on the space of another. Food bowls were fastened to their houses and their insulated wooden structures were stuffed to overflowing with straw—a crawl-in hole hollowed out in the center. Thirty-two dogs—two teams of fourteen and four alternates—called the area behind her mother's house their home. And that wasn't including the two litters of puppies with their mothers in the barn. Summer and winter, the training was much the same. Only a change in diet delineated seasons and whether the sled had runners or wheels. Training didn't stop just because the snow was disappearing.

Almost nine a.m. and a bleary light spread across the horizon. Sunrise. Late by most standards but this was Alaska. Raven stood at the edge of the dog yard and watched five young men walk among the dogs retrieving food bowls. They were fed in the dark under spotlights, the food stored at freezing temp in the barn close to the house. Meals were thawed in the house the night before for all of the following day's feedings. The dogs were primarily fed the BARF diet—Bones and Raw Food—high in natural protein. Salmon, guts and all, was a staple. Chum salmon that spawns near river mouths was always in ready supply. It was lower in oil but an excellent source of omega-3 and vitamin B12 and called dog salmon because for years it was dried and fed by mushers. She followed tradition and it felt good to be making use of the old ways and seeing positive results.

She loved the research that went into raising the better dog—the better racer. A lot of her knowledge came from her father. She had been his best pupil and often wondered what he would think of her today. Would he approve of her racing? She thought so. It had always felt like unfinished business when he died. A true talent snuffed out way too soon. But even she couldn't chase away his demons—the persistent depression that led to straying from his marriage and eventually to a gun to the head that left a wife and two children, ten and sixteen, to pick up the pieces of a fractured life.

She'd left Aunt Uki's at six a.m. to help feed the dogs

at her mother's. It was demanding work—you couldn't put off feeding an animal. She hadn't gone inside the house until now, and no one had heard her come in even though it was after nine. Her mother's front door was always unlocked. The door to E.J.'s bedroom remained closed, and she walked on down the hallway, and through the living room to the kitchen. Her mother liked to sleep in most mornings. So, per usual, it was a cup of the rich black stuff all by herself. This morning she heated milk and mixed in half and half—like the chicory she remembered from New Orleans. Had she been semi-consciously reliving that summer so many years ago when she spent every waking hour with probably the most handsome man she'd ever met? She gave a slight shake as if to dispel dwelling on the past. She knew she was puttering, doing anything but thinking about her soon to be problem. A problem that touched a lot of lives. A problem she didn't know how to fix. But if she made the wrong call, the results could be punishing—devastating to someone very dear to her.

Chapter 6

If only a person had hindsight when it was needed, Ben mused later. Would he have done anything differently if he'd known the impact of that day? Would have known that he'd think back on that first day of flying to his new job like a memory loop without an end? He marveled at fate or coincidence or the Navajo's Coyote or the Hopi Kokopelli—both tricksters in Indian lore. But, again, that was hindsight. That phenomenon that made one so very much smarter via distance and looking in rear-view mirrors. Yet, he believed it wasn't a trick but something a bit more predestined—and that sounded just like his Tewa grandmother. For starters, that day had been a long one. He'd been grounded in Seattle—for a day and a half. Why? The weather in Anchorage, of course. A freak storm had blindsided airline personnel and instead of getting out the day before at a reasonable time, he'd spent the night next to an escalator, squashing his six-foot two-inch frame onto the narrow bench that was meant for temporary storage of baggage.

Supposedly he would be missing the tundra's Cold Season—if he could trust the write-up in Wikipedia—by one month. The Warm Season started March 17, a month from today, but no one had told the elements in Seattle that winter should be tapering off. Stranded in the sprawling, under-heated Sea-Tac airport, even being inside was cold. The light parka might keep the wind out, but it wasn't warm. He had been in the air for two days but it seemed longer. There was no way to fly diagonally from Florida to Alaska quickly. Julie had left him at the airport in Orlando the day before yesterday, left him in the sun and warmth of the semi-tropics to board a plane taking him to full-blown winter. They'd spent the night close to the airport because his flight left at six a.m. But there wasn't any sleeping just a lot of talking and a lot of lovemaking. It was difficult to be separated so soon in their new marriage. Was she having second thoughts? He hoped not.

At six a.m. the airline handed out vouchers for breakfast. The air around him was soon filled with the scent of waffles, bacon, coffee and he couldn't keep his stomach from growling. He'd just come back from the restroom where even a generous dousing of water couldn't tame the cowlick at the crown of his head. His dark hair insisted on sticking straight up. The lightweight parka wadded up under his head hadn't done his coif any favors, but as a pillow it was probably better than any use as a jacket.

He was feeling virtuous for having walked past a Cinnabon vendor when an airline representative rushed up.

"Dr. Pecos, my apologies for the interruption but I need your help. We have you as a frequent flyer for the Government—Indian Health Service. Is that correct?"

"Yes. I'm actually on my way to Alaska now to work in a temporary position for the agency."

"This is perfect. No, I don't mean your inconvenience but I think you can help. We have a bit of a problem. This weather delay has messed up a lot of things—for one, we have a child—ten to be exact—who has just landed in Seattle but the guardian who was meeting him here in order to escort him to Anchorage is stuck in Anchorage herself. The woman who brought him this far has already left the airport and we haven't been able to reach her. Children under the age of fourteen according to airline policy, cannot be unaccompanied. I'm sure you see our dilemma. We can't send him back and we can't send him on. Would you offer to accompany him here in the airport while we're waiting for his flight to Anchorage? Then boarding with him? You're on the same flight."

"Of course. Not a problem."

"Great. Thank you so much. Wait here; I'll bring him over. I'm sure he's starving; could you take him to breakfast? We expect to leave before lunch so this might be the last food-call."

Ben nodded and watched as the attendant hurried away, returning with a tall-for-his-age child wearing crumpled jeans. A sweater stretched out at the neck reached almost to his knees and was wadded up around his elbows. Ben realized that this wasn't the haphazard dressing of someone poverty-stricken but more of a uniform of sorts. Like baggy shorts. This kid was cool and walked with more than a little swagger. The interesting thing was, he was a

Native. Alaskan? Maybe, but there was a hint of something else and a smattering of Anglo for sure.

"Dr. Pecos, this is Zachary Allen. I'll leave you two. Be sure and get a good breakfast. Take your time. We won't be leaving for another two hours—maybe more."

She handed Ben Zac's boarding pass. "And here's another breakfast voucher. Thanks again, have a good trip." They watched as she disappeared through a door marked Employees Only.

Ben smiled at his new traveling companion and offered an outstretched hand. It was grasped by a smaller one and a pair of bright, unblinking, brown-black eyes met his. Ben was struck by the maturity and self-confidence. It was Ben's experience that kids much older didn't have this one's poise.

"Do you prefer Zac or Zachary?"

"Zac. Are you a real doctor?"

"Yeah, pretty much so, but I can't like put a cast on your arm if you break it, and I can't do anything about stomach aches or snake bites."

"So, what do you do?"

"Sometimes people hurt where you can't see it." Ben pointed at his head. "I treat illnesses of the mind."

"How do you do that? That sounds like magic."

Ben laughed. "Well, I listen to what's bothering them and help them to find answers—their own cure to their own problems."

"Do you like that?"

"Yes, I do. I feel good when I can help people."

A slight nod from his companion. "What happened to your hair?"

"I slept standing on my head," Ben deadpanned and

got the result he wanted. A slow smile spread across Zac's face and then he laughed.

"Can I have two waffles with extra syrup?"

"Sounds good. I'm going to add some bacon to my order. You, too?"

Another affirmative nod. They were standing at the back of a line at an IHOP wannabe some twelve hungry people deep—over half were with fussy children. Ben knew he didn't envy the tired parents in front of him. He guessed that would probably be him someday with Julie and one or two kids in tow. He was glad they both agreed to wait awhile before starting a family. He knew they needed to feel some permanence in their lives and not fear a separation at the whim of the government whenever it suited someone's startup schedule.

The line moved quickly and Ben carried a tray of waffles and bacon to the nearest free table.

"I'm going to get some coffee. How about some juice?"

"Orange?"

"Coming up." Ben walked to a sidebar, poured a cup of very black coffee from a carafe that had probably been there for a while, filled a quarter of his cup with half and half, and fished a box of orange juice out of an ice-filled bucket.

One of Zac's waffles was already half eaten by the time Ben sat back down.

"Good?"

A nod and a mumbled "yes" didn't seem to slow the waffle-to-mouth movement already in motion. All those bottomless pit jokes from his own childhood came to mind. Kids could eat. At ten, this was only the beginning; teenagers would put consuming two measly waffles to shame.

Finally, even the syrup had been spooned up and the plate scraped clean. Ben gathered Styrofoam plates and plastic utensils and headed for the trash.

"Another orange juice?" This time a shake of the head. Ben refilled his coffee and sat back down. "Are you on spring break?"

"Yeah."

"Anchorage is home but you go to school in the lower forty-eight?"

"In Bellingham, at the Lummi Nation School. Do you live in Anchorage?"

"No. My home is far from here, but when I was your age I lived on a reservation in New Mexico." Ben shared Pueblo stories about growing up. Zac was a good listener. Ben was impressed by the ten-year-old's detailed questions.

"Do you play sports?"

"Yeah. Basketball mostly but soccer when it's warm. I'm on the middle-school team—Lummi Eagles—'cus I'm tall."

The two hours before boarding passed quickly. Before the last call, Ben loaded up on snacks, paying attention to adding some fresh fruit to the pile. He put the cache in his briefcase but shared some peanut butter cracker sandwiches first. After all, it'd been two hours since they had both eaten.

The plane was full. Ben let Zac take the window seat before squeezing into the unpopular middle one. Knee-room was almost nonexistent and the three-hour plus flight wouldn't be pleasant, but Ben had to admit it was worth it—he was thoroughly enjoying his unplanned traveling companion.

By the time they landed at Ted Stevens International Airport in Anchorage, both apples, all the bagged peanuts and one Kit Kat bar were history. A restroom stop and a short wait at the baggage claim and Ben walked Zac to the visitor area. Ben's connecting flight had been delayed so he'd be able to make certain that Zac's escort was waiting for him.

Even at a distance he recognized the woman standing behind the roped off visitor's area. The years, if anything, had only enhanced her beauty. He didn't have much time to dwell on memories because Zac had pulled away to sprint toward the woman ducking under the rope to grab her in a bear hug.

"Raven, good to see you." Ben handed her Zac's duffle and small suitcase.

"Zac, please get us a baggage cart." Raven watched him walk to the rack some thirty feet behind them, then with lowered voice said, "I hadn't thought this would be the way you'd meet, but I see you've had some time to get to know your son."

Ben didn't even take a deep breath, but felt a numbness spread across his chest reaching finally to his fingertips. Then he heard an intake of breath, his own, before expelling the air that was filling his lungs in a long, muted, whoosh of sound. Son? He didn't even need to question it. The truth had been right in front of him. He still couldn't say anything; he just stared at Raven. Was he waiting for some comment? Something that would explain, make the tension less awkward? With all the ramifications he knew more would be coming—just not now.

Raven's gaze was steady. "We're staying in Anchorage for a few days but will be in Moose Flats by late Wednesday. We need to talk." Ben nodded, and placed Zac's bags on the cart he'd just pushed up.

"Looks like we'll get to see each other again."

"That's cool." Zac's smile was genuine. But, then, so was Ben's.

Chapter 7

This wasn't a case of someone slapping a paternity suit on the unsuspecting and possibly innocent. At some level hadn't he known? Looked at the young boy and thought this could have been me—a Native of mixed ethnic background, tall for his age, bright, a touch of swagger, the ability to converse with adults ... still the shock ... he'd lost ten years of his child's life. He'd let a child down, let alone his mother. And that had been his fault. He'd ignored the calls, the messages begging him to get back in touch. They had seemed a little melodramatic. Just something an eighteen-year-old would do. And he hadn't known, hadn't cared enough to interrupt his life to find out. And she couldn't have told him, lured him back because of a child, a sense of owing, not one out of love. If nothing, Raven was proud.

And it wouldn't have worked, not as a couple, but he could have helped. Put grad school on hold and taken responsibility—and risked resenting being cornered? Pushed into a life with a woman he didn't love and a family on the way that needed more than he had to give. Zac had turned to wave before walking through the electronic doors leading to the parking area. A wave before the doors slid shut putting a barrier between father and son. Father? It sent a jolt through his body and made him catch his breath again. Painful. Especially because of his own lack of a parent during formative years. Interesting how history repeats itself. So, what now?

He knew, in those moments, his life would never be the same. His life and Julie's. Julie. He had to tell her, try to explain, be honest about the callous, lack of feeling—lack of respect, really, for a young girl who had to shoulder a tremendous burden all on her own. It had been a summer of sex and drinking and partying. Twenty-four, a Masters degree under his belt, acceptance into a Ph.D. program in psych—his world was just opening up. And Raven was two months out of high school facing a life with predetermined constraints. Her freedom, her ability to choose a path in life, not only just curtailed, but taken away. There wasn't any good way to spin the story.

He walked back to the terminal to wait for his flight. When his itinerary listed "connecting flight from ANC to Moose Flats via local air transport", he had no idea that meant a two-seater, fixed-wing cargo hauler. The pilot was one of those old, wizened types that looked like they'd survived a World War, and all those wrinkles hadn't come from just living on the tundra. The leather jacket was vintage and long johns peeked out from the torn pocket of well-worn jeans—Levi's from another century.

"Clouds have lifted. Not half-bad weather finally. Won't be flying all the way on instruments anyway." The grin showed a number of missing teeth.

At any other time all this might have instilled a lack of confidence but today, too much had happened already. Flying into clouds with some hippy yahoo seemed like a minor concern compared to becoming a father. And everything *was* fine—Ben stored his luggage in a bin in the fuselage, strapped himself into a not too uncomfortable seat and even enjoyed takeoff looking down at the snowy landscape. That is, all was well until Pete decided to buzz a herd of caribou. Ben kept his mouth shut but didn't enter in on the whoops and hollering and absolute manic joy of the pilot.

"Don't get to do that much anymore. Time was you'd see all sorts of wildlife from up here."

"This is my first trip up this way. It's beautiful."

"And rugged—dangerous and cold—but I've lived here all my life. Well, all but for a few years serving Uncle Sam. Wouldn't trade it, but I don't like what's happening to it now. There's no going back, either. Climate Change has screwed us. This past winter the sea-temps rose and the water got so hot the salmon started dying. And that means a whole way of life is dying, too."

"Yeah, one problem leads to another. The state is anxious to find alternatives—new ways to challenge residents, support them, show them a different way of life. Actually, I'm here as part of that plan." Ben explained the opioid/drug clinic and the type of programs he'd be introducing.

"What if it's too late? The problems I'm seeing should

have been addressed fifty years ago. You got your work cut out for you, doc, that's for sure."

They flew along in silence for a while. Ben had known the job wouldn't be easy. And maybe he felt more than a little resentment that the seriousness of his work was now overshadowed by the revelation of his being a father. Catastrophic events shouldn't come in pairs.

"Hey, doc, we're getting close. You want to put a little money on whether I'm going to set this machine down on the runway or slide right off the end? I got a couple twenties here that I'm willing to wager that I'll put this baby bird down on a dime, ice be damned. You in? You got a chance to win, you know, I'm only right fifty percent of the time." A loud cackle of a laugh followed this admission.

"Sure, count me in." Ben thought he could feel a couple twenties in his billfold sprout wings. He had a distinct feeling they were probably in lieu of a tip. But when in Rome … appeasing the locals had advantages. Who knew when his path might cross old Pete's again?

As he guessed, Ben was handing over two twenties before he even unloaded his luggage. He had to admit that Pete was a marvel with an airplane. At least the twenties bought him help with his bags as the two men walked toward the small square metal building that served as a terminal.

"Hope Iris has got a pot on. Coffee ain't good, just black and hot. Hey, where you staying? Doesn't look like anyone knew about the change in the flight schedule. I'm here until she's unloaded and fueled up. Why don't I give you a ride to wherever you're staying?"

"Actually, I don't know where that is."

"I'll make it easy for you—there's only one place it

could be. Visitors without family local get to bunk at Aunty Uki's. Used to be she had the only two-story house within a hundred miles but that ain't so anymore. She's got five rooms—a couple she lets out on a semi-permanent basis. Those semi-perms got their own bathrooms."

"I suppose I could call her and find out if anything's been set up."

"Well, welcome to the real world or at least the one up here. No phone service—not from National carriers, that is. Only GCI Alaska. Lots to get used to, but you'll get the hang of it. We're not bad, just different." Pete guffawed loudly. "So, how 'bout my just driving you by Aunty's? It ain't far from here—hell, nothing's far from here." Another loud snort of a laugh. "I keep my dually out back. Good for hauling. It's going to come in handy if they go to moving this village inland. Gotta keep an eye out for any way to make a buck. It's got a plow on the front so I don't figure we'll get stuck."

"I'd appreciate the lift." Ben was a little surprised that E.J. hadn't met the plane, but it was a day late and it wasn't like he could text him. Figuring out the phone service had just made it to the top of his to-do list.

"Here we are."

Pete was right; it wasn't far—straight for two blocks, a left turn, and another left and they were sitting in front of a sky-blue, two-story house with a wraparound porch. Flowerboxes hung in front of each window; empty now, but he could imagine the colorful spots of color come spring. Dormers jutted out above him in what must be an attic and gave the place a coziness for so large a structure. Snow on the shiny, silver aluminum roof and a dusting across the front sidewalk—it was a living Hallmark card.

"You go on up and say hello to Aunty. Give me a wave if she's holding a spot for you, and I'll bring your bags."

There was no need to knock, Aunty Uki burst through the front door both arms outstretched. A bright red plaid scarf slipped back over a coil of black braids that nestled at the nape of her neck exposing an inch or so of plump shoulder at the edge of her parka. It would be difficult to determine age, Ben thought. Dimpled, unlined skin only showed a myriad of fine wrinkles around sparkling brown-black eyes.

"Give me a hug, now. I must be the first one to welcome you to Moose Flat. Well, the second if we count ol' Pete." She leaned around him and waved to Ben's pilot turned taxi driver. "Don't just stand there, bring his bags on up." Then turning back to Ben, "Coffee? A cup of hot tea? Something with a little more kick to it?" Pete chose that moment to plop both of Ben's pieces of luggage down on the porch. "The choices for you, Pete, are coffee or tea. I don't want any planes flying over my house with a tipsy pilot."

"Gonna save you some trouble, Aunty. I gotta get back out to the strip and make sure that plane is ready to go. I'm back to Anchorage tonight. Doc, I'm leaving you in good hands—just make sure she keeps both of them in her own pockets." A thunderous laugh as he dodged the swipe that only just missed his shoulder.

"Dirty old man." But it was said in fun and Ben could tell that the little give-and-take wasn't the first go-around for the two. Pete wished Ben the best, shook his hand again, and walked back to his truck.

Ben picked up both bags and followed Uki into the house. And what a step back in time was. A player piano

in one corner, claw and ball footed dining room table
with high back chairs in another, and every inch of wall-
space covered with framed prints or oils or just newspaper
clippings presenting a pictorial history of Moose Flats.
Ben quickly decided on where he'd spend his first free
afternoon.

"I've got you in one of the upstairs front rooms.
They're my favorite. You'll face the street and have your
own bath. There's a schedule on your door, but breakfast is
served once at six and then again at seven thirty. Just let me
know your choice the night before. I post the menu on the
kitchen door every evening. It's easier to eat here. I can add
board to your room rent, if you want. We only have one
restaurant in town but I can recommend it. And one coffee
shop. Both buy my baked goods. Well, I should say 'our'
baked goods. My sister and I have a little business—the
Two Sisters Bakery—so I better be able to recommend the
food." She smiled, "This is a small place, Dr. Pecos, you
know, the 'I scratch your back, you scratch mine' mentality.
But that's what makes a village work."

"I understand. That's my background, too."

"I imagine E.J. will be by in the morning to take you to
your office. You might be used to something a little more
formal. I hate to say it but you got the short straw without
even being here to draw."

"Don't think I'm following." And Ben wasn't. Riddles
and metaphors seemed to be favorites around the place.
And everyone knew everything about each other's business.
But Ben was more or less used to that, too.

"Pastor Mike of the Unitarian Baptists has offered to
loan you his office. He's off to the lower forty-eight for the
summer—going to talk some people out of their money.

You know, lobby for Native Alaskan rights and program support. I think he has the ear of the Christian Right."

Ben couldn't stop thinking that Unitarian Baptist was an oxymoron. He was familiar with both groups and he couldn't see them united—in any way. "I'm sure the church will work fine."

"Well, you'll have a secretary—guess they don't call them that anymore, do they? Marie's been around longer than I have and her knowing everyone will come in handy. Let's get you settled now, and then why don't I bring up a plate of smoked Coho and some of my whole wheat toast. I still think a cup of hot tea would hit the spot. Fortifies the body against the cold."

It all sounded good to Ben. He was beginning to realize that it had been an awfully long day. As soon as he figured out how he was going to call Julie, he wanted to get unpacked, take a long-overdue shower and hit the sack. His new landlady let him borrow her phone and with a four-hour difference in time zones, Julie was just getting ready to go out to dinner with some of her new work associates. A shared 'I love you' and the promise of a call the next day and Ben hung up missing his new wife and dreading the conversation that was inevitable. How many ways could you say 'I have a son' and not have it be a shock?

Chapter 8

A good night's sleep hadn't been in the cards. After a lot of tossing and turning, he'd dozed off around three a.m. only to jolt awake to the smell of coffee. The kitchen clock said seven a.m. There was a pot of hot coffee on the counter, a note, but no Aunty Uki. There had been a death in the village. A body was found. Apparently, she was a member of search and rescue, and local law enforcement had picked her up to meet up with them when they brought the body in. Her background in nursing gave her all kinds of privileges in an area without a fulltime doctor. There was more homemade whole wheat bread on the counter beside a toaster, and a plate of some pretty sinful looking brownies. He wasn't exactly a chocolate-in-the-morning kind of guy but he was sold after one bite. Her note ended with a promise of a proper dinner that evening—six sharp.

He could have what would probably be his first taste of caribou. She was right. It would be a first.

There was a loud banging on the front door before he'd finished his fourth brownie. E.J. didn't wait for Ben to open up and just walked in after stamping a new dusting of snow from his canvas-topped rubber boots. The handshake and man-hug were welcoming, but Ben felt just a twinge of reserve. The greeting wasn't quite the hearty, couldn't-wait-to-see-you type of personal exchange he'd expected. Yet, E.J. professed to be pleased. He was the one instrumental in getting him assigned to the community project to address the opioid crisis. Still Ben couldn't help but feel there was something he was missing.

"Good to have you here. Any coffee left?"

"Help yourself. I'm on my own this morning."

"Hey man, I'm glad this worked out for you. None too soon, you lost a potential patient this morning."

"How's that?" Ben topped up his coffee and joined E.J. at the table.

"Looks like a probable overdose. Young guy, too—Brant Thomas—a friend of Raven's. Moved back here with her from Anchorage about six months back. It wasn't any secret he had an opioid problem. He'd played a couple seasons for the Seahawks but injuries pretty much ended his career early on. I think Raven thought she could bring him back to his roots and all would be well. She even bought a hundred thousand dollars worth of dogs just to give him a vocation."

"I'm not following. Dogs?"

"Mushers. Out behind my mother's place she's got a dog-box city going—mostly Malamute-Husky crosses. My father was big in the game way on back, taught Raven the ropes from the time she was a toddler. I think she's always planned on picking up where he left off."

"Wow. How many dogs does she have?"

"Not sure exactly. I know there are two teams of fourteen with reserves as mushers and I think she has two or three breeders. Yeah, she went all out but apparently she was in a position to buy a ready-made setup from an old guy who used to work with our father. It's tough work and fast becoming a young man's game. I think Raven needed a challenge and wanted to get Zac out of the city—back to his roots at least for vacations from school—as well as help Brant."

Ben met E.J.'s stare. There it was, out in the open, the reason for the less than all-out welcoming. Ben was beginning to feel he'd been set up. But if so, maybe that wasn't such a bad thing. He'd needed to know, needed to man-up.

"I met Zac."

"Yeah, I know, Raven called me. He's a good kid. Raven's done a great job—all by herself." Ben thought there was a little extra emphasis on this last part.

"I didn't know ..."

"Or didn't care to find out? I know she tried to let you know."

"I'm not going to make excuses. I would like to believe that I'd have done the right thing."

"Hindsight is pretty fool-proof, isn't it? But the question is what now? How will you step up and help raise a ten-year-old?"

"I guess that's what Raven and I need to discuss ... and Julie. I'm married now."

"That's a complication."

"Doesn't need to be." Ben felt like crossing his fingers.

He honestly had no idea what Julie's reaction might be. He knew her to be a compassionate, caring person but would that be different if the circumstances were this close to home?

"It wasn't Raven's idea to bring you here. Besides the family drama, you're best for the job."

"Thanks for the vote of confidence." Ben realized he sounded a little snide.

"I mean that. Am I pissed about what you did to my sister? Yeah. But it's up to you two to work out. It was just up to me to put you in a position to get involved. I'd given up on Raven doing the right thing. That doesn't mean that I won't be watching—I don't want either one of them to get screwed over … again. Zac needs a father. And not someone who suddenly shows up only to disappear again. Let that be a warning. You and Raven have a lot to decide. Now, we need to go take a look at your office."

"Give me a minute." Ben rinsed his coffee cup and put it in the drainer. A warning. How did he answer that? He wasn't here to screw over anyone, but he was fast getting tired of being blamed for something he knew nothing about. What was his place in Zac's life now? How was he expected to make up for ten lost years? He wondered how many other people knew he was Zac's father? Others might not be as reserved as E.J.; Ben was beginning to feel the weight of a target squarely on his back. Should he be looking over his shoulder?

"We can walk. Day's a little gray, but what's new. At least there's no precip forecast. We're only two blocks away." E.J. waited by the door while Ben grabbed his parka from his room and came back down stairs. "You've probably heard that the good reverend took a six month leave of absence—guess he's calling it a sabbatical—anyway the church is picking up the tab and giving him what's described as 'meaningful' work to do in the lower forty-eight. He's supposed to come back with money to move the church and maybe another building or two. We'll see. I'm pretty used to promises and no action. Alaska can easily slip into an 'out of sight, out of mind' category. But lucky for you, you inherit Marie. Probably fifty percent of what she'll tell you is hearsay—maybe even just plain gossip, but the other half will be useable and necessary background info. Trust her. Your bullshit meter will tell you if something doesn't ring true."

Ben wasn't certain he had a BS meter. Guess he'd find out.

+ + +

The church was a treasure. The building only hinted of its use by the five-foot-tall hand-carved cross and a religious-themed totem beside the double doors. Inside, stylized red and black Haida art filled the walls of the entry and church proper. Pews were hand-carved depictions of tundra animals with a preponderance of bears, eagles and seal. Ben could only imagine the work it would be to move and preserve all he was seeing. It would almost require specialists to dismantle the dais, two podiums, pews and all the hanging artwork. This was a miniature museum and many of the carvings had to be ancient.

Ben stood at the back taking it all in. He couldn't help but feel he was seeing the last of an era. Could this setting be replicated? The murals on the walls of the choir loft would be lost. And the carved steps that led down onto the main floor—salvaged? Reworked, varnished and replaced in a building built to identical specs? What kind of money would it take?

His musings were interrupted when a door at the back burst open and a small, roundish woman with bobbed, thick black hair streaked with gray bustled toward him.

"Oh, Dr. Pecos, I meant to be out here to greet you but Pastor Mike called. It's always something. He wants fifty of our hand-painted Sunday bulletins sent to him as quickly as I can get them on a plane. And he wants a bio and picture of the artist. My nephew is the Haida native who painted all these decorations. I know the Pastor doesn't want to lose any but it pushes the cost of moving and restoring this building sky high. But look here." Marie pointed to a discolored line along the wall some ten inches from the floor. "This is what happened last fall when this end of Moose Flats flooded. This is a water stain; it isn't permafrost. We thought our lovely little church was a goner then. And I do think it hastened the sponsoring church's dedication to saving this treasure. Oh dear, I'm rattling on so. E.J., take Dr. Pecos back to the Pastor's office. I'll be back as soon as I can."

"This way." E.J. walked to what looked like an add-on, an annexed alcove with walls and a door as ornately decorated as the nave. "I should have checked. Not sure what kind of condition the office is in."

It looked great. Someone had boxed and stacked the Pastor's belongings to one side next to what was probably a closet door. Ben thought he would be correct if he guessed that Marie had been hard at work to make room for him. Even one small book case had been emptied. The entire space was an easy four hundred square feet and the building itself had probably originally been part of the block of municipal buildings that he saw when he walked up. Looked like the village utility services had the building directly in back of the church with what might be the jail to its right.

Inside, it was like being in another world. The Pastor's office was perfect. Ben slipped off his parka and hung it on a hook beside the door. And he meant it. He'd worked in far less inviting surroundings—once a sponsor had squeezed a desk into what had been a broom closet.

"I'm going to leave you and check in with the Chief of Police. Raven and Zac will be back this afternoon. I need to pick them up. She's going to be upset over Brant. Oh, I almost forgot; there's a potlatch in your honor at the gymnasium tomorrow night. Should be some good eats, and you'll get to meet the movers and the shakers." This seemed to be funny, and E.J. followed the announcement with a shake of the head and a loud guffaw. "Later."

E.J. almost ran into Marie on his way out. "Slow down. This is still a house of God," she called after him. "That boy hasn't changed—he was rowdy in the fifth grade and still rowdy at thirty-something. I used to teach in the elementary school 'til it got to be too much. Parents don't support you. They expect the moon and stars and don't invest in the outcome or help in the journey." A shake of the head and then, "Plus, I got too old. Just couldn't keep up anymore. You may think Alaska's different, remote and all, but we've got a lot of the same problems that plague the lower forty-eight. Can I get you anything? I'm even good at coming up with a cup of tea mid-morning and one of your landlady's brownies from the Two Sisters. Their bakery is just plain out of this world."

"I can attest to those brownies being special—I've

already had four this morning. But I just need to put a few things away and get my laptop cranked up. I'll be linking up with Indian Health Service, as well as the University of Alaska, Anchorage. I'll make sure you have a list of contracted support institutions and a master copy of all passwords."

"Great. I look forward to working with you, Dr. Pecos. You've come at the right time to do some good for our village. We need you." With that she walked to the door, then stopped and turned back. "I meant to point out that the door in the corner there leads to a conference room. I imagine you'll make good use of it. I've ordered a new white board and viewing screen, but who knows when they'll get here—it'll probably be at least a couple more months … after the thaw and barges can get up the river. Sometimes it's just too expensive to fly in our supplies. We make yearly shopping lists—more like wish-lists. But it's a quiet place to work. Out here, you'll get all the noise of the workmen—if we're to believe that the dismantling of the church will start next month. But you'll be spared back here. My office is through that door." She pointed to the front of the office. "We don't have an intercom. Leave the door open and we can yell back and forth. Now, I'm out of here." At the door she tossed back a "remember, yell if you need me" before disappearing into her office.

Ben fought the urge to walk over and shut the door to Marie's office. He wasn't used to fish-bowl exposure. At least he had the conference room for private consultation. Addiction and its accompanying problems weren't topics many would be comfortable discussing in front of others. It always made getting group meetings started a challenge. At least the rooms were spacious. Both the office and attached conference room offered space enough for up to twenty—maybe twenty-five in the conference room alone. No, he'd had far worse accommodations.

He emptied his briefcase, connected a surge-protector to the wall outlet behind him and plugged in his laptop. He hadn't noticed a laptop on Marie's desk but surely she had one. Or maybe she depended on the electric typewriter Ben had noticed. He couldn't believe it, an honest-to-God typewriter. There were things in Alaska that made him feel like he was at the ends of the earth—the lack of technical devices was one of them. He wondered at how well equipped the schools were. Probably not very well. He knew coming here that a part of the problems he would be addressing with the younger generation included the lack of a useable education—a lack of preparation to take on college, let alone technical school. Hadn't he read that the state's graduation rate was the fifth worst of all fifty states? A shocking statistic but one he knew he had to address.

And Ben knew the reasoning well—if you didn't plan to ever leave your village, why prepare for an outside world? You'd join your family in fishing and that would be your life. But now, with that life disappearing, there was an emphasis upon schooling that had never been there before. It was going to take money to turn that around, offer opportunities where none had existed. And hadn't he read that the current governor was slashing funds for education? Shortsightedness when it came to education always seemed like some sort of Russian roulette with children's lives. How could anyone not see bankrolling a child's future as a bigger investment in the village as a whole?

Ben sighed; he was struggling with a little bit of

what-have-I-gotten-myself-in-for angst. Unrewarded and underfunded programs were often cancelled before any positive result was realized. He didn't want his program to end up just another disheartening attempt to improve the lives of Natives—a lot of work that ended in failure. Surely the need for a clinic spawned by the opioid crisis was critical enough to garner the money and attention it would need to survive and prosper. But he didn't kid himself, tribal politics could be brutal. Changing times didn't equate to changing beliefs.

He pulled out his desk chair. He had a full day's work ahead of him. First, a notice to attract interns for the summer. The University of Alaska, Anchorage, had indicated an interest. As most schools state-side, the psych department welcomed meaningful opportunities for its graduates. Those hoping to enter a Master's degree program in the fall could get some rare, hands-on experience—with pay. Preference would go to Alaskan Natives but not stop there. He'd try to recruit two young men or women, maybe three, if the need was there. This was the part of his job he truly looked forward to. It wasn't that he thought of himself as getting old, early thirties was still young; but it was a way to stay in touch with a younger generation.

Chapter 9

He hadn't visited his frozen friend in two weeks. E.J. assured himself that he'd been busy. Did it make a difference? It wasn't like the object of his attention was going to get up and walk away, be angered at being ignored. So, why was he beating himself up about not making his way out on the tundra to sit next to a dead body—one he knew nothing about—and ... what? ... meditate? He guessed that was as good as any explanation. He was offering solace and in return getting the quiet time to reflect. There was something about the blank slate of all-white surroundings that kept his attention focused inward, on problems more immediate to his own life. He pulled the wolverine-lined, seal-fur hood closer to his face. One more plus of nature that was fast disappearing—fur that didn't freeze. Even if the wolverine got wet, its fur stayed dry due to the natural oils in its coat. And fur seals? Another soon-to-be victim of climate warming? Alaska's Pribilof Islands were the breeding grounds for two-thirds of the world's fur seals. Canada had declared them endangered but that didn't protect them from the elements, the disappearance of their habitat. More change no one was prepared for.

He sat on the snow machine and stared at his inert friend. Yes, he could call him that—a friend—but did he know it was a him? Something about the nose said masculine, what little of it was exposed seemed overly large to be feminine. Perhaps, the bigger question to ponder was why hadn't he reported finding the body? He was fairly certain it was a white man. And that had its own set of problems—implications of possible racial improprieties. White men weren't easily trusted.

Ethnic cleansing took on new meaning in the frozen north, out where he grew up away from the big cities. Here the white man was viewed with suspicion. He could only want one thing—money. Maybe it meant fracking, stealing what lay beneath the tundra, or expanded fishing rights raping the ocean for salmon and other fish of high-market value. And when it came to finding a body, who would E.J. report it to anyway? The felons who made up the community police force? All answering to a Chief of Police who was in love with his own voice and authority. Five deputies all with criminal records who had their jobs because no one else wanted that work. In fact, if he wanted to be truthful, there were few men of the right age and temperament to be a police officer, in all of Moose Flats, who didn't have a record. Granted most had served time or were on probation for drug improprieties, not killers but still not law-abiding either.

Some of the jail time had been served because of domestic violence, maybe the number one problem in his village. It wasn't too long ago that his mother would show up with the occasional black eye or bruised arm. E.J.'s stepfather was an exacting man. He could take his belt off and slash it across E.J.'s backside faster than a man cracking a bullwhip over a team of mules. Wasn't that the reason he'd left as a teenager? Ran away with the help of church members—and vowed never to return. But things were different now. His stepfather worked in Spokane or Tacoma six months out of the year. He was a small engine mechanic in high demand—a man from a different world who'd made it on the tundra.

He knew his mother was relieved to have him gone a part of the year. Ahnah Takanni would turn sixty next summer. And finally life was easier. Ed Johnson was a good provider. The money he sent home each month had bought a house and two snow machines, and helped Raven get through school and set up a business in Anchorage. Being half white meant Ed could pull some strings for his adopted family. Set them up with jobs in the city or pay for college. E.J. couldn't forget that; he owed his undergraduate education to the largess of his stepfather. It was just the man's demons, the lashing out, hurting those close to him that he couldn't take and hear over and over the excuses his mother made. He was helpless as a boy to intervene—but maybe not so helpless as a man.

Yet, an older woman alone was not an enviable position to be in. Not out here. After his father committed suicide, she lacked protection—the kind E.J. was too young to provide. He shouldn't have been surprised when Ed Johnson showed up as a suitor. He was a widower with a good job. Childless himself, he convinced his mother that a ready-made family was welcome. Yeah, right. In fact, E.J. wasn't absolutely certain that his mother had actually married Ed. He remembered she fought to keep his father's name so that she would have the same surname as her children. Did anyone care if his mother was married or not married? A piece of paper couldn't really change the dynamics of being in love. Or the raw truth of simply being together out of convenience.

He turned his attention back to the nose. Maybe it didn't make a difference what ethnic group this anomaly belonged to. Well, yes, and no. His state was sixty-five percent white. Natives accounted for maybe fifteen percent. The other twenty percent was a mixed bag of Black, Hispanic, American Indian, Pacific Islander, and Asian. This was reversed in Moose Flats. The majority of residents were Native—seventy percent or more. Whites were limited to the Pastor, his family, several teachers, the owner/operators of a half dozen fishing boats, bank personnel—the list was varied but not that long. What made a difference was the fact that Whites held positions of power within the community. His coming back as a Native lawyer gave him clout—the respect of the elders. He knew he was the village's favorite success story after Brant Thomas. And, he knew there were those who would try to curb his power—play to the novelty of a Native with a degree, but not to the seriousness of what he might accomplish.

And he knew he was expected to stay, supervise the village's transition. Plus, there would be no ducking out once plans were completed. He would be expected to remain a voice for the community, marry and raise a family on the tundra. Provide for his mother as she aged, his sister and her son as they sought to fit in. But should Zac remain? Isolated by the harshness of climate? A young man who showed academic promise and was somewhat of a soccer prodigy? Maybe the unanswered question, the elephant in the room, was whether or not Ben would step in and help.

E.J. smiled. Lots of ifs and a couple maybes. But what did it say about him that he did his best thinking in the company of someone who could never answer—to contradict or agree? Still there was something to be said about having his own private listening ear. He laughed out loud, then waved to his friend, started the snow machine and turned toward the trail some half mile away.

+ + +

The binoculars were trained on the lone snow machine as it turned and approached the trail. Scrub brush acted as a snow fence, a foil that concealed the occupant in the ATV bundled against the paralyzing cold, a hood obscuring all of the face but the scarf wound three times across nose and mouth. Wasn't the first time that the tundra had yielded something unusual.

Still, it was odd that an individual would come to this same spot several times a month and just stand out in the snow, risking frostbite to stare at the ground. What could be so interesting about open tundra a couple miles outside the village? Perhaps, that needed some investigation. Could it be that the tundra was already giving up its secrets? Before a final thaw exposing its dirty linen, so to speak?

Safeguards needed to be taken. The right people needed to answer for this, if, in fact, it was the body that had surfaced—in February, in the dead of winter, without provocation or coaxing. But wouldn't the onlooker recognize the dead? Recognize and sound the alarm?

It would be dangerous for the discovery to become common knowledge this early. Someone would have to answer for this misdeed. So, why shouldn't it be the one who discovered the body? He could take the fall. Unknowingly step up and martyr himself. He was good at that—pompous and all-knowing; the one in charge. Intruding where he wasn't wanted or needed.

The safety was off the 700 series Remington Sendero but the gun remained leaning against the vehicle's instrument panel. It would be too hard on the man's mother to lose him, too. Besides, it wasn't needed; there was a better plan.

The driver reached for a camera and wiped the telephoto lens with a cloth. It wasn't the first capture of candid shots from this distance. This was proof. No one would question that it made sense to suspect the person who knew where the body was, visited it regularly, and kept it covered.

Once the relationship was revealed, no one would doubt that the photos had captured the killer. It would be very, very difficult to disprove. All circumstantial evidence but all very damning. A smile played above the scarf causing the eyes to squint. This was perfect.

The camera was gently placed back in its case strapped to the seat. A short wait and the second snow machine bumped over the snow and ice leaving its hiding place and heading back to the village. The police department insignia was obscured by snow.

Chapter 10

Instinct told Ben absolutely nothing good could come from a meeting between Raven and Julie. He secretly vowed to make certain that a meeting never happened—not without him being present. That was safest. He wasn't prepared to face the Zac issue, but it wasn't really as much an issue about the child as it was about the bigger picture—his failure to support Zac's mother. And the fact that he'd never mentioned Raven.

Julie had been engaged before he met her. He knew a lot about her former fiancé—had actually taken a punch at the guy in self-defense one time. And he'd shared stories about a couple girlfriends—just not Raven. Would that give the relationship added importance in Julie's eyes? Make it seem like some secret he was keeping?

If he'd learned anything in life it was that women think

differently. Past girlfriends could embellish the simplest thing, such as a guy giving a neighbor a ride to town, and blowing it all out of proportion. Not that he put Julie in that category of not trusting, but he had to come up with a plausible explanation. Was ten years a good excuse? A reason for not mentioning it? Just too long ago to be pertinent?

Well, it was pertinent now and Ben wished he had a chance to do things over.

So, when the phone call came Wednesday afternoon, he felt cornered. In one week, Julie would join him in Moose Flats. One week. No place to run to, no place to hide. He kept replaying the conversation.

"I can't believe my good luck. The Herald wants me to do a feature on the climate threat to two diverse areas of the States—one, Miami, impacting millions of people and, two, remote villages of Alaska. They want the differences in cultures to be played up. Totally unalike but both literally sinking into the ocean. Can't think of any topic more timely."

"That's great."

"You don't sound very excited. Is everything okay?"

"Yeah, just tired. I'm having to set up an office from scratch and try to bring in two or three interns from Anchorage in addition to starting some therapy sessions here. The need is pretty pressing. Like they've needed all this yesterday. We had another overdose just this week."

"Oh, Ben, I'm sorry. I promise I won't get in the way. I'll probably be staying in Anchorage or Fairbanks most of the time—I'm going to need the amenities of a city. But I can fly over on weekends, and I'll be able to stay in Moose Flats when I'm doing field work. It will be fun."

Ben had kept the call short—even feigned having a

patient waiting for him in the outer office. Julie was smart and attuned to his moods. He didn't think she'd bought into the 'I'm just tired' excuse for sounding distant. He had some thinking to do, soul-searching—planning, really. How did he want to move forward? What would be fair to Zac? To Julie, let alone Raven? As much as he wanted to duck it, any decisions necessitated a talk with Raven. And that would be difficult because of Brant Thomas's death.

Funeral plans fell to Raven and when it came to burying the dead, it took a village. His potlatch was cancelled in favor of a wake—or whatever Natives called a get-together to celebrate Brant's life. A regional undertaker was being flown in from Anchorage. Laying out of the corpse would be left to him.

And bids were being taken by local residents for storage of the body until spring. Usually someone would donate space in his or her garage and then after the thaw, a shovel brigade would flock to the local cemetery, dig a final resting place, and cover it with a mound of stones. The finishing touch would be the placement of a spirit house over the grave.

Even in the snow and cold of winter, the brightly painted, wooden, pitched-roofed structures stood out in stark, yet colorful relief. They struck Ben as dog-houses for mastiffs, then he admonished himself for being sacrilegious. If he were being honest about rites of the dead, the locals here would get a good laugh if told about how his pueblo ancestors honored their dead. Carrying full course meals out to the burial grounds on All Hallows Eve to feed the occupants below only to look the other way when feral dogs and coyotes feasted on the repast. Children were never told it was animals that licked the plates clean.

He still remembered how shocked he was at the age of eight when he and a few cohorts sneaked out to the graveyard while it was still dark to see a ravenous pack of coyotes fighting over scraps of food—all that was left of what started out as some thirty laden bowls and platters. When he told his grandmother what he had seen, she had just nodded and reminded him of the spirit world. Didn't he remember that the coyote was a trickster? How did he know that he hadn't just witnessed the shape-shifting of the dead in order to celebrate a holiday? He didn't have an answer. But, just in case, he never shot another coyote—not even after one had killed five of his neighbor's chickens.

When you didn't know things for sure, you couldn't be too careful. That same philosophy had also served him well in middle school.

What would serve him well now? The truth, he guessed. And then an equitable solution that would be beneficial to everyone. He had started to think along the lines of sharing time with Zac—maybe a school holiday here and there, every other Christmas vacation with a month or so during the summer. Would this be too much? Or not enough?

They didn't have an iron-clad plan in mind, but he and Julie talked of having a family. Starting one in the next five years. A baby and a teenager. Not exactly the ideal. If it gave him pause, what would Julie's reaction be? He needed to have a heart to heart with Raven, and he didn't have much time. He needed some talking points before Julie arrived.

Chapter 11

When Raven opened the door, she stared at him for maybe a 5-count then handed him a five-gallon bucket with what looked and smelled like some kind of slightly rotten slop.

"Gotta get the dogs fed. You can help." She set two more buckets on the porch and closed the kitchen door behind her. "This way."

Ben picked up a second bucket trying not to inhale the distinct fishy odor. The food was warm which didn't help the smell stay contained. So much for stopping by to invite Raven for a cup of coffee and maybe one of the Two Sisters' cinnamon rolls. He hadn't planned on working—at least not while wearing dress leather boots and a three-hundred-dollar, beige, goose down parka.

He should have just continued on to the office and not

tried to do something impromptu. Still, he thought there was merit to confronting the situation and not allow for rehearsed reactions. Wasn't there likely to be more honesty in an off-the-cuff meeting? Not sure he was going to get that chance now.

Raven pointed to the bucket he was carrying. "It's chum, in case you're wondering. Most people just call it dog salmon."

"People eat this?"

A laugh. "Well, not exactly out of buckets. It has a mild taste and less salt than Chinook or Coho—makes it perfect for dogs. But quality is hard to swear by—ok one year, then down the tubes the next. They spawn near river mouths—practically at my backdoor. I pay local kids to bring them to me by the buckets full. We have to add oil though for the dogs and that ups the cost; otherwise, it's cheap high-protein. But between food and housing, the dogs are a super big drain on a bank account."

Ben could tell by the howling that breakfast was a pretty important time of day. He certainly felt welcome. And speaking of that, he had to admit Raven was being nice. She hadn't slammed the door in his face anyway. Maybe all this mess they'd made of their lives could be discussed, solved even, as adults. Calmly, with shared goals. Fingers crossed, but he still felt E.J. had set him up.

"There's a scoop hanging on the wall inside the back door of the maintenance building and more thawed buckets of food to your left of the door when you run out. Take the back two rows. Each dog has a bowl in front of his shelter. A scoop and a half for each dog. Questions?"

"Think I've got it."

"There's an apron hanging in the closet at the back and

rubber slip-ons to put over your boots. Just be careful not to splash any food on you. Eau de Chum isn't something you'd want to wear."

Ben thought he saw the beginnings of a sly smile before she turned to pick up the nearest bucket.

Raven took the front two rows of dogs only returning to the building at the back twice to replenish her food supply. She was quicker than he was ladling out individual meals. She could probably measure out one and a half scoops blindfolded. With the two of them working, thirty-two dogs plus the two 'families' in the barn were fed in under an hour.

"Thanks for your help. I have a couple dogs crated here in the back of the building—recuperating from pulled tendons. They're on low doses of pain-killers, and I need to give them their medication. There're also a couple moms with puppies. I'll join you at the house in ten minutes. My usual handlers will be by to pick up and clean bowls before they begin to exercise everybody; so, that's something I don't have to do. Coffee's in the kitchen."

Ben walked back up to the house. It was cold but not that 'one more breath will freeze your lungs' kind of temperature. This was livable which probably meant spring was truly on its way. He'd helped himself to half and half from the fridge and was doctoring his coffee when Raven came in.

"I'm always glad when that's done. Of course, there's a repeat performance in twelve hours. Zac likes to help then. The dogs love him; he's a natural with them. Mom took him over to the community college library this morning. Not sure he'll abandon the iPad long enough to read a real book, though."

"Growing up is different today."

Raven nodded and pulled a chair away from the dining room table. "I'm assuming you have time to talk? I don't think you came here to help me feed dogs."

"You're probably right." He pulled up a chair opposite and sat down.

"I guess the one thing that I want you to know … want you to believe … is that I didn't plan this. It wasn't my idea to bring you here. In fact, E.J. didn't even tell me what he was planning. I had to find out the night of the presentation to the village council."

"That must have been a shock—I'm sure it dredged up the past."

"Yeah. And it couldn't have come at a worse time. I brought Brant back here at the end of the summer to rehabilitate. I thought going back to his roots would make a difference, reacquaint him with who he was. The dogs were going to be therapy for both of us. Hard work was going to win out over addiction. I was wrong. He immediately found a group of druggies and—" She excused herself and retrieved a box of Kleenex from the kitchen. "Sorry, I thought I had a better handle on all this … you and Zac and now Brant's death."

Ben leaned across the table and put a hand on her arm. "Raven, I'm—"

"Don't." She pulled away. "Whatever we decide it won't be out of pity."

"That hadn't crossed my mind. You've done a terrific job. He's a great kid."

"We don't need you. I hadn't even wanted you to meet him and then of all things he gets stranded in Anchorage at the very time you're coming this way."

"And you don't believe in fate? To risk sounding like my grandmother, you don't think it was meant to be? Something very much beyond our control?"

Raven shrugged. "It's done now. He likes you. I've had to answer a lot of questions the last couple of days."

"I can only imagine. At ten, a father steps into his life … that couldn't be easy."

"At least at ten the gravity of the situation is just a blip—his favorite team losing at Soccer was more of a catastrophe."

"I want to make this right."

"Really? And just what would that look like?" The anger spilled over.

"Whatever you would agree to … something you would want. You set the parameters."

"I've already said I don't want you around. You weren't interested ten years ago; you're not interested now. Oh, maybe you'll go through the motions, say the right things but is your heart into it? Do you want a son?" She stopped to take a sip of coffee, then looked at him directly and held his gaze, "I heard that you're married."

"Yes. I can't imagine Julie not being as excited as I am about the son I didn't know that I had." He felt like he should cross his fingers under the table. In all honesty he had no idea what Julie's reaction would be. There was simply no denying that their lives would never be the same.

"Will she be moving here?"

"Not permanently—not to Moose Flats. She'll be a short-timer like me working on loan."

"What does she do?"

"Julie's a journalist currently with the Miami Herald. She'll be working on a climate change project and dividing her time between Moose Flats and Anchorage."

"Zac's spring break is over in ten days. I don't think much can be accomplished in that length of time."

"That might work out for the best. We don't need to throw too much at him all at once. This will give all of us time to decide on a future—what it's going to look like; what we're going to be comfortable with."

"Ten-year-olds are resilient. I just don't know about me. It's been just the two of us the entire ten years."

"On his airline ticket his name was listed as Zachary Allen. I assumed that meant there was a Mr. Allen."

"I gave him my father's middle name—Thomas Allen Takanni. When he started school, I just left it as a last name. Fewer questions."

"There's a part of me that wishes that he had my name."

"And there's a part of me that's glad he doesn't. You don't deserve a son with your name. I resent you coming into his life; I resent you not being there from the start."

"I don't blame you. I didn't get back in touch when I should have. I was an immature twenty-four and—"

"Took advantage of an eighteen-year-old?"

"We were young adults, but consenting ones."

"I thought I was in love with you. You were my forever and then you weren't. For a long time I hated you. I hated the burden of a child, the change in my life's plans, the feeling of being caught and forced to work at whatever I could to just get along. If it hadn't been for my mother and Aunt Uki, things would have been unbearable."

"And that's exactly why I want the future to be promising—a fulfillment of dreams, not one of feeling stuck in something unbearable. If Zac is comfortable, I want him to visit, maybe spend a summer, or a part of one, in Florida whenever he can."

"I won't let you take him away from me."

"No one is going to do that, Raven."

"I'm afraid he'll like you better. You'll buy him gifts, fail to discipline him when he needs it—" She wasn't even trying to stop the tears as they rolled down her cheeks. "I'll be the tough guy and you'll be the easy one, the one he'll run to every chance he gets. I've had friends in situations like this. It's never good."

"Then we'll make certain that it is."

"How?"

"I don't know yet. We'll learn together how to do it—how to make it right. I want the three of us to sit down—you and Julie and me. She'll be here Wednesday. We'll carve out time to talk—maybe not reach any conclusions but get a start on what we want, what we think will work for all of us. We can do this."

Raven shook her head, reached for a Kleenex and blew her nose. "I'm not so sure. I wish I shared your optimism."

Chapter 12

Wednesday came all too soon but gave him two more near sleepless nights to worry about a meeting with Julie and run through a narrative that would somehow not paint him as a total villain. He discarded the 'too young to be responsible theory', and the 'too ego-involved in career at the time to even notice what was going on around him' let alone return phone calls from a former girlfriend—that explanation, however true, really painted him as a villain.

He strongly resisted referring to Raven as a brief summer fling. In fact, he dropped the word 'fling' from his vocabulary all together. They'd spent a lot of time in the sack and maybe it hadn't been much more than that to him, but again, one of those things he couldn't mention.

As awkward as this was going to be for Julie, his instincts and training warned him not to belittle a sister—

indicate in any way that he had used an eighteen-year-old for his pleasure. He had to walk a fine line between 'no, I wasn't in love with her but I cared', and 'yes, I want to do what's right—for both of them.'

And he knew he had to convince Julie that the decision was going to be a shared one—her input as well as his.

+ + +

Julie's arrival coincided with the ceremony for Brant. The burial had been postponed because Brant's mother was coming from Oregon and the weather had made travel dicey. Ben's welcoming potluck was on indefinite hold. But that was okay. It had given him time to establish his office and a schedule of events—community sessions to discuss solutions as well as problems.

So, now at three o'clock in the afternoon in foggy, near-darkness, he was watching Pete bring his two-seater in for a landing. He'd borrowed Uki's Outback and they would just have time to toss Julie's luggage in the back and get to the community center for the service. Service was probably a misnomer.

Already the body was tucked away in the garage and adjoining workshop of the mayor along with two others who had passed during the winter when it was too late for any digging. In addition, five other bodies, including three deaths by overdose, were languishing on shelves or in corners in wooden boxes with tight fitting lids in the out buildings of several parishioners. It was a service that the church provided free of charge.

Ben hoped someday he'd stop being shocked by how things were handled in this state. Alaska took a little getting used to.

He thought of home, the Pueblo with its cemetery flanking the village church. Its white-washed crosses, uniform in size and spaced evenly in rows, were decorated with wild flowers or never-fading plastic daisies or roses. In New Mexico a backhoe could still dig a decent sized burial plot even in January.

With a twinge he thought of his grandmother. Would friends still be tending her grave? Removing the ever-opportunistic weeds and wild thistles from around the white cross? Would the cross receive a fresh coat of paint when needed? But weren't these things his responsibilities? And when would he be able to go back? Certainly not in the foreseeable future.

Alaska felt so remote—removed from civilization. He sometimes had to remind himself that he was still in the United States. He needed to plan a trip home, maybe a trip that included Zac. The high, dry mesas of New Mexico were his heritage, too. Ben felt a little buzz of excitement at the thought of bringing his own son to see where he had grown up. But lots of things had to be decided before that could happen.

He didn't know how happy he would be to see Julie until Pete dropped the steps and helped Julie out of the plane. He didn't wait but rushed to pick her up, swing her around and whisper—probably one too many times—how much he'd missed her. The kiss was long and arousing. Intimate enough that a slightly embarrassed Pete cleared his throat and declared he needed help with 'this here luggage'.

"You feel good; you taste good … I'm beginning to regret a prior afternoon commitment. I think we should just go back to my room." Ben tossed Julie's luggage in back of the Outback and opened the passenger-side door then leaned in for one more kiss. "Do I tell you how much

I love you? I mean enough?"

Julie nodded and laughed, "I think I have the picture. I'm beginning to think a little separation is a good thing."

"Maybe it's because Miami seems like it's in another world—not like we can just jog over and see each other whenever we want."

"I'm here now and will be for the next month or two. It was a great stroke of luck that this assignment opened up."

"You know you don't have to go to the celebration of life for this guy—it's not like it was someone you knew."

"But I want to be supportive. It's important for you to be there, and I want to be with you."

He shifted the Outback into reverse, then moved forward on the slick asphalt and left the parking lot. As with all paved roads in the area, the one leading to town had to be replaced or significantly repaired every year. The parking lot was no different. There were no roads out of town, only airways. But maintenance was a good-paying job with the weather as security. The immediate ground around the terminal was clear of the overnight snow; so, Pete must have come in early. Air taxi pilot and ground crew of one—an interesting resume that was probably possible only in Alaska.

Ben found a parking spot to the side of the community center. Most had walked to the auditorium, and he saw several people he'd met. The mayor was leading a group of elders, holding only the outside door open wide enough for one person to pass at a time until the last individual had climbed the steps and entered. This was a community happening and Julie was right, he needed to be there.

Was he worried about some possible showdown with Raven? Yes, and no. He doubted she'd make any kind of public stand. The subject was private—just between the two of them as far as he knew. And, E.J.

He was glad to see that Julie was wearing a double thick down coat with a hood, and the inch-thick rubber soles on calf-high leather boots showed tufts of faux fur lining. He was pretty certain she hadn't gone shopping in Miami for the items but relied on her laptop and a credit card. Once inside she was reluctant to take off the parka and merely unzipped it slipping the hood back. Strawberry blond curls immediately took on a life of their own, tumbling to her shoulders. He knew he was staring but he loved the freckles that dotted the bridge of her nose and scattered across her cheeks. She always looked vibrant and alive to him. And the smile that crinkled flawless skin around her eyes; he'd never get tired of that.

"Sorry, I need to thaw first. My sea level blood is a little thin." But she pulled off sheepskin mittens and tucked a fairly frozen hand in his. "How do you stay so warm? You're actually hot."

"Hey, thanks for the compliment." Ben winked and folded her hand inside his. It felt so good to have Julie with him.

When he looked up, he saw Raven staring his way. She was standing with E.J., their mother and a group of five people who must be Brant's family. Zac was nowhere around. Probably best. A ten-year-old might have problems with this kind of ceremony. And Ben had no idea if Zac considered Brant his father. He wasn't sure how long Brant had been in the picture. But when Zac's friends did things with their dads, what explanation had been given to Zac's having a fatherless household? Despite the conversation with Raven, he reminded himself that there was a lot he didn't know.

However, it didn't mean he could put off telling Julie.

He tried to read Raven's expression but Uki chose that moment to demand that he introduce her to his 'lovely wife'. When he turned back, he could see that Raven's attention had drifted to Julie. No expression only those dark eyes seeming to take in the two of them before turning back to her group. This had to be beyond uncomfortable for Raven. More reason to dread any discussion that the three of them needed to have. And to be honest Ben had absolutely no idea what Julie's reaction would be. He took her arm and pointed toward the back of the room.

As always, refreshments came first. Two single-file lines moved slowly on each side of the folding tables which looked to be offering mostly desserts. Ben talked Julie out of her parka and moved to hang it on one of several pegs next to the door.

"Follow me, there's a couple dishes I want you to try." The nearest line was twenty people deep and Ben noticed that instead of a somber gathering, those in the food line as well as those sitting in the auditorium, were smiling and even laughing. Not the somber event he was expecting.

Even Julie remarked on the lightheartedness that seemed to prevail. "This feels like a celebration of life."

"The village has lived with hardship all its existence. This is a pretty unforgiving environment. We're probably seeing the result of coping skills that have been honed over the years. It would be too easy to sink into depression. Celebrating the positives makes sense." Ben took two paper plates off the stack on the card table next to the food and kept one for himself.

"What do you recommend? Those?" Julie was eyeing a plate of doughnuts obviously fresh out of their store-bought wrapper.

"Not those. The native desserts are not to be believed. Trust me on this."

"You've become an expert pretty quickly."

"Akutaq—Alaskan ice cream—that's what you want to try. I know for a fact that Uki's is made with tundra berries, Salmonberries and Cloudberries. And she doesn't put fish in it."

"A dessert with fish?" Julie had found the bowl full of a purple-red mixture mid-table but put her plate down.

"The original recipe called for boiled fish. Akutaq is a Yup'ik word for 'mixed together'. Every family has its own recipe that's been handed down for generations."

Gingerly, Julie spooned a small amount onto her plate then took a bite. "Oh my gosh, this is wonderful." She plopped another heaping spoonful onto her plate. "Anything else you recommend?"

"I'm told you'll never go to any Alaskan celebration without finding something smoked—like that platter of salmon on the end. I'd suggest trying that." The pink-orange strips of filet were dotted with capers and resting on slices of lemon. How much did a lemon cost in Alaska, Ben wondered. More than he'd want to pay probably. Finally, they were both finished and Ben carried the two paper plates to the closest trash can.

Someone had brought a player and a stack of CDs, presumedly some of Brant's favorites, and music suddenly filled the room. Those who weren't already seated hurried to claim a folding chair. A row of speakers sat on the dais.

The first was Brant's high school basketball coach. He extolled the talents of a young man with promise. The next speaker flashed several overhead slides of a Sea Hawk recruit—a rookie who started his season as a wide receiver who recovered a fumble and dove for a touchdown his very first game. His mother and sister spoke about a loving son and brother who bought them a house and made their life easier.

Raven completed the speakers and spoke of a good friend who struggled with demons and lost. Ben winced. If he'd been here last week or last month, could he have made a difference? It only underlined the need for a clinic. After the ceremony a few gathered to have another helping off the food table. Ben introduced Julie to E.J. and made sure that Uki had a ride home if he took her car. Uki had volunteered for cleanup and then was going home with her sister.

"The house will be all yours until dinnertime." Ben acknowledged Uki's wink and sly smile with a whispered, "thank you."

Then he was in the car with Julie—backing out, turning right on what was Main Street. Julie leaned over and took his hand.

"You're quiet."

"Just reflective."

"There's no doubt about how much you're needed here. Are you worried about meeting those needs? Maybe not having the support of the community?"

"Not really, I guess. The problem has gone on long enough. I think the village as a whole wants a change. I hate to say it but Brant's death made my case."

"Brant seemed to have been well liked."

"Local kid made good. Positive stories help keep kids in school."

"There's something tremendously sad to think of his life ending in his thirties."

Ben nodded as he turned into the short driveway behind Uki's house.

"Was Raven married to Brant?"

"I, uh, don't think so. They had been living together in Anchorage and just returned to the village maybe six months ago."

"Raven is beautiful, isn't she? I mean a little too much ink for me, but in spite of it, she's really striking. I wonder how much of her body is covered with tats."

Don't overreact, Ben admonished himself. This was not a trap to see if he'd seen her naked. Julie was still completely innocent of any details involving his relationship with Raven, but he needed to change that. He gave an 'I have no idea' shrug and slight shake of his head.

He helped Julie retrieve a small bag from the trunk, then carried her larger suitcase upstairs. As usual, the back door was unlocked—another reminder that he was living in a small town. Julie followed him across the living room and up to his bedroom.

"I love this area. Actually, I love the whole house."

"You were expecting an igloo?"

"Don't make fun of me. I'm not sure what I expected— maybe not this level of civilization."

"I'm going to make coffee. Any takers?"

"I'd love some." Julie unzipped her larger bag and was already shaking out clothing and heading toward the closet. "Give me a few minutes. Think Uki might have an iron?" She held up a particularly wrinkled white blouse.

"I'd put money on it. See you downstairs."

Ben was sitting at the dining room table when Julie joined him. "Cups are first cabinet left of the sink. Half and Half in the fridge. Follow me." He pushed back from the table and walked to the kitchen.

"This house is a pictorial museum. Would Uki mind if I recorded all this history?" She pointed to the framed articles on the walls.

"I think she'd be flattered. She's thought of as a kind of local historian."

Julie got a mug out of the cupboard, then set it on the counter, turned and leaned back. "Ben, what's wrong? After that bang-up greeting when I got off the plane, you've been distant. I didn't expect to spend an afternoon in bed, but the idea had crossed my mind."

He turned to face her, "I guess I'm afraid of your reaction to what I have to tell you."

"It can't be that bad." She took his two hands in hers. "Just tell me."

"Then let's get comfortable." He kept her hand in his and walked back through the dining room. "This looks good." He pointed to a sofa with a couple too many throw pillows.

He sank down, turned to face her and just started at the beginning. Grad school, best friend's sister, her eighteen to his twenty-four, three months, lots of hormones, then nothing until the brother recommended him for this job— ten years later. Ten years and a ten-year-old. *His* ten-year-old. A setup? Yes. He could see that now. No, Raven didn't know he was coming. Would he ever have met his son had E.J. not intervened? Maybe years later in some Ancestry. com scenario. But as fate would have it—and, yes, he believed in fate—he met his son in an airport and got to spend time getting to know him without the pressure of knowing he was his father.

Julie sat there, staring at a point in the middle of the

room, her face paler than ever. Then came the questions:

Had he been in love with Raven? Three months was too little time to tell.

Why didn't he answer Raven's calls? He was too wrapped up in grad school and his future—he was callous and young, ego-driven, and blind to those around him.

She never asked for money? Too proud.

Is she asking for money now? No. She's established a business here in Moose Flats and will move with the village when it's relocated.

But surely she wants a trust for her son—a college fund? Whether she does or not, I want to make one available.

What does this do to the family we've talked about having? I don't see that it changes that. Granted a teenager and a toddler might not be the combination we thought would make up our family, but it's doable; we'll make it work.

What do you want to do now? I'd like to work on a visitation schedule. But that depends on you.

When will I meet him? Soon, I hope. He's on spring break so will only be here for a couple weeks. We need to decide on something that might work for next summer.

Finally, the end of questions. Ben waited but Julie just stared into space.

"I'm sorry. I had no idea." He reached for her hand and she didn't pull away.

"I believe that. I know you would never have kept something like this from me. It's just awkward. How much can a ten-year-old understand … accept?"

"I always remind people that children are resilient. In a lot of ways, it was a good thing that we had time together before finding out there was a father/son relationship."

"And Raven? My being here makes things awkward."

"Yeah, I can't dispute that, but the quicker we're all able

to sit down and decide on the next moves, the better."

Julie nodded, but Ben watched as she walked to the window, stood and stared at a gray, bleak landscape. She was slightly slumped against the casement and looked for all the world like someone who had had all the air knocked out of them. She only roused to dab at tears that welled up.

Chapter 13

Y ou certainly weren't thinking of your sister when you brought this Ben Pecos here. Now, there's the new wife to contend with." Ahnah Takanni leaned back against the kitchen sink, arms folded.

"Give it a rest, Mama. I did it for Zac. He has every right to know his father—to benefit from knowing him."

"And you think that's going to happen without a lawsuit? Maybe it gets ugly and Ben demands DNA testing. How will that make Zac feel?"

"Have faith. Ben's fair—honest and fair. They won't need lawyers to work through things, and I don't think it's going to take a DNA test to prove a truth I think he already knows. You worry too much."

"I won't see my babies hurt. You don't have children let alone a wife, you don't understand this mess you've created. Needlessly created, I might add."

"You haven't given them a chance to work things out."

"How do you *work out* ten years of neglect? Answer me that."

"I trust Ben. Yes, I've been angry—but angry with Raven, too. It was her responsibility to do what was right for Zac—to make certain he knew his father. I was merely in a position to bring everyone together. I gave up waiting for Raven to do the right thing."

"How can you know … be so certain that you've done the right thing, as you call it?"

"Zac told me about meeting his dad. He liked Ben; he connected with him."

"Oh, two hours in an airport and he's *connected*. Well, of course, that makes everything A-okay."

"Give it a rest, Mama. I don't need your snide comments. I'd hoped you'd be supportive."

"We'll see. The cake isn't out of the oven yet."

"What is that supposed to mean?"

A shrug and Ahnah Takanni walked out of the kitchen calling over her shoulder, "Help your sister feed the dogs."

That seemed to be the end of that conversation. E.J. grabbed his parka from a peg by the door and waved at Raven from the back porch.

"Need help?"

"Always, but I was just on my way in to save you from our mother's finger-pointing. She means well but she can be a little overbearing. I'm sorry she's reacting this way."

"Yeah, I hope she doesn't upset Zac."

"Me, too." Raven pointed to a row of white buckets lined up in front of her. "Grab a couple and let's go."

"Where's Zac?"

"In the barn playing with the puppies. He's already named one Romo and is begging me not to sell it."

"That's all you need, another dog."

Raven just smiled. "I had the first Romo when I was his age. I think it's good that he has something to take care of, you know, rely on—under the circumstances. And it will make him want to come visit more often. I'm hoping he'll want to get involved with racing someday." She picked up a bucket and walked across the yard.

"Speaking of visits, have you decided what you want from Ben? Have you two had a chance to talk—make plans?" E.J. held open the barn door pulling the weather-lock seal closed behind them.

"No! No plans! I want nothing from Ben Pecos. I don't want Zac near him." Raven whirled and pushed her bucket into his mid-section knocking him backwards against the door. "I hate you. I didn't ask for this. You didn't even give me the courtesy of input. You just decided your read on things was the right one. We started this conversation once before; I guess now we need to finish it."

"Meaning?"

"There are things I will and will not do."

"Okay, like what?"

"I will not share my son. Not after ten years. Not with someone who is really a stranger to me after all this time. I don't know this man … and his wife. I don't want my son buffeted back and forth, maybe getting caught in the middle of one side playing off the other."

"Those are unreal fears. Ben's a psychologist, for God's sake; he's sensitive to the parameters of this whole thing."

"Are those his words? He's 'sensitive' to the situation?"

"Raven, be reasonable."

"Just like you have been?"

"Maybe I assumed too much, but I was thinking of my own childhood, our childhood. We watched our mother struggle after our father died. I watched you mourn the man who had been your best friend growing up; who introduced you to all this." E.J. swept his hand across in front of him to include the dogs. "Maybe you're not saying it but you've come back to avenge his honor—to win, make your mark in the Iditarod. Do what Dad never did."

"Funny but I can't hear any real caring in your voice. Did our father's life, his goals, mean anything to you? You had just graduated from high school when he died—a whole year early with a scholarship to the University of Washington. You left, E.J., you were gone before your father's body was put in the ground. You didn't spend eight years with a stepfather who beat your mother. You didn't have to lock your bedroom door every night knowing that if you didn't, he would attack you. You can't give up caring, pretending these things didn't happen and walk away expecting to reappear and make decisions for everyone. Life goes on; I've *moved* on. I think I've forgiven Ben. I want to believe I have anyway. I only know that I haven't forgiven you."

"You don't mean that. You know I only have your best interests in mind—yours and Zac's."

"Oh, of course, that's why one month from race-day, you introduce a crisis. Embroil this family in something that would take my concentration away from the race, away from a hundred thousand-dollar investment that I've dreamed of making pay off for me and for my father. All these years of planning, and dreaming—it's something that has kept me going. I know now it was wrong to bring

Brant back here, expose him to old habits and old grudges; but I can save myself. I can make being here work for me and continue to make the right decisions for my son. He doesn't deserve a meddling uncle who has never even taken the time to get to know him."

"Take it easy, Raven. That's not exactly fair."

"I'll tell you what's not fair, what people are whispering about—they say Brant was murdered, that he was setup to die, introduced to all the wrong people and tempted by contraband cut with a lethal dose of fentanyl. And you know what else? Every single person repeating that story points a finger at you. You're the killer. Oh, maybe you didn't pull the trigger, but you had him setup to die."

"What? C'mon, Raven, that's bullshit. You know better than that. What motive would I have?"

"Maybe that he beat me." Once again, she held his stare daring him to look away. "You see, there's lots of things you can pretend that you don't know—deny what happened to me, and your mother. But you knew. And your conscience made you try to make amends. You know I'm telling the truth about Ed Johnson. Isn't that why you left? He beat you, too, only you abandoned us and got away. You turned your back on your responsibility. How does that make you any better than Ben Pecos? At least, Ben didn't know he was responsible for a family."

This last Raven yelled after him as he had already turned and handed his bucket to one of the handlers coming in the barn's double doors. He paused and glanced back but decided enough had been said.

He cut diagonally across the dog yard and up the steps to the porch, but not before he had seen a pair of small dark eyes peeking around the partition to the food storage room. How much had Zac heard? Stuff a ten-year-old didn't need to hear. Wouldn't the kid be better off away from this godforsaken place?

Ben was a guarantee that he'd have a good life—all the amenities. He stamped the snow off his boots and opened the kitchen door. Maybe he should make sure that Zac got the chances he deserved.

Chapter 14

Millennials. Pete leaned back against the fuselage of the twin-engine Cessna and watched as three young men pulled bags and duffles from his plane's baggage compartment. Pain-in-the-ass, opportunistic, the world owes me mentality—but they paid well for a plane ride out of Anchorage and a guide. He knew they weren't outdoorsmen, but for the life of him, he couldn't figure out what could be of interest in Moose Flats.

Well, one was here to interview with Dr. Pecos for an intern's position, but the other two? He thought three of their larger cases held camera equipment. Maybe they were with *National Geographic*. Naw, that didn't make sense. However, the oldest of the three flashed newspaper credentials. Still, this wasn't exactly a scenic wonderland. But they were dressed for the cold, must not be their first trip to the state.

"Can we get a cab around here? My cell doesn't seem to work." The tallest young man turned to Pete.

"Where you going?"

"Let me check." He rummaged in his duffle and pulled out an envelope with some scribbling on the side. "A hotel called the U-K. Might be some English establishment. Hope to hell it has a pub."

Pete choked back a laugh. "No hotel, more of a boarding house owned and operated by Uki—that's 'you-key'. Kakee's the last name. Only rental in town. Guess I should refer to it as a B and B—no pub, but the food's more 'an a little good. You won't be disappointed. How long you staying?"

"Couple weeks, doing a story on the race, going to feature Raven Takanni. You know, from the angle of daughter avenges father's record. He's still Alaska's most celebrated second place winner of the Iditarod since the race began. It'll be a nice human-interest piece for the *Times*. That's Seattle, not New York, in case you're wondering."

Yeah, like he'd confuse the two, Pete thought. Might be time to dress the part of a pilot—leather aviator jacket once it got warmer, some kick-ass boots with a side buckle … probably wouldn't make a difference but the grease-monkey flannel shirt and jeans under a dirty parka certainly didn't scream GQ. Somehow seemed to take points off his IQ, too.

"I gotta car in back of the terminal. Be glad to give you a ride." He picked up the nearest black case and duffle. "Follow me."

It was obvious that once they got to the house, Uki was expecting them. A fresh pot of coffee on a warming plate sat in the middle of the dining room table surrounded by a tray of smoked salmon sprinkled with dill sprigs. Probably the very same ones he'd brought her from Anchorage just last week. He'd had a hell of a time finding dill that wasn't shredded and dried in a jar. A plate of deviled eggs and homemade pickles sat next to a foil-lined box of brownies.

He knew whose contribution those were. The other half of the Two Sisters Bakery, Ahnah Takanni. Those brownies were famous. Actually anything those two baked was worth writing home about. Those boys wouldn't be disappointed. He'd try to sneak a brownie when no one was looking.

Uki had propped a note against a carafe of water offering an apology for not being home to greet them and went on to explain that this was her day to volunteer at the library. Apparently flu shots were today's special. There was a copy of her house rules and directions to the rooms set aside for guests ending with a 'dinner at six' and the suggestion 'don't be late.'

Once the young men were settled in, Pete excused himself. He had an hour to kill before heading back to Anchorage, and he needed to finalize plans to fly Raven's two dog teams to Anchorage for the start of the race. It was still three weeks off, starting as usual the first Saturday in March, but he needed the dimensions of the dogs' crates—even the ones that would be folded and placed in the baggage compartment.

Raven was picking up the tab for a commuter-sized plane modified for carrying cargo, and Pete already had plans to pick it up in Tacoma a week ahead of time. Still, he didn't want to leave anything to the last minute. This was a big deal. He'd help her any way he could. He'd watched Raven grow up, and it wasn't easy as an outsider to see the suffering. But she'd made it, gotten away and become successful. He couldn't be more proud if he were her own papa.

And Zac—now there was one smart kid. She'd done a good job raisin' him all by herself. He'd wondered what SOB had abandoned a teenager with a child. There'd be some reckoning if he ever found out.

He drove to Raven's and parked on the backside of the dog yard. Looked like thirty-some dogs were just finishing breakfast. He liked to watch the dogs. Most were Alaskan from the only three breeds recognized as true sled dogs: purebreds like the Alaskan Malamute, and the Siberian Husky with one mixed breed, the Eskimo dog or Alaskan Husky. Only the Malamute was a descendant of the Arctic wolf. Hardy and all heart. Other breeds were seen in the old days—Samoyeds and Chinook—but the Iditarod now only allowed northern breeds to compete. Back in the '80s, a musher named John Suter ran a dog team that included poodles.

That always made Pete smile. Poodles. It was finally ruled that poodles didn't have the undercoat of fur to protect them from the harsh elements, so their fifteen minutes of fame was quickly over. Got 'em on Johnny Carson, though, back in the day. But now the dogs in front of him sported thick coats that made them look like miniature bears. Winter didn't bother them. Mushing almost a thousand miles in nine to twelve days was in their DNA. They could pull a heavy load and just keep on going, steady and sure. But that was a problem. Unless the musher wanted the Red Lantern award by coming in last, the Malamute didn't have the speed to win or even be that overall competitive.

Almost the same problem with the Siberian Huskies. Born runners, immune to ice and cold, team players, eager to please, but just not quick enough to race at the front. Raven's father was one of the first breeders who perfected the cross-bred Alaskan Husky. He'd left his mark on the Iditarod—not with multiple wins but with the knowing that his dogs comprised every team that crossed the line first. His was a special combination of breeds—Malamutes, Siberian Huskies, German Shorthair Pointers, Salukis and his own special contribution, the Anatolian or Turkish mastiff. There was even a plaque in front of the high school that recognized his dedication to the sport and highlighted his contributions.

Ol' Tom's dogs might not be an AKC recognized breed; nevertheless, Pete had hauled enough Eskimo sled dogs around to appreciate their top-notch canine racing abilities. His dogs represented years of research and success, as well as failure, to produce that one type of dog designed specifically for one task—racing. Some breeders had even added the wolf to the breeding mix, but not Raven's father, who felt the wild strain was too unpredictable and took too many generations to breed down to where it added positive factors that were inheritable.

Pete sighed. He missed Tom Takanni. Scuttlebutt had it that Raven had found direct descendants of her father's line of breeding at a racing kennel outside Anchorage, and had bought the bunch outright. He had to admit that would make a good story—maybe those newspaper kids from the lower forty-eight were on to something. With Raven racing it sure added an interesting element. One that got his blood flowing for sure.

In the old days he would fly cargo in and spend an

overnight or two to just hang out with Tom and the dogs. Home was Fairbanks, a big city, so time spent in the village was exciting and challenging, and if truth were known, an insider's perspective on the racers had put a dollar or two in his pocket by way of the bookies. He was planning on making a modest wager this year in his old friend's name by placing five hundred on his daughter.

If he had regrets, it was that he'd let that bastard, Ed Johnson, make a move on Tom's widow. He could understand why Ed won out—settled, a profession that put him in constant demand unlike his own faltering career after the airline strike put him at the mercy of anybody who needed a pilot, from tourists to someone selling home appliances. Big airlines weren't hiring and the independents didn't pay all that well.

But if the rumors were true, Ed Johnson was no catch, being controlling and mean to live with and hellbent on destroying Tom's legacy. A drunk Ed Johnson was accused of twice defacing Tom's commemorative plaque. And there was that time he'd seen the bruises on Ahnah's cheek. A man who would do that deserved to die. But working part time in Washington and Oregon, six months out of every year, gave Ahnah some respite. And some money.

Pete was sure that when every spare nickel went to the dogs, it had been difficult to get ahead. Tom was pretty much married to those dogs. And then there was that rumor about Ahnah's sister not keeping her knickers up and a young Tom fathering a child ... but that was a tale that Pete found hard to believe. Just more gossip aimed at taking down those who were successful. Man, a village could be just plain vicious. There were probably lots of reasons that he lived in Fairbanks.

It was a foregone conclusion that Ahnah wouldn't keep the packs when she lost Tom. So, the dogs were scattered, sold to the highest bidders. Raven was too young to take over her father's program and E.J. didn't care. Pete had watched the family disintegrate. He would never quite get over his friend's death. There had been no warning—one minute planning to participate in the Fur Rendezvous Festival in late February near Anchorage, and then he was gone, found in the barn with a single gunshot to the head.

The coroner immediately ruled it a suicide but Pete always had had his doubts. Yet, foul play didn't make sense either. Easy-going, animal lover, family man, give you the shirt off his back kind of guy. What had he missed? Pete guessed there was just no knowing the inner workings of a person's mind. Even a good friend could be in the dark. If a person had demons, it was tough to run them out. Wasn't the whole village hoping that this Dr. Pecos would be some kind of Pied Piper for the crazies?

"You gonna just hang out with the dogs or come in and get warm?"

He'd been so deep in thought that Raven had walked up behind him and he hadn't heard her. "Got anything liquid in that barn that's on the warm side and brown?"

"Like a cup of coffee?"

"Now you're talking." Pete followed her into the building.

"Uncle Pete, look." Zac was carrying a very fuzzy ball of fur whose hind legs almost reached his knees. "This is Romo. Mom said I could have him."

Zac carefully placed the roly-poly puppy on the ground, then plopped down himself and pulled the puppy back on his lap. "He's really smart. Mom said he could be a racer."

"Mom said *maybe*." Raven interjected. "He needs to grow a little, then we'll start training."

"That's why I can't take him back to school with me. He'll be in school while I'm in school."

"Sounds like a good deal," Pete added. "Both of you getting smart at the same time." Pete squatted down and gave Romo a pat on the neck and then scratched behind one ear. The puppy responded with some licks to his hand but stayed close to Zac. Some pretty strong bonding had already taken place, that was for sure. Looked like Zac had inherited old Tom's way with dogs. Pete only wished his grandfather was around to see.

"Can I tell Uncle Pete our secret?"

"Then it wouldn't be a secret." Raven knelt down to pet Romo. "But go ahead if you'd like to."

"I'm going to be home-schooled this spring so that I can help Mom with the Iditarod. I'll miss a whole month from school."

"Now, I'm jealous. Sounds like something I'd like to do." And he wasn't lying, Pete thought to himself. It would be exciting to take part in the pre and post activities. Anchorage made a big deal out of the race. It got world-wide attention. Surely, she didn't mean Zac would run the race. They had to have age limits on mushers. But to work with the dogs, help with preparations—that would be the opportunity of a young lifetime.

"Maybe my dad will come with us."

"Dad?" Pete looked to Raven for explanation. But she shook her head.

"Now, that's a secret that we shouldn't share. Remember?"

"Oh, yeah, I forgot." Zac looked crestfallen. "I'm sorry."

"Why don't we get Uncle Pete that cup of coffee and a treat for Romo? Maybe offer some chum jerky to Pete, too?"

Pete made his best "phew" face sticking out his tongue and making up-chucking noises. It got the result he wanted as Zac laughed.

"No, Uncle Pete wants one of Aunty's brownies, don't you?" Raven offered.

"I betcha I'd sit up and beg and even rollover for one. Let's go see if I know any tricks." Pete put a hand on Zac's shoulder and they turned toward the barn's kitchen.

Chapter 15

Awkward. That was probably the best word, Ben thought. He and Julie had spent a restless night—lots of tossing and turning and then finally holding. No lovemaking but just taking her in his arms and once again whispering all the words he wanted to say and she needed to hear.

Still, morning came too quickly. His job was challenging enough without this wrinkle—double wrinkle, now that Julie was there.

He had his first possible intern flying out from Anchorage for an interview, and he had an idea that he wanted to run by Marie. He needed Julie to feel at home, have her own place to work from. And he wanted to surprise his wife. He needed something to say 'I'm thinking about you; I want you close to me; you belong here.' Fingers crossed that he was on the right track.

+ + +

A desk for Julie in the corner of Ben's office was Marie's idea after Ben had mentioned wanting to find work space for his wife and sought her opinion. Partitioned off by folding screens decorated with red and black Haida art, whales and ravens and a particularly cute stylized otter, the almost translucent canvases in three frames, some four feet wide by eight feet tall, offered surprising privacy. The space was perfect—a corner all her own—made better by the addition of a four-drawer standing file cabinet and newly constructed shelving above the desk.

Julie was thrilled, and she sensed Ben's hand in setting up her new office. He knew it would be a relief not to have to carry all her paperwork back and forth. She'd still consider Anchorage her headquarters, but a new opportunity meant that she might spend the bulk of her time in Moose Flats.

She'd had a meeting earlier in the morning with the mayor, and he had asked her to sit in on the community's governing board as a consultant. She would be able to share the thinking and planning of Miami's finest lawyers and geophysicists. Invaluable input considering the timeframe for moving the first Alaskan village was fast approaching. But what a study in contrasts—slick Miami with its yachts and glitterati having something in common with a struggling fishing village some four thousand, three hundred and ninety-five miles away.

The gravity of both situations was just beginning to

sink in. This was life or death for two opposite ways of life—one affluent and one barely surviving.

She sank down into a surprisingly comfortable, padded, swivel desk chair. Her job was fascinating, but at the moment more of a lifesaver—it was keeping her from thinking, dwelling on the fact that her new husband was already a father. She couldn't help but think that the thrill of being a first-time parent was already squandered on a situation that he hadn't even known about and now it was shrouded in guilt and what-if's. And she was to become the stepmother of a ten-year-old. This wasn't how she had envisioned her marriage. Or her life.

To be fair it wasn't Zac's fault. He was the one who had really been cheated by circumstances. Not having a father for ten years and the fact that there was one now wasn't necessarily comforting, for anyone. For example, what was everyone's expectations? She certainly knew hers were unclear.

What did she want? Better yet, what would be best for Zac? A traveling, long-distance, step-mother by proxy? That didn't seem fair even if visits weren't for an entire summer vacation and only lasted a couple weeks at a time. No, Ben was a part of her life and Zac was now a part of his. It wasn't just working out the details; it was working out the whole scenario.

She knew she needed to be a team player, shelve any hurt feelings and be a supporter, not an impediment—Ben deserved that and so did Zac. She had the start of a plan. She just needed to give it more thought. It involved making a friend out of Raven and was based on pretty solid female intuition. She just needed the right time to implement it.

She took her laptop out of its case and plugged it into

a surge protector that she carried with her. She'd seen two surge protectors on Ben's desk. Electricity as a steady source would be spotty, she guessed.

Travel to remote areas made her more electronically savvy and Moose Flats didn't instill confidence. She'd read that a lot of villages relied on oil run generators to produce electricity and that equipment needed to be upgraded. With the move imminent, five million in funds to rework the system probably wouldn't pass the fiscal watchdogs. Who would want to invest in a place that was soon to be abandoned?

Just one more in what was probably a hundred everyday problems that would need to be addressed. And made the move something that had needed to have happened yesterday.

If she could find a guide, today would be spent scouting the territory. First, she needed pictures and a tour of the village. She knew that erosion had devastated a part of the community—houses had already been sucked into the river or were balancing on the edge waiting on the next surge of water to slide under. How were people managing? How many families had already moved to get out of the reach of the river? Maybe doubling up with relatives until their town council had concrete answers and a place to start over.

She should set up interviews as well as take photos. Maybe Marie would know of several good contacts—she wanted to talk with people directly impacted—those whose families had lived in Moose Flats for centuries and now had to leave. Human interest—wasn't that what always sold papers? Even those online?

She heard Marie come back from lunch and walked

to her office. Native art, paintings and a hand carved, decorated miniature totem gave Marie's office the feel of a small, but select art gallery.

"I love the artwork. Is it all Alaskan?"

"Oh, it's all from local, that is, Alaskan artists. One more piece and I'll have to relocate." A quick laugh, "I guess I'm doing that anyway. Maybe I'll have more room in my new office."

"Any idea when that might be?"

"The municipal buildings—that includes the high school and auditorium—are on high ground, not in immediate danger; so, I'm thinking we'll go last."

"There have been no announcements? Of who's going first or last? I guess I was expecting some sort of lottery at the very least. I'm assuming that the move will be piece-meal, not all at once?"

"You've got that right. And if it goes any slower, we'll be here for the next Ice Age."

"Why so slow?"

"Try a lack of government funding. People at the top have their heads in the sand—make that the snow—when it comes to global warming. If they don't live with the consequences, see those consequences every day; then, it's out of sight, out of mind. That's why I'm so excited about what you're doing. Getting the word out is the best weapon we have."

"I need to assess the damage to the village and take photos. Is there anyone I could arm-twist into being my guide?"

"Your best bet there would be the Police Chief, Ronnie Pitka."

"How do I reach him?"

"Just walk over. He's in the building behind this one. If there's a cruiser with a dented passenger's-side door, then he's in."

"I'm looking for a dented patrol car?"

"Yeah, the moose was bigger than a fifteen-year-old Crown Vic. Or so he'd like to have us think."

+ + +

The quilted down coat, shearling hat with ear-flaps and lined woolen mittens weren't very much of a fashion statement but they had proved perfect for the moist, but clear day in Moose Flats. Sunrise had been at ten a.m. and sunset would be about ten minutes to six that evening. Not quite eight hours of daylight!

Well, sort of a gray, hazy light. Nothing that screamed out for sunscreen. And the temps? A blistering high of minus sixteen and a low of minus twenty-five. Before she left the office, Marie reminded her that the windchill made it feel like minus forty-one and to bundle up. How could anyone ever get used to this? Live in it? Julie found herself wistfully thinking of Miami.

She rounded the corner of the village government building and saw the Crown Victoria with a dent on the passenger's side sitting squarely in front of a pair of double doors. The building looked small but official with an Alaskan State seal over the entry.

No one was manning the information desk; in fact, there didn't seem to be a chair behind it. Even the single typed sheet taped to the desk's front edge claiming that this was the place where information could be retrieved was frayed at the edges and yellowed. But then in a township of a few hundred, who would need an information "center"?

"Hello there. Ms. Pecos, isn't it?" A burly, solid man whose circumference might be held in place by a corset but whose broad shoulders were challenging the very fabric of his flannel shirt, stepped out of what was probably his office—in stocking feet.

Holding up a red and black striped stockinged foot, he pointed to a kerosene heater just outside his door. "Got my boots wet digging my deputy out of a snowbank. Looks like they might be done." A pair of heavy-soled, leather-topped boots were leaning dangerously close to the stove. "Yep, these are toasty now."

He pulled up a folding chair, sat down and proceeded to pull his boots on. "How can I help you?"

Julie explained what she needed and asked for his recommendation of a tour guide.

"I'd expect you could use some maps, too, am I right?"

"That would be great."

"Well, as for a guide, I think you're looking at him. I've got a couple hours free this afternoon and I could acquaint you with the layout of the village then turn you loose to talk with folks and take some pictures."

"Exactly what I need. I appreciate your help."

"I'm Ronnie Pitka, by the way, but I bet you already knew that." The grin was engaging. "That Marie is a blabbermouth." This time there was an outright laugh.

Julie smiled. "She did give me a name."

"I bet she did … probably made light of that moose that tried to kill me last year, too, right?"

By now Julie was laughing, "I was told to look for a dented patrol car."

"Nothing's sacred in this place. You'll have to get used to that."

He grabbed a fur-lined parka, a hat and scarf and held the door open for the two of them to go back outside. "We'll take my car—it's just a little too far to walk in this temp and I don't much like taking a cab."

"There are cabs?"

"About five but that depends on who has a tank of gas, and that's a fact. Fewer than ten percent of the population owns a car. Everyone relies on cabs to get around—sort of the original Uber community—but it's seasonal work. In good weather, people walk. You may have noticed we're not some sprawling metropolitan area. About two miles start to finish." Another quick laugh and Chief Ronnie opened the passenger side door of the cruiser grimacing when it took an extra tug just to open to a grinding, popping noise. "Moose sure didn't do me any favors."

"Does insurance cover moose encounters?"

"Out here? 'Fraid you're on your own. Finding someone to fix it is the biggest problem. I'd have to put it on a barge come spring to ferry it out of here and God knows when I'd get the car back. No, better to just live with a few bumps and scrapes. Pound out what you can and ignore the rest."

"Life out here would take some getting used to."

"Not if you were born here and didn't know anything else. Let's see, first I'll take you out to the uninhabitable area to give you an idea of where we started. We'll have some walking to do but looks like you're dressed for it. We won't stay out long."

Chief Ronnie followed a snow-packed road that wound along the river, finally pulling over into a wide, cleared spot. They had reached the farthest inhabited point of the community.

"This area has no running water, so no sanitation.

Bathrooms are five-gallon buckets lovingly called 'honey buckets'. It's tough on those left. Several families have had to move in together. Some are still in houses that were originally evacuated due to flooding but with nowhere to go, they've moved back after the water receded. Come, walk with me; I want to show you where our new home will be."

Julie hadn't gone far when she stumbled, catching her heel on a loose plank in the board walk. The tundra was fragile and paths were a rotting grouping of single boards fastened together and wide enough for two people to walk abreast. Only now the wood had deteriorated and was as much a hazard as it was something that offered safe passage across frozen ground.

"Careful. Nothing gets repaired anymore if it's marked for removal anyway. But look over there—across the river—see the lights?"

"What is that?" The area was a couple miles away and it was difficult to determine where the lights were coming from but in the stillness, the hum of equipment was hard to miss—big equipment like earth-movers, she thought.

"Well, at the moment six half-built houses—well, at least the foundations—and the start of a municipal building. Or, our new home. So far, we're just referring to it as the Moose Flats Annex."

"Doesn't seem like a lot—not when you're having to move hundreds of people."

"But it's a start. That's the important thing. It's tangible proof that something is happening. It's hope, Ms. Pecos, that's hope you're looking at."

And a whole lot of despair, Julie thought but didn't give voice to her opinion.

"Let's walk a little closer and take a look at what's left on this side. It's still dangerous so I want you to stay on the walk."

"Has the erosion been sudden?"

"Sudden? Depends on how you define the word, I suppose. It's taken twenty years of melting perma-frost to reach this point. Take that container-condo over there. Family finally had to move. It's going to be in the river this spring. There's no retrieving it now."

Julie looked at the large metal box with a pitched roof and one tiny window cut high, near the roof on one end. The opposite end of the structure was tipping so radically that half the house was not anchored to the ground at all but actually stuck up in the air—a stationary see-saw effect that illustrated the danger and fate all the buildings along the shoreline were facing.

Julie took a number of pictures with the Nikon she almost always had with her, a habit learned in Journalism classes. She made sure she captured the remnants of a life past—a broken plastic trike, discarded swing set, a rusted snow machine on its side, several garbage cans dented and useless.

"Everything in the river's path needs attention now—houses, docks, the playground at the end of the street. The structures a block back from the river's edge will probably be put on hold. They won't be moved until the more needy ones are addressed. But no one wants to admit that nothing can be done without the funding to make the move, and that's at a standstill. Funding has suffered from missed deadlines, lost paperwork to just plain old misappropriation. We even had a contractor with his hand in the till. You name it and it's happened to these people living this close to water."

"There's something incredibly sad about all this. I'm not seeing one building that's not in danger including those a block away. It's only a matter of time, I would think, before all of this area becomes part of the river bed."

"You're right there. Everything you see has been condemned."

"But people are still living in most of the structures—or it looks like they are."

"Yeah, if it can be called living when you're surrounded by mold from the flooding and the drywall has crumbled, maybe the ceiling has fallen in from moisture. It's not healthy but too many people don't have any other place to go."

"And the Annex, the new village, how is it better? It's right over there, maybe a couple miles away. Why isn't it in some kind of future danger?"

"It's on much higher ground for starters, away from the river's edge with a couple hundred acres of tillable land to the back. If it's possible to get fishermen to turn into part time farmers, a new way of life could save hundreds of people—give them a livelihood. Give their children a future. There are plans for field irrigation, and the start of the houses that we can see from here already have electric stumped in and piping for flush toilets that will be ready to connect to a sewage plant planned for later. There's even a structure planned for farming fish. Literally causing the river to detour into that south end of the Annex and feed fifty tanks of spawning fish. You're looking at some brilliant plans that will guarantee a centuries-old way of life will be saved, perpetuated on modern terms—you're looking at the future, Ms. Pecos."

"And I don't see any cargo crates. It sounds like the new houses will be just that—real houses."

"Thanks to the Cold Climate Housing Research Center or CCHRC in Fairbanks. Those guys are funded by the building industry to research in Alaska, try things here and not just borrow technologies from Canada and the lower forty-eight. It's made a difference. It's taken years to get to this point, a handful of new terrain and environment-savvy homes, and we need to continue.

"A lot of things make Alaska different. Shifting soils, for one thing, are a problem in many parts of Alaska. For example, technicians and builders need to be trained to build adjustable foundations. Foundations that flex, if you will. The emphasis needs to be on sustainable, healthy homes. Water treatment, sewage, electrical … it's like we're talking heaven on earth and it's been fifty years in the making. You might be looking at the future, at the start of one, but it's pitifully little and late."

Julie took a few notes and several more pictures before they turned to walk back up the rotting walk to the cruiser. What a downer. If taking drugs ever made sense, then the opioid crisis in this part of Alaska was a no-brainer—it was bound to happen, waiting to happen. How could people live in the conditions she'd just witnessed? Live and keep their spirits up as they watched their way of life implode. Was Ben's clinic doomed? How could he make a difference unless every agency, every government entity made good on their promises? And that meant money. A huge investment.

Chapter 16

The dogs seldom barked at night, huddled as they were in individual, thick, straw burrows. At minus twenty-six degrees and a wind-chill that could penetrate dense layers of undercoat, the dogs had to have a good reason to sound off and leave the warmth of their caves. Raven turned over in bed to listen.

This was warning barking, not the happy greeting barks when expecting food or attention from someone they knew. She quietly stood and began to dress. Something had started that chorus of thirty-odd voices—a bear? Maybe a mountain lion? This would be the first time since she'd returned home that the pack had been threatened by predators. She needed to patrol the grounds daily and make certain there were no mountain lion or bear paw prints outside the fence. If there were, the animals would be coming in for the stored food, not the dogs. But the dogs could turn into food, too.

She had a forest ranger tell her once that no matter what the size, domestic or wild, dogs and cats don't mix. So, maybe it wasn't a mountain lion. But the weak and young were always at risk. A hungry bear? It would be more brazen. Brute strength made them unpredictable and always dangerous. She grabbed the flashlight and shotgun kept by the back door for just such duty and slipped noiselessly out to the porch.

The flash of light coming from inside the barn lasted only a nanosecond—someone needing to use his or her flashlight to illuminate something—but what? At least she wasn't facing a grizzly—the flashlight ruled out four-legged trespassers. But who? Probably one of the kids who helped her. Maybe he'd forgotten something, like his phone. Service might be spotty in the area, but that teenage badge of acceptance was a necessity all the same.

But why wouldn't he turn on a light? Probably because electricity for the barn was produced by the generator that also provided power to the house and several large yard lights. And he'd know better than to upset the dogs and get them barking. No, no one who worked there would come back to the barn in the dead of night. Her helpers were thoughtful; young, yes, but still knowledgeable animal people and considerate of those they worked for. This was danger.

Whoever was in the barn was not someone she knew. She'd bet on that. She took several deep breaths, steadied her hand on the short-barreled gun and kept to the shadows, knowing the cacophony of sound coming from the dog yard would cover any noise she might make. She still had the element of surprise in her favor. And the feel of the gun was comforting. Her father's weapon of choice and if the story everyone told was true, it had been a life-saver not failing her father when he'd needed to face an angry bear. Would it protect her, too?

The fact that the barn was never locked wasn't comforting. Maybe she should change the rules. But who stole anything in a town of a few hundred people who all knew each other? Of course, drugs had led to problems, mostly fights and abuse, but few break-ins. However, no one would even think of looking for money in the barn.

And that was another thing. Had there been recent visitors to Moose Flats? Outsiders that she hadn't heard of? It wouldn't be too unusual for strangers to come to Moose Flats. Just unlikely this time of year. And unlikely it would be tourists at almost any time during the year. It was another story in the spring after the thaw and the river was open to travel and commerce. Not that many visited the remote village even then, but people, like contractors, even hired construction crews from the lower forty-eight, came and went during the year. Sometimes relatives from adjoining villages would visit, but she hadn't seen anyone new.

She stayed close to the building and slipped around to the back. Each partitioned area of the building had a small, two feet by three feet, triple-paned window near the roof line and under the overhanging roof's edge. Another pop of light and she realized that it wasn't someone briefly turning on a flashlight; no, this was someone photographing the interior of the barn. That was the flash of a camera.

Think. Why would anyone want to take pictures of her dog setup? The last flash had briefly illuminated the area of the barn where her office was located. That was strange. What would be of interest in there?

Curiosity, more than fear, took over. She carefully pulled the barn's heavy outer door open and squeezed past, gently pulling it shut. Once she got inside, the office was about fifteen feet to her right. She tucked her flashlight into her belt; she didn't dare use it but moved forward by touch and guided by a tiny stream of light coming from under the office door.

The intruder had something small, probably a penlight, and was keeping it aimed away from the window. Now she could hear the rustling of someone opening a file cabinet and rifling through papers. They weren't trying to be quiet, just fast—open one drawer, pull out what must be a folder, drop it to the floor, go onto another drawer. What could the person be looking for? Dog records? Breeding notes from back in her father's time? Who would be interested in those? And the big question was why?

The office door was open just a crack. In some sort of Wonder Woman move, she would kick the door open, flip the light switch on the wall to her left and keep the shotgun in her right hand, the short-stock butt balanced and steadied between her body and elbow—finger on the trigger. If the plan worked—and that was suddenly a big 'if'—she would have the element of surprise on her side.

The yelp followed by an expletive let her know the plan to surprise was successful. The young man staring at the shotgun had both hands in the air, and he was not someone she knew. Where in the world had he come from? And why was he in her barn?

"Don't shoot."

"And you're going to give me a good reason why I

shouldn't?" Raven decided she might as well have some fun. And this was a kid—maybe mid-twenties, but no older—parka thrown over a chair back, hooded, fleece-lined sweat shirt over thermal, cargo pants tucked into Zamberlan rough weather boots. My God, didn't those start at about three hundred and fifty dollars a pair? This was not a kid strung out looking for something to hock to make quick money. He just oozed pampered preppy from the lower forty-eight. So, why Moose Flats?

"I can explain."

"I'm waiting."

"I'm here to do a story on teams in the Iditarod race. Your story has all the human interest of a feature article. I'm with the *Times*—Seattle *Times*."

"And you had to break in to get what?"

"The door was open. I didn't break in."

"Anyone on this ground, in this building without being expressly invited is an intruder—door open or door locked. And do I have to mention it's two twenty-five in the morning? I think visiting hours end at COB."

"Could you put the gun down?"

"No. We're going to walk to the house and I'm going to call the Chief of Police. If you try to run, I will have every right to shoot you. There are a lot of frontier rules in rural Alaska—leftovers from more lawless times—but trespassing with intent to burgle is a crime. Disturbing, if not vandalizing property," she pointed at the scattered papers and folders on the floor, "is also a crime. I am well within my rights to protect my property."

"I wish you'd listen to me."

"Save it for law enforcement." She moved to the side, grabbed his parka and tossed it to him, watched him put it on—any move to put a hand in a pocket would have gotten him shot; maybe he knew that. Then she waved him toward the door, followed him, gun aimed squarely at his back. They crossed the dog yard and entered the kitchen.

"Sit here." She snagged the leg of a chair with the toe of her boot and pulled it away from the table.

Suddenly the door to the kitchen banged open. "What's going on? Oh my God, Raven what are you doing with your father's gun?"

"Mama, I just apprehended this young man in my office. Call Ronnie Pitka."

"What are you doing on my property? Who are you?" Ahnah, robe wrapped securely around her plump frame, black hair caught loosely at the nape of her neck, picked up a butcher knife from beside the sink. "Do I need to teach you a lesson?"

"Mama, put the knife down. Call Ronnie … now! Use my phone." Raven nodded toward the counter and her phone.

"You're crazy. Both of you. I'm outta here." He pushed the chair back and started to stand.

Raven took a step toward him, the barrel of the shotgun a foot from his chest, but not before her mother had slashed a two-foot slit in the sleeve of his parka. Feathers were bubbling out of the tear and floating haphazardly to the floor.

"Do I need to repeat myself? Your ticket out of here is in a police cruiser or a box. Your choice." He sat back down. "Now, Mama, I don't want any more heroics. Call Ronnie."

Ahnah put the knife down and reached for the phone, dialed the local emergency number, and put the phone back on the counter. There was no dispatcher but her address would show up on the Chief's phone and he would waste no time in reaching them. Ahnah picked up the knife before pulling a chair out from the opposite end of the table. She placed the knife in front of her, sat down, and kept a hand on it.

In a township with one paved main street less than two miles long that was kept more or less clear of snow in the winter, law enforcement could move in a hurry. Ronnie Pitka didn't even knock but just burst in the back door, gun drawn.

"Good God, who killed a goose in the kitchen? We talking nefarious wildlife or something on two legs like this here stranger?"

"That one." Raven pointed at the kid sitting in front of her with one hand but kept the other on the shotgun.

"Listen, I can explain all this. It's all a big misunderstanding. I just—"

"For starters, you just need to stay seated. I'm going to start with the basics. Name, home address, and purpose for being on Ms. Takanni's property." A quick look at Raven, "I'm assuming you haven't gotten this far? Don't have a name, or do you?"

Raven shook her head, mentioned the dogs sounding off at about two-fifteen and finding this young man rifling through the files in her office.

"Guess we're all going to hear the story at the same time. Floor's all yours." Ronnie Pitka holstered his gun and leaned against the counter. "I bet you have new respect for Alaskan women. She hurt you with that knife?" A shake of the head. "Then let's get this show on the road."

The young man turned to face the chief. "My name is

Andrew Cook. I live in Seattle. I work for the *Times* and I'm on assignment. I can show you my press badge."

"So far, so good—but I didn't hear any explanation for trespassing. Need to do a little better."

"I needed background for my story. This article is going to be a coup for the local musher—woman makes good on a promise to her father after twenty years. That's just about loaded with human interest and a little fame for you." He glanced over his shoulder at Raven.

"And you were looking through my files ... for what?"

"Anything. I need to impress my boss. I need a scoop, as they say, everybody and their uncle is covering the race. I have to have the angle, the one that will sell papers. Cut a guy some slack, I'm on your side."

"And that's an f-ing lie." This time the man who burst through the kitchen door already had his hands up. "I'm Dwight Rowland, I traveled here with that piece of scum. And I know for a fact he's being paid under the table by PETA. You want to know what he was looking for? Records on dogs that have been injured during a race or even practice—especially dogs that have died. There's a big push to shut down the Iditarod."

A muttered expletive and Chief Pitka just shook his head. "We don't need people from the outside telling us how to live, contradicting centuries of surviving in a place most would think was hell—a little on the cold side, but still hell. Dogs keep us alive, keep us in touch with our neighbors, deliver food and medicines, save lives ... who are you to tell us we're wrong? You have a problem with the Iditarod? We're just showing off, calling attention to what a team of finely tuned animals can do. How their talent is needed in this place and we depend on it. I've heard enough to take you down to the station. And you? What's your part in all this?"

"I also work for the *Times*, but no PETA for me. I personally think they do more harm than good. First, racing greyhounds in Florida and now the sled dogs. But they're well organized on a national level and prey on assholes like my former friend here. How much did they pay you to get dirt this time?"

A shrug and shake of the head, but no comment. Raven was finding it difficult to hold back her anger. Hadn't she stayed away from the lower forty-eight so as not to have to deal with crime? Always watching what she said or did? Making sure she had a permit to carry? But this was home and her home had been invaded.

"Who's that?" Zac stood in the hallway door, pajama top on backwards, rubbing his eyes. "You're really loud." Then glancing at the pile of feathers on the floor, "Oh wow, who'd you have to shoot?"

"Zac, let Grammy put you back to bed. Chief Pitka is just leaving. Nobody got shot—that man's coat just sprang a leak." Ahnah kept a straight face but winked at Zac.

Zac looked skeptical but let Ahnah take his hand. "Goodnight." He followed his grandmother into the hall.

"Okay, then, that should just about wrap it up. I'll be holding our young felon here on the charges of breaking and entering. Mr. Rowland, you can check on your friend's bail in the morning when everyone's back at work. Now let's all get some sleep."

Chapter 17

Ben had gotten up early, seven-thirty, and headed downstairs to the kitchen. The least he could do was make coffee and let Julie stay in bed a little longer. Maybe he'd try for some extra points with breakfast in bed. He'd asked Uki for a couple of Two Sisters' famous cinnamon rolls and he hoped she'd remembered. His mouth watered just thinking of them. He knew they were bound to become Julie's favorites.

He looked at the lineup of mugs next to the coffee pot. Four new ones. The place was filling up. His intern interviewee had come in with two other young men yesterday afternoon. Two more bedrooms were taken but this morning, the second floor was deadly quiet. Maybe everyone had already gone out. He guessed that Uki had stayed late at her sister's and would be sleeping in. Both of the women seemed to take great joy in looking after Zac. Ben liked to see that. He wasn't picking up any signs of emotional problems that Zac might have. He pretty much fit the bill of a normal ten-year-old—with a newfound surplus of family.

"Hey, I wasn't going to wake you. Thought I'd get some coffee going first. And look what I found—breakfast." He held out the plate with two gigantic cinnamon rolls. "You're not going to believe how good these are—and still warm."

Julie stood in the kitchen doorway. "I'm famished. Those look beyond good. What's on the agenda for today?"

"Well, depends on whether you have plans—need to work, get some more photos?"

"Not until later. I'm sitting in on a Council meeting at two. I have some questions about the Annex that I need to get answered, and then I'll try to spend a couple hours in the office after that. So, ideas for this morning?"

"Yeah, I need to set up the finances for the program. I've submitted a budget that's been approved. I just need a copy to forward to IHS. Indian Health will be matching funds. This program is getting a lot of attention, as it should. Like everything else in the community, it's been a long time in coming. Plus, I'll be interviewing the intern today, and it would help if I knew what I can spend. E.J. knows the particulars, and I just need to sign off on what I'm going to need from my end. I was hoping you wouldn't mind tagging along to E.J.'s office. I kinda like you with me." He said this last after leaning in for a kiss.

"Sounds like a perfect morning."

"Hey, sarcasm and cinnamon rolls don't go together." But he laughed, grabbed her around the waist and this time the kiss lasted a lot longer.

+ + +

Julie struggled to find the words that would adequately describe E.J.'s office—the popular but vastly over used, 'Man Cave', didn't do it justice. It was somewhat isolated, taking up a wing of the municipal building at the far end right next to the community utilities office.

But aside from an orderly desk, the room looked like he lived there—right down to the daybed with wadded flannel sheets and down comforter half on the floor. A change of clothes had been casually thrown across the back of an office chair, a bowl of something that had included fries, half-eaten, sat on the floor, and three pairs of boots had been haphazardly tossed in the corner. She noticed the four beer cans in the trash and wondered how he got away with having alcohol within village limits—hadn't she read that the borough was dry?

Alaska didn't have counties, and boroughs had strict rules about drinking. And she was pretty certain that Moose Flats was dry because it wasn't connected by road to a 'wet' village. But, then, she'd also read that isolated communities could make and adhere to their own rules. Alaska could be a little confusing.

E.J. quickly cleared a space for them to sit. Two chairs were piled a foot high with books and folders and the small conference table had several more stacks next to a laptop and printer. E.J. was saying something about never trusting someone with a sterile office. As much as the clutter bothered her, he seemed to wear it like a badge. Men. If she had to try and work in surroundings like these, she'd be crazy in under an hour. And she'd never find anything.

"I'm so glad the two of you stopped by. I want us to

bury the hatchet as long as it's not in each other's back."
He held out a hand. Ben and then Julie each shook it. "I
need to apologize for the office. As you guessed I spent
the night." A wave of his hand took in the mussed bed.
"Worked late and didn't want to wake everyone up getting
in. Come to find out they had a little excitement in the
middle of the night at the dog yard. Guy paid by PETA
was caught going through Raven's office files in the barn."

"Is everyone okay?" Had Zac been in danger, Ben
wondered.

"Yeah, between Raven wielding Dad's old sawed-off
shotgun and Mama ripping his jacket with a knife, I think
he got the fear of God put in him. Apparently, Ronnie
Pitka did a pretty good job of defusing the situation and
bringing the guy in on breaking and entering charges."

"Did you say PETA? What's of interest to that group
out here?" Julie felt she'd missed something.

"I guess shutting down dog racing wasn't enough
to keep them busy. They got the State of Florida to put
shutting down their tracks on the ballot and thanks to a lot
of misleading advertisements, the residents voted tracks
out. Ninety-nine percent of those voting to abolish dog
racing had never been to one. But a few pictures on TV
of dead or injured dogs and that's all it took. So now the
Iditarod and like races have their attention."

"But dogs have been used in Alaska for hundreds of
years. They've been a major part of life up here. Aren't we
talking apples and oranges? One, the difference between
people surviving or not, versus something just for sport?"
Julie was astounded. How could a centuries old way of
life be targeted by a group of sometimes misinformed do-
gooders?

"The kid caught with his hand in the files, literally, had been paid a few thousand to prove Raven's dogs were being mistreated. He was looking for records of injuries and illnesses, as well as deaths. PETA is going to make good use of the publicity surrounding the race over the next few weeks to call attention to what they claim is 'unconscionable cruelty'. Raven doesn't need this. It's so much more than just a big investment of money—her heart is in this as well as a promise to our father's spirit."

"What can be done?" Ben asked.

"Always tough to go up against a well-organized group. They've already hit at fringe group support. The Chicago Auto Show is facing a protest over Iditarod sponsorship, Chrysler and the Philadelphia Auto Expo are two more auto shows being discriminated against just because of their support of the races. They shut down New York's AKC Museum of the Dog last month by staging a protest. It's not just here or in Anchorage, and it would seem they are willing to pay people to make felons of themselves to uncover what might be useful information."

"I hope the guy you brought in isn't my wannabe intern?"

"No, this guy is legitimately with the Seattle *Times* sent here on a legitimate mission to do a feature on Raven—how she's carrying on the legacy of our father. It just turns out that he was getting a little extra to do this group's dirty work. It would have been a great story. As a child Raven was devoted to the dogs and to Dad. When he killed himself, she was never quite the same again. She struggled for years, first withdrawing, becoming a recluse, dropping out of school—she's come a long way, Ben."

"I remember she didn't think much of her stepfather—

even had some problems with him."

"Ed Johnson is an SOB. I always thought he molested her in addition to beating up my mother."

"And that's why you killed him?" Chief Pitka boomed out from the doorway. No one had heard him come down the hall.

"What are you saying? Me? Nobody's killed him. He's in Washington State—Tacoma, I think. He's due back the first of April. You know that; he's been doing it for years."

"Sure, E.J., he's not even supposed to be here. That's a good story or should I say 'cover up'? Damn well made it all the more convenient, didn't it? Nobody'd even look for him for six months."

"Chief, I have no idea what you're talking about."

"Well, guess these photos will help jog your memory." The chief handed him a manila folder thick with glossy prints. "Got these photos and an anonymous tip of just where to go to find your victim."

And in that moment E.J. knew who his frozen listener was and why no one was looking for him. He was *supposed* to be gone, working out-of-state. For someone committing a murder it *was* perfect cover, but his death might have been natural, too. Why was anyone pointing a finger at him?

E.J. fanned through the ten or so photos taken with a telephoto zoom lens of some sort. Actually, they were pretty good—details that made him and his actions unmistakable, like covering up the nose when it had become exposed. And the Wolverine lined hood on his parka was like wearing a name-tag. But who was taking photos? And why?

"Who's the photographer?" E.J. handed the folder back.

"Like I said, Mr. or Ms. Anonymous. I got to questioning

people around town and quite a few folks had made a note of your visits. You should know that in a village this size somebody's gonna take an interest in a man who regularly disappears out on the tundra—no gun, no fishing poles, or buckets of bait—just a grown man in a snow machine, parks it on the tundra and takes off for a stroll in sub-zero weather to the same place sometimes twice a week. Now, you think that doesn't set some tongues a waggin'? But it was your mother who got us involved. Poor woman was afraid that you were contemplating harming yourself. Your neighbors felt it was their duty to call her attention to what was going on. Your daddy put a gun to his head, so why couldn't suicide run in the family? She was about beside herself with worry. She had no idea you were making sure a death was covered up. She was in shock this morning when we showed her what we have."

"You showed Mama these pictures?"

The chief nodded. "She was the first to blame herself. She knew she was wrong to let you see ol' Ed beat her up—that had to have left a lasting impression on a child. She thought at the time helping you escape by going to school in the lower forty-eight would be the answer. But I guess when you came back last fall, you had it out with Ed? Some knockdown, drag out shouting match?"

"Zac was still here—hadn't left for school yet, and Ed was threatening a whipping because, according to him, the dogs' buckets hadn't been cleaned well enough. I simply intervened."

"It's my understanding with some threats of your own, what you'd do if he ever laid a hand on Zac—that about right?"

E.J. nodded. It hadn't been pretty and he'd meant it.

Funny, if he'd known who his frozen companion was, he wouldn't have visited. He would have thought 'good riddance' and ignored the body. Sure seemed like Ed was getting the last laugh.

"Still doesn't say I murdered him. Yeah, I'll give you circumstantial evidence but that's not good enough to pin a murder on me."

"Oh, come on, E.J. You're the lawyer. You had motive— even you can't deny that—and you were photographed not only going directly to where the body was but then keeping it covered with snow, hidden from view. If old Ed had wandered out in the snow and froze to death, there wouldn't have been a reason for all the clandestine maneuvers."

"So, how long before you have an autopsy report? Murder would seem easy enough to rule out." Ben had kept quiet long enough. Things didn't look good for E.J., but there was nothing conclusive … yet.

"Dr. Pecos, with all due respect, stay the hell out of this. I gotta serious crime here on my hands and the likely killer denying it. I don't need you taking sides."

Ben stepped back. Last thing he needed was to antagonize the locals. He knew he needed all the support he could get to not only open a clinic, but maintain it by attracting participants.

"Let's go back to the autopsy. I take it you've exhumed the body?" E.J. interjected.

"Working on it. Should have it out by late today. Four days of ten-degree high temps and the ice is pliable—still tedious work though. Chip and pray we don't tap into a body part. I got five guys out there working on it. We've basically uncovered just enough for a positive ID. Elijah

Kane, undertaker, pathologist, primary care—whatever you want to call him—is coming back out from Anchorage on this afternoon's supply run. He's got some paperwork to catch up on but we'll get him to take a look at Ed. And he might as well get the death certificate recorded for Brant—make sure the right people at the State Department get the lab report. Any death not attributable to natural causes is a pain in the elbow. In the meantime I'm going to lock you in one of my cells. It's getting damned crowded. Already have a felon … but we'll manage. I'll let Ahnah know to bring over meals for two. You need cuffs or can we just walk around the corner all peaceful like?"

"It's not like I'm going anywhere. No need to take up another space in the jail."

"That's beside the point. I'm doing this by the book. You never know who's going to be looking over your shoulder. The more Federal funding we ask for, the more we need to keep our noses clean. Nobody gets special treatment—a suspected murderer is just that and rules are rules. I'm not going to recommend bail."

"Then, give me a minute with Ben. I need to give him a copy of his budget for the clinic and a list of the contacts from the village."

"I'll be right outside the door."

E.J. waited until the chief went into the hall and shut the door behind him.

"I know I have no right to ask, not after the way I got you here, but help me?"

"I'm a shrink, not a PI or a lawyer—"

"I'm the lawyer but sitting in a cell greatly diminishes my access to evidence that would prove my innocence."

"I'll do what I can. Just answer me one thing—"

"No, Ben, I did not kill Ed Johnson."

Chapter 18

How are you going to help?" Julie and Ben walked back to their shared office.

"Not sure. For starters, I'm going to wrangle my way into Dr. Kane's autopsy. I need some outside perspective on the opioid crisis and to find out what exactly killed Brant. Plus, I'm thinking of setting the doc up to speak to the community. I know there are questions out there, and he's the perfect candidate to provide answers. In the meantime, I'll see what I can find out about the death of E.J.'s stepfather. The body should be over at the clinic waiting on the doc."

"It made me sick when they talked about threats to Zac. Sounds like more than one person is better off with Ed Johnson out of the picture," Julie said.

"Yeah, I don't look forward to helping families deal

with domestic violence. It's so difficult to find equitable solutions. Problems run deep—a way of coping that transcends generations. Some of these behaviors are learned and more than tough to unlearn."

"How are you going to prove that E.J. is innocent?"

"I wish I knew."

"Do you believe him? That he didn't kill his stepfather?"

"Yeah, I do. But first, murder in general, has to be ruled out. It'll be easy if the death proves to be the result of natural causes. That's going to be the best outcome. If Ed Johnson was murdered, I don't know where I'd start to try to help E.J."

"It's getting late, I need to get to the Council meeting. I should be back here by mid-afternoon."

"Meet you there. We're on our own tonight for dinner. Uki's propane hookup is leaking—at least that's what her note said. Let's eat at the Bearpaw tonight. The village's one restaurant is supposed to have the best moose stew in the territory. Hey, what's with the nose wrinkling? Don't knock it if you haven't tried it."

The outpatient clinic was one room off a short hallway with an office attached, squeezed into a corner of a building that had once been planned as a sizeable health complex. As part of a bigger community plan to provide real health care—someday even including dental—the building had been halted when moving the entire village became inevitable.

Then, as the plan to move took center stage, enticing qualified personnel like an MD became impossible. So, manned by a retired nurse, his landlady, and a couple on-call deputies with EMT training, Moose Flats made do.

Ben was fast learning the challenges that the village faced, and a lack of medical facilities didn't make his job easy. How many OD's could have been reversed if care had been available? At this point there should be no looking back; the future held all the answers.

The Annex plans included a two-thousand square foot clinic complete with two day-surgery bays, five exam rooms, a lab, a pharmacy, and a separate hospital wing that could house ten beds. A dental clinic, if voted in, would fit in an adjoining building to the side. The facility would be shared with three villages and included the services of a traveling PA or NP depending on money for personnel. He knew the village council was hoping the amenities, along with new houses, would entice the Moose Flats population to get onboard—support the move and learn to adapt to a new way of life. But it wasn't going to happen overnight.

Interestingly, the current clinic in Moose Flats was relatively new. And the building costs had been astronomical—especially for a poor village now needing to start over and spend even more money on another new clinic. No wonder the state was dragging its feet on funding. According to E.J., it had taken a year to complete the building in front of him.

And there was no way to cut corners, save money and still have a solid structure. Building on permafrost was slow-going and expensive. Alaskan building contractors had a saying, "If it's frozen, keep it frozen; if it's thawed, keep it thawed."

'Thaw stable' was a term heard over and over—how much ice was in the foundation material? If the ground beneath a building was going to repeatedly thaw and freeze, the structure would be in serious trouble, to the point of being uninhabitable.

The tundra was made up of silty soil and not the granite bedrock of Alaska's mountainous regions. Ben had read that permafrost earth was not permanently frozen but was soil that had remained at below thirty-two degrees for twenty-four months or more. This minimum requirement described 'newer' soil. Some permafrost in Alaska had been there since the last Ice Age. Ground over permafrost freezes and thaws every year—winter into summer and back. Elevating structures was one answer to maintaining a permafrost base.

Contractors had chosen to elevate the current clinic, one of the only structures in Moose Flats that hovered above ground. Twelve steps led up to a porch-like landing before double-doors opened to the inside. There was a notice next to the bottom step proclaiming the structure to have been designed and erected by the Cold Climate Housing Research Center, the CCHRC—the same group already a part of the planning of the Annex and the new clinic.

The door was unlocked and the hallway was devoid of any decoration or furniture. Ben tried the door to the exam area; it was open, but the room was empty. Sparsely equipped, there was an exam table, glassed-in cabinets containing everything from Q-tips and gauze to tongue depressors and alcohol next to a desk, a file cabinet and a supply closet. The bare necessities. There was something depressing about the clinic and Ben reminded himself not to ever need medical care in Moose Flats. The place didn't instill confidence.

"Help! Is anybody there?" The frantic call broke

through his reverie and Ben backtracked and pushed open the outside door. Uki and two men with deputies' badges pinned to their parkas were carrying an inert third man with Chief Pitka bringing up the rear.

"Thought I might find you here. It's that kid who broke into Raven's barn last night. Help us get him upstairs." Officer Pitka held the door open.

"What happened?"

"Found him collapsed in his cell about fifteen minutes ago when I locked up E.J."

"Shit, we're losing him." One of the deputies ripped off the kid's parka and heavy sweater. "Put him on the table."

Ben and the chief stood against the wall trying to stay out of the medical team's way.

"Was it some kind of medical emergency?" Ben heard one of the EMTs humming *Stayin' Alive*. He'd heard that doing compressions to the tune would maintain the ideal rhythm of one hundred plus compressions per minute. Still, it seemed odd to hear the song.

"Allergic reaction near as I can tell. Ate lunch and collapsed. Kid's wearing a medical bracelet—you know, the kind that's supposed to give you peace of mind 'cause it lists everything that could kill you. I wasn't there, and well, somebody wasn't paying attention. Uki, did you or Ahnah take lunch to the jail?"

"Neither one of us. My kitchen's out of commission and Ahnah is helping Raven with the dogs today. The Bearpaw is serving meals. I have no idea who took the food over. As you know, Chief, they always let the inmates order from a menu. I can't imagine the allergy thing wasn't mentioned."

"Well, the doc will be able to tell us the culprit but

little good it will do now. Time wasn't on our side. We picked you up and got here as quickly as we could. Too bad Doc Kane won't be in for another hour. We're just not equipped out here to handle emergencies. The Annex will be a lifesaver—literally."

The EMT closest to Ben was shaking his head. "He's gone. As much as I see death out here, I'll never get used to it. This was just a kid."

"A kid who'd already gotten into trouble—probably because of money. I'd love to pin his death on those PETA folks," the chief continued.

"This the one who took money from PETA to try to get some dirt on Raven's dog setup?" Ben asked.

"Yeah. We wouldn't have known about that if the kid's sidekick hadn't ratted on him. You'd think those people would have better things to do than mess around with our way of life. I don't know of one musher who's ever mistreated his dogs. Not saying it's never been done, but not to my knowledge. If they wanted to do something constructive, they should investigate horse racing."

"Too much money in that sport." Ben offered.

"Ain't that the truth. We won't have women in fancy hats prancing around Anchorage holding mint juleps at the start of the race next month, that's for sure; but it's the way we celebrate a sport that's a way of life—one that we depend on."

Ben thought he'd struck a chord. These people valued their way of life—were fiercely proud of their accomplishments, let alone their survival by adapting to a country too harsh for most. Kind of gave new meaning to the word, 'macho'.

The chief shrugged and leaned against the wall. "Not

saying life's fair but sometimes the stupidity and fragility of it all just slaps you upside the head. There's a momma and a daddy out there somewhere going to take this hard. Guess we need somebody to tell that pal of his what's happened. He'll know how to locate his parents, as well as his boss at the paper. Be good if the Seattle *Times* does a nice write-up. Nobody needs to mention the PETA angle."

"I don't think the kid here was talking to his fellow journalist. The other guy met Pete at the airport this morning, skipped breakfast, and took the red-eye to Anchorage. Couldn't get out of here fast enough. So much for helping a friend. Even though he swore he was clean, I think he was afraid he'd end up like his partner—guilty by association—and locked up, too," Uki said.

"Damn. Nothing's ever easy. I'll give Seattle PD a call. Hate to push off work on another department but they'll be the best ones to handle it. They can officially notify the parents or whoever the next of kin might be."

"Gotcha. Let me know if I can help." The deputy added, "I'm assuming that you'll want to get the body back to Anchorage as quickly as possible?"

"Yeah, sooner the better. I'll let Pete know after I get word on who's going to be meeting the plane." The chief sighed and then roused himself, walked to the door and looked out. "We gonna have room to bring in ol' Ed? I understand the boys have got him out of the ice and starting to thaw. Should be on their way now."

"There's another metal table, actually a gurney, folded up against the back wall of the supply closet. It's the one that Doc Kane usually uses for autopsies—easier to wheel in and out of cold storage." Uki opened the closet door. "Still there. Glad to see it hasn't been moved. You waiting on the doc?" She turned to Ben.

"Yeah. I think he could help me with my clinic plans. I'll just set up a time to meet with him later; his day turned out to be a little busy."

"Hey, ol' Doc Kane can walk and chew gum. He'll probably talk with you right here. He's not one to waste time. But he's a good man to work with. Straight-shooter. Just the guy you want on your team when you set up your clinic. Villagers trust him." The chief added, "I'd like to see him move here on a permanent basis once we get the new clinic over at the Annex. Uh-oh, sounds like the guys are here with Ed. Ben, you want to lend a hand?"

Ben stepped out on the landing with the chief and watched two men park a snow machine in front of the clinic and unhook a travois that appeared to be a foot-deep trough made of a plastic material. The body was wrapped in canvas but the signs of thawing were evident.

"Had him in the garage with a heat fan at about plus thirty but he's still got a ways to go before he's room temperature." The deputy who had driven the snow machine pushed the container up to the bottom of the steps.

The chief propped the door open as Ben walked down the steps and took the back of the container and the other three aligned themselves, two in the middle and the chief at the head. Maneuvering up the steps took the greatest amount of pushing and pulling effort, but finally the box was resting on the clinic floor.

Uki suggested moving the body of the reporter to the gurney and rolling him into the hallway outside the exam area. "It'll be cool here and Doc Kane can help with the arrangements to get the body back to Anchorage later.

Let's just leave Ed the way he is."

"I'm going to go back to my office. I'll leave a message for Pete to bring the doctor there." Ben said good-bye and walked back to the church.

Chapter 19

Ben didn't have long to wait. He'd just had time to reschedule the interview with the possible intern, leave a message at the airport for Pete to bring Doc Kane to his office, and have a second cup of coffee when Marie called out that the doctor was coming up the walk.

"Welcome to America's Outback where we lose people faster than we can bring them into the world. I'm Elijah Kane." The man in the doorway walked toward Ben with his hand outstretched. He was short, a head shorter than Ben's six-foot two frame. The dusting of fluffy, gray hair that ringed an otherwise bald head was only revealed after he'd taken off a stiff-brimmed, leather Aussie Breezer hat with a chin-strap. "I've been looking forward to meeting you. You're a boon to this community—setting up a clinic for addicts is just what the doctor ordered. And I mean that literally."

"Doctor Kane, good to meet you. Unless I can get you a cup of coffee, let's walk over to the clinic."

"I'm good to go. I understand I'm looking at two deceased individuals? Both males?"

"Yes, one is a local and has apparently spent most of the winter on the tundra in a prone position. The other is a recent visitor—supposedly here as a reporter/ photographer for the Seattle *Times* getting some background on dog racing."

"I keep forgetting that the big day is coming up. Only a couple weeks away. I hope Raven does well."

"You seem to know this community fairly well."

"Been coming out here for more years than I care to remember. I have five villages along the river who have had access to my services. It'll be nice to have a co-op health care center and hospital one of these days. I admit it's a touch of modernism and convenience that I've longed for."

In five minutes both men were walking up the steps to the clinic. Ben helped the doctor roll the gurney, with Andrew Cook strapped to it, in from the hallway and place it in the middle of the room under a bright ceiling light.

"Should be a clipboard in that first drawer. Can you hand it to me, that is, if you don't mind a little work as my assistant?"

"Not a problem; I'd like to feel useful."

"Good. Then, first off, I'll ask you to record the time and date at the top of the first form."

Ben followed directions and filled in the information.

"Do we have a name for this individual?"

"Here's what the EMT's filled out. Looks like this is Andrew Cook." Ben smoothed out the single folded sheet and clipped it to the clipboard in his hand, then stepped back to watch as the doctor loosened the straps and began his examination. A quick inspection of nasal passages, mouth, throat including a cursory palpitation of the salivary glands beneath the jaw and the doctor put his instruments in a tray and stood back.

"Constricted airways—caused by rapid swelling of tissue in the throat. My guess is a reaction to nuts—the common peanut is probably the bad guy. But I can't imagine Mr. Cook here wasn't careful. He was concerned enough to wear the bracelet. But as quickly as his airways shut down, and with no way to reverse the reaction, this is quite believably the result of a severe peanut allergy. I'll know more when I can get lab results back. Of course, I'm sure his parents will want an independent test and diagnosis done. I sure hope we're seeing the end of this death threat. Research today on preparing children to handle the allergy is extremely promising. Give me a hand and we'll put Mr. Cook back in the hallway."

Ben made certain the gurney's legs were locked and the straps across the body tightened before opening the door to the hallway. "The deputies will take him over to the airport later. I'll let the chief know he's ready. He should have a body bag that we can use."

"Oh, and before I forget, I need to finish up the paperwork for Brant Thomas and get some copies made. Got the original of the lab report here. This is one sad story. This guy had all the potential in the world—just couldn't handle fame. But it's still odd that he'd be clean for months and then OD. It was like he was targeted. The heroin was cut with enough fentanyl to kill three men.

And interestingly enough, there were no other deaths. If a group was doing drugs that night like everyone's said, then there would have been other deaths. As a rule these druggies share their loot. Guess we'll never know the exact circumstances. I'm just going to slip the lab report in the first drawer here and make sure the chief gets a copy later. Okay, who's next?"

"Ed Johnson. Someone else you probably know. He's over here behind the desk—still thawing out."

"Chief shared with me who it was. Ed wouldn't win the popular vote for best liked, but he made a rough life pay off. He was a good provider and he was a talented mechanic. I want to think he meant well, just couldn't cope with life's stressors. Yeah, I know what you're thinking—that doc's letting the guy off the hook for beating his wife and his stepson. But believe me, there's no excuse for that. None. I just like to see some good in everyone. Maybe if we'd had your help earlier ..."

"Domestic violence is often rampant in villages so far removed from help when just surviving is stressful and iffy. I want to believe that the Annex will be a change factor, but it will take time and the right personnel."

"Does that mean you aren't volunteering for the job?" Doc Kane asked.

A brief picture of Florida flashed before Ben's eyes—sun and ocean and cities with all the amenities. Could he live in Moose Flats? Even the Tewa Pueblo in the Jemez mountains of New Mexico was a thriving metropolis in comparison—right off the highway, a short sixty minutes to Albuquerque. "I don't think I'd be a good fit. I want to volunteer my help and I'll let Indian Health know that, but not on a permanent basis."

"Can't blame you. You're a young man on his way

up—don't let anyone bury you out here or in a place like this. Watch the government; they're good at overlooking individual needs just to meet perceived needs that will make the collective look good. It's all just politics. And if anyone owes anyone favors, you could get sacrificed—don't let it happen."

"I think my wife will keep me out of the Moose Flats' of the world. We hope to raise our family without the harshness of the environment working against us."

"I hear you. I'd probably still be married if I'd chosen the lower forty-eight for a home. Now let's see what secrets ol' Ed wants to give up."

Ben lowered the exam table and the two men lifted Ed, canvas wrapping and all, and placed him in the center. One on each side, the men slowly and carefully unwrapped the corpse.

"Well, would you look at that."

"Suicide?" Ben was looking at a good-sized hole in the chest.

"Not unless he could shoot himself in the back with what was probably a deer rifle. Judging by where he was found, I'd say ol' Ed was in the wrong place at the wrong time. When it comes to feeding your family, it's often shoot first, ask questions later."

"So, you're saying accidental?"

"Could be. I could make a case for that. Though I'm probably going to put 'undetermined' on the cert. It's easy to imagine up here—somebody out hunting, sees something move in the mist and fog, takes a shot from long distance, then can't find the deer and thinks he's missed and goes home—yeah, it's happened before. Many times, if you want to know the truth. Weren't we just talking about the challenges of living out here?"

"You know, they're trying to pin a murder rap on E.J. Takanni. Seems like he knew about the body but didn't report it. There's surveillance video and photos of E.J. visiting the corpse on several occasions—even making certain it remained covered."

"You don't say. No, I hadn't heard that. Interesting theory. There's a part of me that says just desserts, another part of me that feels sorry for the widow, and finally a part that says killing another human being is just plain wrong."

"Any idea how far away the shooter was?"

"A good distance. The idea of mistaking a human for a deer has merit. And most of the old boys up here are sharp-shooters. They've been shooting at animals or fence posts all their lives. Even if they're fishermen, a little red-blooded meat can always tide you over. It's even nice to take a break from seal or walrus once in a while."

"But you also think someone could have murdered him?"

"Someone could have cooked the kid's lunch in peanut oil, or fed a fatal dose of drugs to Brant—these might all be murders. But proving it? You'll play hell. There's a certain element of protection to living out here especially if you want to get away with something."

"That's encouraging—at least, I think it could be for E.J."

"Then don't overlook the jealousy factor. A local kid returns with a prestigious law degree and the Village Council welcomes him with open arms, discusses his becoming mayor, gives him carte blanche to beg for federal funding to move the community—you think feathers haven't been ruffled? He's seen as pushy and cold, more interested in putting money in his own pocket than helping others. Remember this guy left, moved to the lower forty-eight, stranded his mother, abandoned his sister and turned his back on his heritage. That isn't easily forgotten or overlooked."

"Wow. Small towns."

"Yep, this ain't Kansas, Dorothy, or actually, maybe it is."

"So, if I wanted to help E.J., any idea of where I'd start?"

"Yeah, stop before you start; don't get mixed up in the drama. Keep your nose clean. Get a clinic established, help with the move, and stay away from the Sherlock business. Don't cultivate enemies. You stand an excellent chance of doing good up here—changing lives, saving them, too. That's your primary goal. Keep that in mind."

Ben wished he didn't think Doc Kane had a point.

Chapter 20

You have to admit motive and circumstantial evidence are awfully convincing."

Julie was just finishing her bowl of moose stew. "E.J. is in a tough position."

"Yeah, and if local sentiment is as biased as the doc says, no one is going to spend a lot of time trying to change that."

The Bearpaw was beginning to empty after having had every table taken over the dinner hour. Ben hadn't lied to Julie, the food was outstanding. Fresh bread, crusty on the outside, doughy soft on the inside and a salad whose lettuce was actually crisp were perfect compliments to the moose stew.

He'd just asked for the dessert menu—hadn't he seen the next table over from theirs sharing a gigantic piece of carrot cake? And he ordered a latte, no flavoring. Wooden-backed chairs, each painted a different color, tables with spotless white linen—it wasn't just the food that made the place inviting, this was as cozy as any mom and pop restaurant in the lower forty-eight.

"I'm thinking of stopping by to talk with E.J. after dinner. I'd be interested to see if he can explain his actions—at least, why he didn't report the body when he first found it. Let's show up with an extra piece of carrot cake and see if he's up to talking.

+ + +

"This is the pits." And it was—ten by ten, no window, sink and toilet in the back corner and a bunk bed that had probably been manufactured for a child, one not over five-foot-five tall. E.J. was right—not the Hilton of incarceration.

He'd placed the carrot cake on the only table in the room—and calling it a table was being flattering; it was a fold down piece of lumber pressed upright against the wall, with a single 'leg' that unfolded and propped the two-foot square table top horizontally to the floor. One accidental nudge with a foot and the cake would be splat on the not very clean cement cell floor. "Any news on what killed Ed Johnson?"

Funny, Ben thought, there are those moments when you know someone is telling the truth and with that question, E.J. placed himself beyond suspicion—at least, with him. Ben shared the 'undetermined' verdict of the doc and noted that very likely that was the truth. The killing had been a simple mistake.

"The fall is rutting season for deer. It would have had

to be someone poaching, which would explain why no one followed up and found the body—or maybe they did and didn't want to be brought up on murder charges. Could explain covering the body. But what was Ed doing out on the tundra? It had to have happened in September or early October. I'll ask mama when he left or was supposed to leave. I know he always shipped his clothes and tools before the river froze so he wouldn't have had much more than a shaving kit for travel. Anything found with him?"

"Not that I know of. But I haven't had a chance to talk with Chief Pitka."

"Wouldn't he have flown out of here with Pete?" Julie asked.

"Basically, that's the only way. It's about four hundred miles to Anchorage over the tundra without roads, or under an hour by plane. That gives you the choice of a grueling, multi-day trip by dog sled or the relative comfort of one of Pete's flights. He's been known to hand out a piece or two of moose jerky every once in a while."

"I'm not certain; I don't think Julie's tried the jerky, but I watched her lick the bowl after finishing her moose stew at the Bearpaw earlier."

"Don't make fun of me, it was really good. But you're saying a plane ticket should have been found on his person?"

"At least Pete's log or the passenger roster at the terminal should have Ed's name. As you can imagine, moving to the lower forty-eight for six months isn't a spur of the moment decision. He's been doing it for years. Isn't likely he's going to skip a step."

"Wouldn't your mom know what his plans had been?" Julie asked.

"Definitely should. Talk to her; I'm sure Ronnie

Pitka has told her the body was identified. She'll be going through some stuff. It's a mixed bag—Ed wasn't easy to live with but I can't imagine even in the worst of times she would have thought he would be murdered or accidentally shot. He's been in this area long enough to be a native almost—he knows the dangers of wandering out on the tundra—especially that time of year."

"So, we're back to square one—are you saying that you believe it was probably accidental?"

"Yeah, and not just because it gets me off the hook. He was harder on his family than his friends. I honestly don't know of anyone he ever got cross-wise with. To the outside world he was Mr. Wonderful. He supported cake sales for the church, always helped build the booths for the PTA bazaar, fed a neighbor's dogs if they had to be gone overnight. Nobody paid him; he didn't ask for money. He helped because that was the kind of guy he was, community first."

"So, now the tough questions—why didn't you report the body when you first found it?"

"Can we go with because I'm stupid?"

"No, because I don't believe that." Ben said. "Not you. Not Mr. Cool, always in control E.J. Takanni, ace prosecutor—"

"Enough." A snort of a laugh. "You flatter me. After I found the body—actually, all I ever saw was an exposed nose—I checked to make sure no one was missing from the village. There were no reports of a local wandering off or even a visitor unaccounted for. I thought it was some contractor or do-gooder from the government, snooping around, wanting to make money on a village in distress. We'd had a fake moving company take money from residents just last year. But even they weren't murdered."

E.J. pulled the carrot cake closer to him and picked up a fork. "Hey, either one of you going to help me with this?"

"Had some earlier. Good stuff, I recommend it. Julie? You want to help E.J.?"

"No way. But thanks."

E.J. took a couple bites and then put his fork down. "I honestly thought this person had gotten disoriented during that early fall snow and ice storm that grounded air travel and put a halt to building for over thirty days. Never once did I think there had been foul play—that's why I still don't. This is treacherous country. It's easy to run afoul of the environment. I was busy here; it was easy to forget about the body when I wasn't looking at it. So, no action translated into a wait and see approach. Besides … and here's where it gets weird, I felt a kinship with the body. I had a listening ear that didn't talk back. It was sort of comforting. I could think things through, listen to my solutions by voicing them out loud without interruption. A sounding board, if you will."

"Yeah, that's weird. Not something the average person around here is going to understand," Ben admitted. "Don't know why the chief is so hell-bent on pinning this on you, though."

"It's no secret that the chief has had his eye on my mother. He always steps in when Ed is away and makes certain that Mama has supplies. I'd never thought of it as romantic, but with Ed out of the picture, it might turn into that."

"Then, you'd think he'd support you, her son," Julie said.

"Not necessarily. I think he wanted Mama to leave Ed, or at least bring charges for the violence. But she's tough and it was a matter of pride—she really thought she could help Ed, understand his demons, be there for him. In this village, he made her a rich woman and paid for Raven's schooling and business, and yes, my schooling, too. Money is a powerful thing out here. People can put up with a lot for a few comforts. I encouraged her to think through any move—not make a rash decision."

"I don't think the tundra has a corner on putting a high value on money. Julie and I had planned on visiting your mother this evening. If I get the chance, I'll ask a few questions, but now might not be the time. Anything you want me to say for you?"

"Let her know I'm thinking of her and that I'm sorry that Ed passed in this way."

Ben turned back at the door. "You know, it just dawned on me, wouldn't she have known something was wrong if he wasn't sending money each month while he was supposedly working in Tacoma?"

"He often drew against his salary and left six-month's worth of living expenses in the local bank with extra for emergencies. There had been problems before of making timely deposits; so, they had established this approach. Before I forget, thanks to both of you for the carrot cake."

Chapter 21

Two cabs were parked in front of the Takanni's house. As word got out, Ben was sure Ahnah had a steady stream of well-wishers and support from the community. He thought he'd seen the church van parked on a nearby side street. Raven met them at the door with Zac close behind. Ben could see that the living room had eight to ten people standing around Ahnah, who was sitting on an oversized, tan, leather couch. Two rugs in the center of the room were honest-to-God bear skins with trophy-sized moose antlers above a brick fireplace that appeared to be more for looks than actual use. The ubiquitous platter of smoked salmon and basket of bread crisps were centered on a split-cedar log table along with a stack of plates and a tumbler holding cutlery. Two cakes, one half eaten, were on a dining room table in the adjoining room.

"Hi." Zac stepped around his mother to stand squarely in front of Ben. "You want to see my puppy? His name is Romo. He lives out in the barn with his brothers and sisters."

"Sure. I want to say hello to your grandmother first but then I'd like to meet him. Can Julie come?"

"Who's Julie?" It wasn't said in a mean way, just curious, but Ben could kick himself for not introducing the two of them in a different setting. He hadn't thought ahead, prepared for a first meeting. He should have realized that Zac would be at the house. He had been more apprehensive about Julie and Raven interacting.

"I'm Julie. I'm your dad's wife." She held out her hand. "I'm very glad to meet you."

Zac shook her hand, then stepped back, "Do you have any kids?"

"No, I don't. I don't have a puppy either. That's why I'm looking forward to visiting with you. I'd like to learn about taking care of a puppy."

"I can show you. You'll like Romo."

"I'm sure I will."

"I'm going to go out to the barn and help feed the dogs. Don't forget to come meet Romo."

"We won't." Zac walked back through the living room, turned and waved before pushing open the kitchen door and disappearing outside.

Ben watched Raven while Julie was talking to Zac. She seemed relaxed, fine with what was being said. Probably too soon to feel relief but it was a positive start. For a first time together—so far, it wasn't as uncomfortable as he'd thought it might be.

Julie turned to Raven, "I really am looking forward to meeting Romo."

"He's crazy about that puppy. I'm glad he has something to occupy him and keep him from being underfoot. He's doing better with Ed's death than I expected. Not too many questions—at least, none that I haven't been able to answer." A shrug and a rueful smile, then Raven added, "I didn't know what to expect—what he might be curious about and how much I should say."

"Usually the less, the better. Take his lead and only offer an explanation that answers the question, nothing extra. I'm sure you're doing fine."

"I hope so."

"What was his relationship like with Ed?" This might not be the best time to ask, but Ben was curious.

"Spotty. Sometimes Ed would take him fishing, other times completely ignore him." She paused. "I tried to make certain that Ed wasn't too controlling—ask E.J., Ed seemed to have pretty set ideas on what made a man and what didn't. And his discipline could be harsh." She glanced at the dining room table. "Excuse me for a minute, looks like we're out of plates."

Ben noticed how tired Raven looked. Her tattooed chin lines seemed to pull her face downward toward her chest. As she stepped away to put plates on the buffet, he noticed the ink across the back of her neck above her shirt collar. He wasn't a fan of facial or body mutilation—well, maybe that word was a little strong and he knew the tribal history of female chin stripes. They signaled a young girl had reached puberty and they also served years ago to protect women caught in enemy raids on their village. If her tats showed she already belonged to a feared leader of one of the villages, she might be spared. In more modern times, tattooing came under scrutiny by the outside world and was discarded as a ritual by most Alaskan people.

Raven's becoming a tattoo artist was rekindling what had once been an important part of native lore discovered to have existed some thirty-five hundred years ago in the Arctic, only to be shunned and prohibited by Western colonization in the nineteenth and twentieth centuries.

And the resurgence didn't start and end with Raven. Studies of original symbols had become a part of modern Native history classes. Indigenous people realized what they had lost. Ben didn't know too much about the art but remembered a triangle meant an iceberg and the female sun and male moon figured predominantly in almost every inked scene.

Raven was bringing back a lost art—yet, she wasn't just a tat artist, she was an historian fighting the efforts against her grandparents' generation to wipe out an entire culture. He admired her for that. The young girl he remembered had not only taken on the responsibility of raising a child but was an important contributor to preserving and celebrating a cultural renaissance.

Raven had disappeared into the kitchen but returned with two mugs. "Here. The two of you looked like you might need something to warm up." Raven handed a cup first to Julie and then to Ben.

"Thank you. I appreciate you making me feel welcome." Julie said.

"I want all of us to be fair with each other. And fair to Zac. Yeah, I'm upset but I want solutions, not more hard feelings. And I don't blame you. I can only imagine the shock of finding out about Zac."

Julie nodded, "I want this to be a positive opportunity for Zac—whatever we decide that's going to be."

"I agree. Oh, Mama knows you're here but the church

deacons are a little long-winded. I'll make sure you get a chance to talk to her the minute she's free."

"What is this? It smells heavenly." Julie was stirring the liquid in her mug with a stick of cinnamon.

"Spiced Chai. Brown sugar, ginger, cardamom, cloves, bay leaves, fennel seeds, peppercorns and cinnamon."

"Unless there's a copyright on the recipe, I'd love to have it."

"I'll text it to you."

"When does Zac go back to school?" Ben asked.

"I'm keeping him with me until after the race. We'll be leaving for Anchorage with all the dogs and a couple sleds week after next. Pete already has a cargo plane rented and ready. I think Zac is old enough to enjoy the races and learn something about our state's history."

Julie took a breath. This was a perfect time to put the plan she'd been thinking about in motion. "I was sorry the reporter was actually a PETA informer. I'd like to make that right, if I could. My strong suit is really being a feature editor, having started out in newspapers as a copy writer. I'd like to write that feature about your racing history and your hopes for the Iditarod this year."

"That's really thoughtful," Raven conceded.

"I have some clout with a couple big papers and if I can't get a feature in print, I'm sure my boss would back me up and use his leverage. I just think it's a story that needs to be told. Lots of human interest. I'd like to interview you, photograph the dogs, possibly use some photos from your father's racing days—that sort of thing. I want this to be your story told from a woman's point of view—a Native Alaskan point of view."

"That's generous and timely. It would be a help to

emphasize the cultural history of dog sled travel. Maybe shut up the PETA people."

"I wouldn't count on that. They're everywhere and some of the TV ads are misleading but stark enough to woo people to their side. There's nothing like the hint of an animal injured to get people to overreact. But I think counteracting the bad press with something heartwarming might soften PETA's impact."

"When would you like to meet?"

Another breath, now was the time for part two of her plan. "I was thinking I could get information and pay you for your time if we talked while I got a tat."

"Hey, isn't that a family decision?" Ben was slightly alarmed. A tat? Julie?

"No, it's a 'me-decision'. One I've been considering for a while."

"Can we, at least, talk?"

"Probably not if you expect my decision to change."

"Do you know what you want? I have a number of catalogues we could look at."

"That sounds perfect. I think I know what I want but I'm not totally sure."

"Maybe you could tell me where this tat is going to go?" Ben interrupted.

"It's more fun to guess or play a little game of hunt and find." Raven barely suppressed a smile. She was obviously enjoying this, Ben thought. Maybe it wasn't such a great idea to have his wife interact with the former girlfriend.

"Are you free tomorrow? I'll be writing two stories with close deadlines and need to get started on yours in order to get it published before race-day."

"I'll make the time. I usually finish light roadwork with

the dogs by eleven. Meet me here at the house. I could probably spring for lunch." Then Raven did smile, directly at Ben, and winked before turning back to survey the living room. "Ah, looks like the crowd has thinned. Let's go talk to Mama and then you need to meet Romo. I know Zac is waiting for you."

+ + +

Breakfast was more cinnamon buns. Julie was pretty certain that they would find her thighs and stay there. She needed to get back to the gym. Ben left to work at his office around nine and Julie stayed behind to organize her notes on the Annex and the upcoming moving day. A quiet hour and a half all her own was a gift. It always amazed her how much could be accomplished when there were no interruptions.

Even though she would prefer to walk, she called a cab. She just didn't have the weight of winter clothing to ward off windchill even in short distances. Everyone warned her that if she wasn't bundled up properly, she could freeze, at least get a serious case of frostbite, just walking from one house to another across a street. She checked her phone for the weather—minus nine. Yeah, it was time to call a cab.

The cab was prompt and drove down the block, past the church before turning onto the first residential street then continued to the last house on her right. The Takanni residence really formed the outskirts of the village.

She heard the dogs as she got out of the cab and turned to pay the driver the twenty-five-dollar fare. She added a tip and asked for a receipt. A short four block drive and she was out thirty dollars. It was just one more expense of living in Alaska. Everything seemed so outrageously overpriced. A meal for two at the Bearpaw was an easy sixty dollars—add a couple beers and that was twenty dollars more and their website touted the restaurant as 'mid-range'. Thank God, she was still on an expense account.

The door opened before Julie reached the front steps. Raven in short sleeves was showing off some beautiful ink work.

"Oh, wow, I like that one." Julie pointed to a ten-inch feather whose tip dissolved into a flock of black birds flying toward her right shoulder.

"Ravens. That one is my signature image and my very first tattoo."

"I had been thinking of a feather but one that has a quill tip to represent my writing."

"I like that. I think every image, no matter how many or how few you have, should represent something from your life. In the Celtic religion, the goddess Morrigan is represented by the raven. She's known for courage and power. But let's find what works for you. Follow me."

Julie hung her parka, scarf and gloves on a peg by the door and pulled off the heavy fur-lined boots. The house was warm or maybe that was just in comparison to the outside. Either way her heavy wool socks felt comfortable.

Raven walked ahead and pushed open the last door in the short hallway. "I've taken over one of the guest bedrooms. All my stuff is here. I sold the business furnished but had duplicates of some of my tools."

Other than being black leather, the chair that took up the center of the room was identical to a dentist's chair—it reclined to almost prone, the head rest was padded and comfortable, arm rests were wide and perfectly situated; a moveable tray on an outstretched 'arm', and a bright enclosed, vertically moveable light hanging from the ceiling completed the dental office 'feel'.

"This is perfect."

"I still have to convince my mother. She's been able to rent out this room and misses the extra cash."

"Do you get much business from the village?"

"More than I thought I would. I get teens from Moose Flats and surrounding villages. I'm hoping to open a storefront in the Annex."

"That would be great."

"Here, take a look at these sketches. I just searched tat art feathers and found some pictures you might like." Raven handed Julie an iPad. "And this notebook is all my own artwork. You'll find quite a few of mine include feathers. It's a popular Native symbol. See if any of these catch your interest." She placed a three-ring binder on the tray.

"I do want the feather to have a Native feel and end in a quill as I mentioned."

"You may find exactly what you'd like. Feathers mean everything from trust to freedom. So, you go ahead and look and I'll make us some Chai tea and lunch. I have the makings of ham and swiss sans on homemade rye with a side of potato salad. Any takers?"

"Count me in. I didn't even realize I was hungry until just now." Julie carried Raven's binder to the dining room table. "I see a couple designs already that I like."

By the time lunch was over, and Raven had poured two more steaming mugs of the aromatic Chai, Julie had found an exact image of what she wanted—a five-inch long, multi-colored, stylized feather decorated with turquoise and coral beads. Very Native and very New Mexico. She'd given some thought to a Dolphin in honor of Florida but something that reminded her of Ben's home just seemed right. Besides, her friends would have teased her mercilessly about having a portrait of Flipper on her body. She handed the iPad to Raven.

"Color! Oh, I'm so glad you want something other than plain black." Raven saved the screen image to pictures, then hit the print button and pulled a copy out of her printer's tray. She studied the drawing before rolling her wheeled stool to the side of the chair. "Now, the sixty-four-thousand-dollar question—where are we placing this feather? Over the coccyx?"

Julie laughed. "I saw a number of pictures of art over the tailbone, but I want the tat to show. What do you think? Ankle? Top of my foot?"

"Your choice. Either would look good. I'm hoping your schedule is clear for this afternoon. I think we're looking at around three hours—will that work?"

"I told Ben I'd meet him at the Bearpaw around five."

"Perfect. Let's get started. Ankle or foot?"

Julie chose the outside of her right ankle. "Is this going to hurt?"

"I won't lie, yes. Not a debilitating pain, but somewhere on a scale between a cat scratch and amputation—no, I'm kidding. I'll use numbing creams and that will help. Shoulders are one of the best areas with a little more muscle and a tautness that provides a good surface. The top of the foot can be painful because of the lack of padding. Ankles are somewhere in between."

"Hmmm, I think you just sold a shoulder."

"Sure? It's probably a good choice for the first one."

Julie nodded, "Yeah, here would be good." She slipped her shirt off, pulled her arm out of her sports bra strap, and pointed to her left shoulder.

Raven nodded, "Good choice." She pulled the tray closer to the chair and opened a chest of what looked like pens, tips, tubes and grips with a box of six small bottles of colored ink in the back. The machine, with its own power supply, had a tray of its own that sat to the side. Raven pulled the foot pedal closer to the chair, positioning it near her right foot before slipping on a pair of latex gloves and beginning to clean Julie's left shoulder.

"We really didn't have a chance to talk at mama's last night. But I want you to know that I know I've been wrong. I've been angry—at everyone. For starters, at E.J. because he brought Ben here without my knowledge. I wanted the introduction of Zac to his father to be under my control. I didn't want to be forced into a situation that might go very wrong. Ben spending time alone with Zac in the airport on his way here was a godsend, or as he pointed out—it was fate. I guess I also believe that there are no coincidences. But it was natural, no preconceived ideas of what either one should feel. No embarrassing 'do I hug him or shake his hand?' moments.

"The result has been Zac honestly liking Ben—proud to have a father who is supportive. The fact that Ben played soccer as a kid was the clincher. Did you see how Ben's set up one end of the barn with a goal complete with net so Zac can practice being an attacker? Zac practiced the Back Heel move for an hour yesterday. He's needed this. And I want to thank you for understanding. Like I said, I know it was a shock and you didn't sign on for a ready-made family."

"I won't lie—it's been a challenge. But I admire what

you've done for Zac; he's a great kid."

"I think you can understand why I don't want him to lose his heritage—his father's or his mother's. I want him to visit a Pueblo, meet relatives, connect with that part of him. In the meantime I want him to understand the dog races and life on the tundra."

"I think the best story is one that features the close ties you had with your father. That will be the hook to get readers interested. Do you mind if I ask questions about him?"

"No, I want to pay homage to my father. It is the major reason why I'm racing. I want people to know of his contributions to the sport and especially to this race."

"I plan to do exactly that."

"I'm sure I feel so strongly about Zac knowing his family because I lost the bigger part of mine at just his age."

"I know you were close to your father, as a daughter you raced with him? That was unusual—his interest in getting you involved and not his son."

"It just wasn't E.J.'s thing. I helped with the dogs every chance I got. E.J. was planning his escape from a way of life that he felt was killing him—at least killing his chances to reach his goals."

"Tell me about the races you shared."

"I rode on short races around here between villages and on sled trips to deliver medicines and food. I was never on the Iditarod. You can imagine how thrilled I was to find my father's pack's bloodlines at a kennel outside Anchorage—and for sale. I'll be able to put the dogs up there when I go back to race next month. It's a large kennel, a tourist attraction in that they offer tours and sledding classes.

They were consolidating their lines and after keeping a nucleus of breeding stock, they were offering the younger dogs for sale. It was one of those meant-to-be moments when I found out."

"I'm going to sound like Ben, but it's true, there are no coincidences. This is a terrific opportunity. Tell me more about your father. He was important in the village—I know people looked up to him. His racing prowess was envied by many in the sport. It must have made his death that much more shocking—to everyone."

"If it was a suicide, you're right, it made no sense."

"If?"

"In eighteen years I've never mentioned this to anyone, but maybe now is the time to talk about Zac's grandfather."

Raven paused but continued the tiny brush strokes that were beginning to form the outline of a feather. "I'm going to ask that you don't repeat this—it's not something that I want to see in print."

"You have my word."

"I was the one who discovered the body. I had gone out to the barn after supper that night to play with a litter of two-month-old puppies. My father was in his barn-office, in his favorite lounge chair. Sometimes he'd even fall asleep out there and not come back to the house until morning. I heard what proved to be a gun shot. I called out to him but when there was no answer, I knew right away that something was wrong. I remember just standing there in the doorway. There was blood everywhere; a part of the side of his head was missing, and I knew he was dead. I had learned about death at a young age because of the animals. Sometimes an elder dog was lost due to illness or accident or just old age. Sometimes my dad had to put those dogs down. Puppies even had accidents. Sometimes one would be accidentally smothered in the whelping box.

"But this was the strange part. My father was still holding the gun—the revolver everyone said that he had used. It was balanced in his lap, against his knee and clutched in his right hand. I was the one who took the gun out of his hand and laid it on the floor between his feet. Then I crawled up into his lap. My mother found me hours later fast asleep.

"You'll find all of this in the police report. What you won't find is that my father was left-handed. The point where the gun was held beside his temple was on the right side. It is simply not logical that a left-handed man would have shot himself from the right side holding a gun in his right hand."

"You didn't tell anyone? Share your suspicions with your mother?"

"I was ten, in shock, and scared. My life was changed forever. Honestly, it wasn't until years later that I began to dwell on what I had seen. And, by then, it made no sense to dredge his death up. His body had been cremated. Unless there were pictures taken, which I doubt, there would have been no proof and even then, what did it really prove? Nothing I said or did would bring him back."

"Was there anyone you suspected? Anyone you thought might have killed him?"

"I hated Ed Johnson so much, I blamed him. He moved in six months after my dad died. E.J. left for school in the lower forty-eight that next year. Even Aunt Uki went away to nursing school. I was pretty much alone. Ed sold off the dogs and my mother didn't stop him. Everything I loved was gone. I begged to go away, too, but Mama said she needed me with her. Years later when she let me visit E.J. in the states, that summer I met Ben, I had planned on staying away—never going home again. I had hoped that E.J. would help me. He knew I had to get away from Ed."

"Ed molested you?"

A nod. Raven took a deep breath before continuing, "I think Mama knew and I think she knew I would try to stay with E.J.—that it wasn't just a visit. Looking the other way was often her answer, instead of confronting problems. Getting pregnant changed everything. I had to come home. Later Ed bankrolled my schooling—I finished high school and went on to college. I was able to get a degree in graphic arts and later get my license to tattoo. He paid for E.J.'s schooling, too. I call them guilt degrees.

"Ed's working in Tacoma part of the year made being here bearable. When he lifted a hand to whip Zac, I thought Mama would kill him. Looks like someone beat her to it."

"So, you think Ed was killed? Not mistaken for a deer?"

"Again, nothing can be proved. I guess I suspect E.J. — he has many reasons to want him dead. Life was intolerable for him that year before he could get away. Ed was not one to spare the rod when it came to discipline, even with a teenager. He slapped E.J. around more than once. When E.J. came back last year, his fights with Ed were epic— verbal, but bordering on getting out of control. I've never seen two people who should not have been in the same room together, let alone, live in the same house."

"You really think E.J. killed Ed?"

Again, a nod. "Rumor has it E.J. killed Brant, too— that he gave the lethal, fentanyl-laced heroin to Brant."

"I find it so difficult to believe—E.J. risking everything. His career, his very life."

"He saw what each man did to the women in their lives. Domestic violence is rampant. I think E.J. just snapped. To be fair this time when he came back, he supported his family."

"Ben needs to know this. E.J. asked Ben to help him. I understand that the chief won't even discuss bail, wants to keep him locked up."

"If Ben can come up with something that will get E.J. off, that's great. I love my brother; I don't want to think he did it but I understand if he did. I'm glad Ben's helping him."

"Then I'll see what I can do."

"I'm going to be finished here in half an hour, and then I think we need a break. First, to get some feedback on my masterpiece, but also to enjoy the plate of brownies that Mama left on the counter. Have you ever had one of her double dark chocolate creations?"

Julie laughed, "I'm wearing a couple on my thighs as we speak—along with a couple cinnamon rolls. The brownies are beyond delicious, but I don't need more."

"I can't tempt you with even a couple brownies?"

"I'm going to be good, no brownies."

"Well, I'm just going to send a couple with you. I can't imagine Ben would turn one down. But let's finish this feather. I can't wait to see what you think."

The finishing touches took longer than thirty minutes, but finally, Raven shut off the machine and put the liner tool on the tray. "Let's go take a look." Julie walked with Raven to a pink ceramic tiled bathroom off the hallway with a large gilt-edged mirror above a sink. Julie shut her eyes, turned her shoulder toward the mirror and opened them.

"Oh, it's perfect. Raven, I love it." Julie gave Raven a quick hug before turning back to admire the silver feather with turquoise and coral beads. "It's even better than the picture."

"I'm so glad you like it. But, before I let you go this afternoon, there are a few things I want to go over. In two to five hours, I want you to put a very thin coating of coconut oil on the area but only after you've gently patted it down with a damp cloth. Use warm water and wring the cloth out thoroughly. You don't have to re-cover the area unless clothing will rub against it. In your case, a light gauze dressing on the shoulder will be fine. No Vaseline or anything with petroleum jelly. Any lubricant should be light to the point of being non-existent. I've put together a tat survival kit. No guesswork. Here's everything you'll need for the first week. After that, moisturize as needed and you're done. Oh, I meant to add some ibuprofen. Not that you'll need it, but just as a precaution. I think Mama keeps some individual packets in here."

Raven opened the medicine cabinet above the sink. "Here we go." She reached up to retrieve several packets only to dislodge a bottle of eyedrops and a zip-lock bag of towelettes from an overcrowded top shelf. "And she could use a bigger medicine cabinet." Raven put the items back on the top shelf and dropped the things for Julie into a small plaid cloth bag marked with Tats4Two in gold lettering.

"Your business?"

"Past tense. It was a lot of work. Most of the time I don't miss it." Raven helped Julie with her parka, checking to make certain the tat was still covered. "Call if you have any questions. I'd like to take a look at it in one week. I'm so glad you like it; now, if it just passes you-know-who's approval."

Chapter 22

Ben was frustrated. He'd interviewed the student wanting the intern job only to find out he wouldn't be able to sign on for the entire six-month tenure. He'd taken a secondary position in Fairbanks as a school psychologist and it started the first of July. Ben was wondering if he'd been too optimistic thinking he could offer college credit, a reasonable stipend for six month's work, and have takers.

There was a time he would have jumped at such an opportunity, but this wasn't his generation. And not everyone wanted to work in a less than stellar environment. Not being able to easily and economically bring a car to Moose Flats turned out to be a huge impediment. Two miles of paved road and they had to have a car? Ridiculous.

The office was closing in on him. He needed a break, a little change of pace. Now would be a good time to see if Ed Johnson had booked his flight to Anchorage with Pete on his way to Tacoma and, if so, when. He called the terminal and waited while the receptionist, turned ticket taker, paged Pilot Pete who called him right back saying he was out delivering supplies but would be back in his office in thirty minutes. Meet him at the office then.

The cab was prompt and Ben took a chair in the hall outside Pete's office fifteen minutes before he was due back. His assistant brought him a cup of coffee just as Pete walked through the door.

"Dr. Pecos, to what do I owe the pleasure?"

Ben explained his trying to establish a timeline for Ed Johnson's whereabouts which would help to narrow the date of his death.

"I don't have to look at the log books to tell you when he was booked. September twenty-four. When he missed his flight, I called Ahnah and she apologized, but said that Ed had decided to take the barge so he could stop at another village on the way. He was leaving a little early to be able to navigate the river before it began to freeze over closer to the last of October. He'd be calling me to make arrangements to be picked up in around ten to fifteen days from that destination. Apparently, that village's brigade of snow machines had only two in working order leaving eight not running. Ed was taking parts and spending a few extra days repairing them. When he didn't call for a pickup, I figured some bush pilot had given him a lift over to Anchorage or maybe even down to Juneau."

"Had he done that before—not used you as primary transportation out of Moose Flats?"

"A couple times if my memory serves me. Two years ago and the year before that. As a mechanic, he was in demand. Lots of villages up and down the river took advantage of his skills. I bet he was booked three years in advance."

"Let me ask your opinion; do you know of anyone who might want Ed Johnson killed or do you think it was a hunting accident, mistaken identity?"

"Could go either way. He beat another man's child and drove him from home, who knows what he might have done to the man's daughter, and God knows his wife had enough black eyes over the years to make for some bad blood. I know there's a lot of abuse, even today, but that don't mean it's not looked down on. And one other thing, long as I got you here and as long as we're discussing men mistreating women." **Pete shuffled his feet and wouldn't make eye contact. When he did, his face turned hard. "I've just heard something else about you, Dr. Pecos, and it's been on my mind.** I take a dim view of your callous, privileged ways—casting aside a pregnant eighteen-year-old and just moving on. How are you any better than an Ed Johnson who beat the shit out of women? Is it any more acceptable to dump and run? Ruining a young girl's life just so she won't be baggage in yours?"

Ben was stunned. "I had no idea that Raven was pregnant."

"And didn't care enough to take precautions? Just willing to take chances?"

"Raven thought that she was protected. It didn't work out that way."

"And now there's a ten-year-old boy who's been without a father for all those years. No, let me say, I don't respect you one bit, Dr. Ben Pecos. Surprises me that someone hasn't taken you out—like that brother of hers. You're the one E.J. should have shot."

That seemed to end the interview. He didn't need to be trying to prove anything to a bush pilot who was reacting to ten-year-old, secondhand information.

Ben put his notebook away and walked out the door. Shaken? Yeah. Threatened? Yeah, that, too. Law out here was what people made it, not something cast in stone or supported by a government sanctioned court system.

+ + +

"C'mon, just a peek?"

"It has to stay covered for at least forty-eight hours. It's not very pretty now, a little red and roughed up, but I think you're going to like it. Listen, we have much more important things to talk about."

Five o'clock and the dinner crowd hadn't arrived yet. The Bearpaw was cozy and inviting even with its flaming red walls—hadn't he read somewhere that the color red made a person hungry? In this case, it just made the place sort of artsy and whatever was being prepared in the kitchen smelled fantastic. It wasn't his imagination; his stomach had growled. The waitress said it was venison meatloaf, or fresh salmon with a blackberry glaze from last year's berry crop; a tossed salad was fifteen dollars more. The cook was running late, though, and it'd be a twenty-minute wait if they wanted either the venison or the salmon. So, they put in an order, one venison/one salmon, added a glass of good red, and requested a table close to the fireplace.

"Here's to date-nights." Ben clinked his wine glass against Julie's. "Now, what's this about important information?"

Julie told him exactly what Raven had shared and waited for a response.

"Wow. It doesn't do E.J. any favors to have his sister think he's guilty of two deaths—neither one has been proved a murder, but both are suspect. And her father's supposed suicide? Any proof would have been lost over the years, but it raises some serious questions."

"Such as?

"Well, for one, I'm having a tough time believing Raven's story of discovering her father's body."

"Why? What reason would she have to make up a story like that?"

"That part I don't know, but for a ten-year-old to notice and try to correct a right-hand versus left-hand shot pattern pushes the boundaries of believability. A kid just wouldn't be that savvy. And, if she were, why wouldn't that information be passed on? To the police chief, if not her mother. It just doesn't ring true."

"Raven seemed so earnest. I never once thought the story might be fabricated. She was pretty convincing."

"I don't doubt. A child's memory can sometimes change over the years—the emphasis of one aspect over another. Sometimes things become 'true' that actually weren't. But I would have thought Ahnah would have noticed the right versus left trajectory of the bullet. There's got to be an autopsy report somewhere. I'm going to check with Elijah Kane. I'm not sure he was the pathologist back then—how many years ago did it happen?"

"Eighteen, I think."

"Even if Doc Kane wasn't involved, there would have to be a record of the autopsy somewhere. Most states have public health laws; I'm just not sure about Alaska.

Unexpected, sudden or violent deaths usually have to be examined by a state medical examiner. I can contact Alaska Department of Health and Social Services. However, Alaska Native tribes are sovereign nations; with Tom Takanni being a Native, perhaps, any reporting was inter-tribal only. In the lower forty-eight there's a government-to-government relationship with the United States. And eighteen years might have precluded the kind of reporting I'm talking about."

Ben paused to nod a greeting to Chief Pitka, who had just entered the Bearpaw with one of his deputies. Stopping at Ben's table, the chief asked if Ben could stop by his office in the morning. He promised it wasn't anything earthshattering, but he had some questions that he thought Ben could help with. Ben asked if ten would work; he knew he was free then.

After agreeing, the chief excused himself, said he was sorry to butt into their conversation like that and took a table just two in front of Ben and Julie. Within five minutes, he was joined by another man in uniform.

"Before I forget I need your word on something." Julie lowered her voice to a whisper. "If you check the records, and talk to anyone about it, please leave Raven out of it; don't even mention her name. I told her I would tell you but no one else."

Ben agreed; he'd only take a look at the records—no names and no discussion. Two salads, both with blue cheese dressing, cut any further conversation short. Once again, the crusty bread with dipping oil was his favorite. It was better than dessert ... well, almost. But once he'd tasted the venison, he had a new favorite.

How could the food be so good here? He never once

could forget that he was in a remote village of maybe six or seven hundred people in rural Alaska and this restaurant was every bit as good as anywhere he'd eaten in the lower forty-eight. Berry cobbler and coffee topped off a perfect meal. And based on the smells coming from Uki's kitchen that morning, the cobbler was a product of the Two Sisters Bakery.

Lingering over dessert, conversation turned to Julie's story on the upcoming race. She had already made plans to attend the opening ceremony. Ben shared her excitement about the Iditarod. She'd talked with her boss about what papers might be interested in her story on Raven and had emailed several synopses. She needed pictures—dogs and equipment. And wouldn't overlook that adorable two-month old litter in the barn. That would get attention. Ben nixed one of Zac feeding the dogs. He was always a little wary of children being in print. God knew there were enough problems with people posting family pics online.

The sound of the crash was so loud and explosive, Ben actually jumped before scrambling out of his chair to turn toward the source. Officer Pitka was writhing on the floor clutching his throat amid gutturally gasping. His breath was literally coming from his lungs in jagged and uneven bursts of air. My God, what had happened? The man couldn't breathe. Ben rushed to help the deputy kneeling beside the chief. The other man was phoning for backup. The first deputy jerked open the chief's shirt collar and propped up his head by wadding up the man's down vest. Ben thrust it under his head and neck making certain that the chief's airways weren't cramped shut. Suddenly, the chief reached out and grabbed Ben's arm.

"Don't trust … target on your back." It was only a

whisper through barely moving lips.

Ben looked down quickly. Had he heard correctly? Had that been meant for him? There was no telling. The chief had seemingly passed out, upper body slumped to the side, head lolling forward.

By the time Dr. Kane and Uki came through the front door, and after some twenty minutes of chest contractions alternately applied by the deputies, the chief was gone.

"Bring a car to the back door. Let's get him to the clinic." Dr. Kane was directing all activity. "And bag everything on this table, everything he might have taken a bite out of. As of now, that's evidence. Save the liquid in the water glass and bag the glass itself. Ben, would you mind collecting all this and bringing it by the clinic?"

The Bearpaw's owner, Jimmy Whitehorse, was ushering other patrons out before locking the front door. "I'll help." He returned from the kitchen with a large carboard box and several plastic containers. "This should hold everything. And here's a couple pair of gloves—compliments of the cook."

Ben and Julie both put on the latex gloves and then carefully began collecting food from the chief's partially eaten meal.

Julie paused, "I'm still in shock. What could have happened?"

"I'm going to go to the clinic with the body. I need to talk to the doctor. Do you mind taking the car back to Uki's?" Julie shook her head and Ben took off the gloves and handed her the keys. "I'll try not to be too late."

+ + +

Finally, it was just the three of them; Ben, the doctor, and the inert body of the chief on a gurney between them. The coffee maker was bubbling away in the kitchen area.

"How about something a little stronger? Something to put into that coffee?"

Doc Kane opened the bottom drawer of his desk and pulled out a bottle of Old Bushmills. "Fresh out of whipped cream and brown sugar, or we could have a hell of an Irish Coffee."

"This will do, thanks."

"You'd think we had ourselves a serial killer out here—a real Ted Bundy of the Yukon. Think about it. The chief is number four in a very short period of time. We've had Ed, Brant, the PETA kid, and now the chief. Doesn't instill confidence, does it?"

"Not when the chief whispered a warning just before he died, something about my having a target on my back. Any idea what happened?"

"He didn't choke on anything. We didn't miss out on a chance to apply the Heimlich. My guess is heart. He'd had some problems before—had a stent put in, if my memory serves me correctly. I remember he was hospitalized in Anchorage for a week or so, maybe three years ago. I don't know if he was currently sticking to his diet or exercising like he should, but this is another death that can be easily explained if it's heart trouble. I just think the coincidences are adding up. I guess I'd take his warning seriously if I were you."

"Pete was still here late this afternoon, want me to give him a call? I'm assuming you'll need to get the body to Anchorage?"

"Yeah, that would be helpful. Tell him I'll meet him

here in time for the red eye and then I'll give you a ride
back to Uki's."

Chapter 23

Ben was up at five-thirty. He wasn't looking forward to seeing Pete again, not after yesterday. But the least he could do would be to help Pete and Doc Kane load the chief's body on the flight out. Once again, the hallway at the clinic had acted as refrigeration. But it took the three of them plus two deputies to get the body, gurney and all, down the steps and into a police van.

"With the chief gone, who has jurisdiction over E.J.? As in, who has the authority to either keep him locked up or release him?" Ben asked.

"I'd say under the circumstances slap an electronic monitor on his ankle and turn him loose," one of the deputies offered.

"That makes sense. I honestly believe that he's not going anywhere. I'll stop by on my way back to my office."

Ben couldn't wait to tell E.J.

"Let me know as soon as you know something." Ben gestured toward the body. "I'm hoping it was his heart. I'm not ready for a serial killer in Moose Flats."

"I agree but just the same, you be careful. And thanks for your help." The doc shook his hand, then followed the body up the steps and into the plane. Pete stayed quiet but nodded good-bye before making his way to the cockpit.

+ + +

Ben had no idea if E.J. had eaten breakfast but he brought two cinnamon rolls in a bag and two paper cups of black coffee sitting in the console of Uki's car. Once again, his landlady had let him borrow transportation.

It was eerie walking through the chief's empty office on his way back to the jail. He still couldn't believe that the seemingly robust man was gone. Did he have any idea what he'd do if it had been a murder? He only half-heartedly believed the doc's serial killer theory. So far, every death had an explanation, from the first victim being mistaken for wild game, the second having an allergic reaction, and now to heart failure. All great cover-ups. Or not?

E.J. was by himself. Someone had given him his phone back and he was sitting on the bottom bunk texting.

"Hey, what's this I hear about my keeper buying it?"

"Yeah, in the middle of a fantastic plate of meatloaf. Information moves at lightning speed around here."

"Cleaning lady had the details this morning. Supposedly his heart? He'd had problems before. And it wasn't like he didn't weigh two-eighty."

"That's the doc's guess but he doesn't rule out foul play.

Honestly thinks we might have a serial killer in our midst."

"Surely that's a joke?"

"I don't really think so—Doc Kane isn't given to levity concerning his work."

"I don't even see a connection among the deceased. Different motivations."

"As long as we're on the subject, who brought lunch in for the PETA kid?"

"Usually it's something my mother puts together but that day the Bearpaw made it a box lunch. I'm sure Mama sneaked in a brownie or two and Raven was the one who dropped off the two boxes with an extra one for the chief."

"Do you remember what you had?"

"Chicken salad sandwiches, tossed salad, and a soft drink."

"The doc thinks the kid succumbed to a nut allergy—was there any dressing for the salad?"

"Vinaigrette. Good stuff, I've had it before."

"It'd be nice if there were samples."

"Hey, you know the trash with the lunch leftovers might still be in back unless the cleaning lady emptied the bin. Sometimes she does, but not always. It's not like setting garbage on the back steps is going to smell in these temps. Maybe attract a bear every once in a while, but that's about all."

"If you put this on, you can help me find the stuff."

"Electronic monitor? I'm free?" The whoop of joy probably startled workers three offices away.

Ben nodded, "Well, I'm sort of your new keeper, but I have the code to open the cell and I bet I can get your word not to leave town. Right?"

"In spades. I'm not going anywhere."

"Then let's take a look at those lunch remains." Ben punched in the code and slid the cell door open. "Here's the monitor. Right ankle, just tight enough so that it doesn't move around a lot."

"I'll grab a couple zip lock bags from the kitchen. Go straight down that hall, meet you on the porch."

The container was actually a half-sized dumpster close enough to the building that someone didn't have to wander out in the snow in order to toss out garbage. No wonder it wasn't emptied regularly. Ben decided he could wait for E.J. and not go diving himself. E.J. would be able to identify the lunch remains better than he could. And he was right. It took E.J. about one minute to retrieve two cardboard boxes, stuff them into plastic bags and return to the porch.

"You think this is going to be helpful?"

"If a food stuff in here does contain nuts, it will give us the origin."

"But not who put it there—even if it was on purpose. I don't remember the kid mentioning being allergic to anything. And I'll be honest, I didn't notice a medical bracelet. I'm really inclined to say his death was purely accidental."

"Yeah, me too. I'm kinda going through the motions for Doc Kane."

Ben gave E.J. a ride to his mother's house and stayed long enough to see Ahnah embrace him, saying over and over, "I know you're innocent. I know you didn't kill Ed." She didn't even try to wipe away the tears.

Ben didn't intrude. He excused himself and drove back to his office. He'd put notices up around town—on the church bulletin board, the make-shift gym at the high school, in the front window at the Bearpaw—announcing the first meeting of a parents, teachers and friends against drugs. He had no idea if he'd have anyone in attendance, but it was a place to start.

He wanted any solutions to come from the community, not dictated by him. Uki had promised to get with Marie and make sure he had coffee and some kind of treat. If the group was too big, Marie had said he should move out of the conference room and use the main floor of the church. She even promised to do a little dusting in preparation.

There had been a request to RSVP with Marie's office phone listed on the flyer. Ben needed to see if there had been anyone signing up.

He had barely reached Marie's door when she called out, "I just counted twenty-two replies—you have a crowd for tonight."

Ben felt more relief than he wanted to admit. This was his first interaction with the village at large. E.J. offered to sit in but they both decided that it might not be a good idea. He was still not cleared of a murder charge, and E.J. was aware there was more than a little distrust of a local-turned-lawyer coming back to tell the other locals how to do things. Doc Kane had been right, there was always a mix of pride and jealousy when someone was able to better himself. Ben was glad he didn't have to repeat gossip about how the village felt about him.

So, Ben was on his own. Julie was busy with her feature on Raven and the dogs but it might be awkward having her sit in anyway. Native people didn't like to talk in front of strangers—at least non-Natives. His Pueblo heritage put him in a position of trust. He hated to admit it but E.J. had probably chosen the right person to bring an anti-drug program to the tundra and open a clinic.

He'd spend the afternoon organizing handouts, sign-up sheets, and refreshments. He had several workshops planned but offering them depended on what the group was interested in and might need. Sign-up sheets would indicate interest and nothing was cast in stone at this point. Without overdoing the statistics, he had a number of fact sheets covering everything from Narcan to drug-caused medical conditions. Sometimes those were an eye-opener, but often not of interest. An addict losing his teeth to meth wasn't a deterrent.

There was a 'closed' sign on the Bearpaw—out of support for Chief Pitka? Maybe. But probably because of possible health issues. Any unexplained death had to be investigated to help support what the autopsy might find. The Bearpaw could be a crime scene or simply the unfortunate, unplanned final destination of the deceased. It'd be next week at the earliest that a definitive cause of death would be known. At least this would slow rumors that the death was in any way related to the food. But that meant Ben was on his own to get something before the seven o'clock meeting. He'd just finished a couple hours of paperwork when there was a knock on the door.

"Come in." Marie must be out. She usually announced any visitors—not that it was needed but it seemed to fit her idea of what an administrative assistant would do.

"Thought you could use something hot." Jimmy Whitehorse stood in the doorway holding out an insulated food carrier. "There's enough moose stew in here for the missus to have a bowl later. Oh yeah, and some bread—fresh baked this morning according to Ahnah Takanni."

"Fantastic. I was beginning to think I probably wouldn't make it to the end of the meeting before I fainted from hunger. This is perfect. I think you saved a life. And Julie will be thrilled. That's her favorite dish."

"I also brought some finger foods for tonight's meeting. I needed to use up some perishables since we're closed for a couple days. It's nothing fancy."

"That's great. Leave an invoice with me and I'll see that Marie cuts you a check in the morning."

"Naw, this one's on me. My contribution to the community. We've needed you or someone like you for a long time. I'm hoping what you have to offer will be well received."

"I hope so, too."

"Um, doc, do you have a minute?"

"Sure, pull up a chair."

"I don't have time to get comfortable. I just want to share a FYI."

"Something I can help with?"

"Um, I don't know. Brant Thomas was a good friend of mine. When he came back here, he was clean and had been for awhile. The night he died we both had gotten pretty wasted—booze, not drugs. Brant had passed out by midnight but he was alive. I tried to get him up to go home but he was too drunk. Doc, somebody injected Brant with that fatal dose laced with fentanyl. He was not using. Plus, he couldn't have lifted a syringe, let alone inject the contents that night. I'd swear on my mother's grave someone killed him."

"Have you talked to anyone about this?"

"To the chief. He listened and took some notes. Asked if I had any idea who might want him dead. Said he had his own ideas—might have a couple people that he needed to question. That was it."

"Is that the only person you talked with? No one from the family? Friends?"

A shake of the head. "I tried to talk to Raven but they had been kinda on the outs and she brushed me off. She didn't seem very torn up over the death in the first place. Guess she spent a lot of money to get him back here and then the two of them just couldn't make a relationship work. I only talked to her and the chief. Nobody else's gonna listen. Once an addict, always an addict; and I don't have proof just a really strong overpowering gut-level sense of 'I know'. And that ain't good enough to get anyone's attention—and make them want to do something about it."

"Without saying too much, let me share that you're not alone in questioning Brant's death and a couple others. No promises. As you know it's difficult to prove. But there are people keeping an ear to the ground. If you hear of anything or suspect someone of knowing something, I'd appreciate your letting me know."

"Thanks, doc." A sigh, "I don't feel so crazy anymore." He grabbed Ben in an impromptu bearhug. "You're the best, doc."

Ben walked Jimmy to the door and reassured him that he'd stay in touch. Interesting. Doc Kane could be onto something. But, if so, were others in danger? And what was the common thread among the deaths? If there even was one.

Ben walked back to his desk and scooped out a bowl of stew, warmed it to piping hot in the kitchen's microwave, and tore off a generous chunk of homemade bread before carrying everything back to his desk. Julie would be thrilled. This stuff was good.

Chapter 24

The meeting was a success. Not that Ben felt comfortable patting himself on the back when that success was borne out of desperation and a pervading sadness. Everyone who attended had been touched by the opioid epidemic. Every single person. Husbands, wives, children—everyone knew, or was related to someone, who had died. The discussion over what would serve their best interests went on well past the meeting's scheduled ending.

After the initial discussion of current problems, the conversation turned to questions about the future. What would the clinic be like? Who would man it? Would there be one central person in charge? What workshops would be the best preventatives? Who should go into the schools? Was there money for hiring professionals? Were middle school-aged children too young to see a video on the ravages of addiction? The questions were well thought out and the answers full of hope.

Only half of the attendants had RSVP'd; another twenty-five or so just showed up at the door. No one was turned away, and the worst thing to happen was running out of Ahnah's brownies. He couldn't have wished for a better start to his community plan.

+ + +

Ben spent the next three days putting the finishing touches on a proposal that he would submit to IHS. The budget was, perhaps, the most important aspect and the most perplexing. It was a positive that he would be planning a clinic from the ground up; it was off-putting to think of how long it might be before the building would be started, let alone finished. Ben knew all too well how quickly momentum could be lost. His contract placed him in Moose Flats for six months. He'd be back in Florida mid-July. It wasn't enough time. He'd commit, plan, design, and then disappear. He needed to bring E.J. into the planning. In the meantime, Ben had to make certain there was a timeline for goals. He'd made an appointment to meet with two of the lead contractors from the Annex the next day.

But, he had another issue. The chief's body had been taken to the State-run morgue in Anchorage—to wait in a long line of other cadavers in cold storage. Anchorage wasn't the only understaffed, overworked, space-challenged pathology lab in the United States. From the Midwest to the coasts, space was at a premium in almost every facility but, sadly, so were pathologists and other support personnel. Reports had to be researched, documented with photographs, and recorded. The Bearpaw was going through that level of scrutiny at the moment.

The chief's death was listed as 'special interest'—which simply meant no conclusive evidence had been recovered to give a cause of death. When Dr. Kane called Ben, he was just getting off a ten-hour shift. Ten hours. That would be torture, Ben thought. And the doc needed Ben's help. He wanted him to collect everything from the chief's desk, his car and the room he had rented from Uki. Ben asked what he should be looking for and Doc Kane said he didn't know. Ben was to just box up everything—right down to pencils, his coffee cup from the breakroom, any meds—anything the chief had touched was eligible for collection and testing.

"So, what are *you* looking for?" Ben was confused. This seemed like some scatter pattern search where he was flying blindly.

"I wish I knew." The doc sounded beyond tired. "The family has chosen to have a private autopsy. The body will be flown to a lab in Washington state--Seattle, I think. It seems the chief had a sizeable life insurance policy that requires a definitive cause of death to pay out. Needless to say, the family would like things expedited. This is going to cost them thousands, but if you weigh that against the two million dollar pay out, it's not that much."

"And no ideas of cause? I'm sure you've completed a preliminary examination?"

"Yes, but we lack the sophisticated lab here to look at everything. We'll catch run-of-the-mill poisons, for example, but something sophisticated might get by us. That's why I need everything—literally everything the chief touched or ingested."

"Let me know when you get things collected, then put them on the next flight here. I appreciate this, Ben."

"And you take care." Ben clicked his phone off and put it down the desk. He didn't have time for all the running around but the ramifications of a possible intended death, a murder, were huge and could potentially involve a number of people. And something told him to keep quiet—gather everything the doc had asked for but not tell anyone why he was doing it.

If there had been foul play, no one was talking about it, no what-ifs anyway. Heart attack seemed to be the culprit according to the grapevine. And if anyone asked what Ben was doing he could always say the family had requested the chief's belongings be sent to them. And the doc had stressed the urgency. It was always too easy for things to disappear—someone cleans up, throws away empty containers that might hold clues, for example. Which jolted his memory. He still had two zip-lock bags of lunch box remains that might shed light on the PETA kid's death. He'd mark them separately and send them off to Doc Kane along with the chief's belongings.

Ben got up, gave the first five pages of a summation of last night's meeting to Marie to type up, put on his parka and walked across the parking lot to the chief's office.

Today the information desk was manned and Ben explained to the young man on duty that he had been asked by the family to collect the chief's belongings. No problem. The young man even helped Ben unfold, open and tape the sides of the three cardboard boxes he'd taken from the storeroom.

The chief's office had been kept locked. That was a plus. At least it discouraged anyone with 'help yourself' inclinations. The office was spartan—the stapler was lined up with a three-hole-punch, which was next to four pens, all on an immaculate blotter that covered half the desk. OCD tendencies came to mind.

He found the chief's coffee cup in the first desk drawer on the right and after donning latex gloves, put it gingerly in an envelope and then the packing box. Next was a portable radio, three packages of typing paper, a tightly closed bag of what were probably Ahnah's brownies, one whole, one half-eaten, two packages of unused markers, replacement light bulbs; by now, Ben was beginning to fill a second box.

He solicited the help of the young man from the information desk to separately stack folders from the filing cabinet on a side table. Someone from the office would need to go through those and decide what might be priority or contain highly private personnel information that couldn't be shared and needed to stay.

He had seen the chief's cruiser out back and asked for the keys. Again, no one seemed to question his gathering of personal effects. The car yielded a heavy wool plaid scarf, seal skin gloves, a bottle of Excedrin, two pocket-packs of Kleenex, and that was about all. His credentials were clipped above the visor and Ben left those. Likewise, the glove compartment and the console both held only job-related articles—a flashlight, GPS equipment, a tool kit—not things Ben could really explain taking. Whoever inherited the car would expect those tools to be there.

Uki luckily hadn't touched the chief's room on the first floor of her house. He'd apparently rented the room for several years, but it wasn't obvious the stay had been a long one—the room was as spartanly furnished as his office. No pictures of family even. There was something kind of sad about that.

The adjoining bath was private so Ben emptied the

medicine cabinet first. More Excedrin, three prescriptions, one for high blood pressure (did that prove a probable heart attack?), shaving cream, razors, box of Band-Aids— nothing stood out as suspect, at least not to Ben.

Articles of clothing came next and called for two more boxes which Uki managed to come up with. Finally, he was finished. He taped and marked contents on what was now five full boxes, carried them downstairs, called Pete, got his estimated time of arrival in Anchorage for later that afternoon, and lastly left a message at the Anchorage coroner's office for Doc Kane.

He hoped it hadn't been a wasted day, but it seemed he was getting everything done but his own work. He'd just have to get an early start in the morning.

Chapter 25

I can't believe I'm going. But it makes perfect sense. My press pass will get me into almost anywhere. I rented a two-bedroom condo on the south side before I came to Moose Flats just so I'd have a home base in Anchorage. It'll be great for Zac. Fifteen satellite TV channels, a gym and pool on premises, four-star restaurant and ice cream bar. He'll be in heaven. At least he won't be stuck with strangers while his mom's racing. The minute Raven suggested I tag along, I knew that would give me invaluable material for my feature."

"I'm jealous."

"Oh, Ben, I wish you could get away. I'm taking a leave from the Moose Flats Council on climate change and relocation. I didn't mean to let them down but supporting Raven has their approval. It wouldn't hurt the reputation of Moose Flats to have an Iditarod winner."

"I'd love to tag along, but I feel guilty taking as much time as I do away from my job. I spent three hours collecting and boxing up the chief's belongings to send to Dr. Kane day before yesterday. The workshop and discussion were so successful, I need to capitalize on the enthusiasm and get the attendees involved in something else as quickly as I can."

"Well, I'll miss you."

"Oh, sure. You're going to be too busy for that." But he grinned. He was glad she was excited about the journalistic opportunity, but he was most thrilled she seemed to want to spend time with Zac. That was a true plus, and all her idea. "When do you leave?"

"Raven is still in the middle of preparations here. The race is the first weekend in March, three weeks from Saturday. I overheard her tell Pete to plan on being there with the dogs set up ten days out. That means we leave in five days. She doesn't want the dogs to lose weight or get out of condition. Keeping her animals in top shape is challenging. I'm going to start working with her here so that I can help later on."

"She's not paying you with more tats, is she?" Ben was half-way kidding.

"I haven't heard any complaints about mine." He'd only gotten glimpses of the feather on her shoulder and actually had to admit it was well done.

"And you probably won't—at least not here. Raven's talented. Have you planned your article yet? Like a title?"

"It's not original but until something better suggests itself, I'm calling it 'The Last Great Race.' It's truly a one-of-a-kind competition. Combine history, some of the most beautiful scenery to be found anywhere, with danger, human interest, and insane cold to be endured over one thousand miles of unpredictable terrain and you have the Iditarod. I'm drawn to it yet I'm repulsed by it—but no one can deny it has everything, evokes emotion for sure."

"I suppose every musher has his or her own recipe for winning."

"I could write volumes on diet and preparation—on the road work and conditioning alone. I also want to include the breeding behind Raven's dogs—her father's contribution. Raven certainly isn't the first woman to run the race and won't be the first to win, if she does."

"Do you think she has a chance?"

"She's worked hard for it. Right down to deciding which trails she'll run at night."

"At night? That doesn't seem wise."

"Sometimes it can give a musher an advantage. Depends on the dogs and what they can endure. If you push the dogs too early, they won't perform down the trail later."

"What kind of weight are they carrying? I remember seeing sleds loaded—piled high with supplies."

"There's a fair amount of equipment required. For example, an artic parka tested to below zero tolerance, the same for a sleeping bag are both must-haves. Then basic tools—ones you would expect would be necessary, an axe and picks—plus snowshoes and boots for the dogs. All this before you figure in the weight and amount of food for human and dogs. Edible supplies have to last for up to three weeks on the trail."

"Did you say a woman has won before?"

"First female winner in 1985, Libby Riddles."

"I think this is a terrific opportunity for Zac to see history first hand. And I'm glad you'll be there as an extra set of eyes. Ten-year-olds can get into trouble without even trying. But are you sure you want to baby-sit? In addition to everything else?"

"I'm considering it prep work—for when he can spend time with us. It's a great opportunity to bond. He's an easy kid to be around; I'm going to enjoy being with him."

+ + +

Ben hadn't heard from Doc Kane, other than a thank you for sending the chief's belongings, and for the two bags from the kid's jail box-lunch. He didn't hold out hope that proving nut oil was the culprit would make a difference—another untimely mistake, probably.

Not having heard didn't mean anything sinister. He wasn't going to panic. Probably nothing more than Doc Kane was still waiting in line for the new pathologist to examine the chief's body and that the private lab was at capacity. Private labs were also more than likely overworked.

Still, Ben was feeling pressure to find out. Natural death or murder? He couldn't forget Jimmy Whitehorse and the accusation that someone had taken Brant's life. It wasn't easy to just sit and wait. He'd never been known for having patience—not when more human lives might be at stake.

Between winter on the tundra and the death of the chief, E.J.'s plight had cooled somewhat. No one was pushing for a conviction or to lock him up again. Even Ahnah wasn't pushing an investigation into her husband's death. But, then, it would only put her son into focus again.

Judging from her welcome when he got home,

reopening the case would never happen if it depended on her to do it. It did seem odd that she wouldn't want closure—was it an accident?

Pretty much everyone seemed to accept E.J.'s explanation of just being curious with his visits to spend time with a body that didn't talk back and had decided Ed was in the wrong place at the wrong time, the victim of an accidental shooting. But to Ben her silence raised questions.

Wasn't this what he had hoped for? Quiet time with no pending crises. So why did his grandmother's saying pop into his head? The quiet before the storm. She had always had a sixth sense when it came to impending doom. He had to stop thinking that way. That was overblown—doom? What even gave Ben that idea? Yet, there was a nagging feeling of something being not quite right.

He'd had three calls about individual, private sessions after the community meeting. Three out of forty-nine in attendance. He wished there had been more, but this was a start. He knew building trust would not happen overnight.

All three new patients were young men in their twenties, in so many ways the age group most threatened by the opioid crisis. Men afraid to leave and panicked about staying. Knowing that if they left, they lacked the skills to get a good-paying job in the lower forty-eight without training, and schooling would take money that they didn't have. Catch-22 didn't even begin to describe their dilemma.

The one bright side to building the Annex was that it would provide good jobs for all who wanted to work. The downside was that money could only lead to more drugs. And the good jobs weren't permanent—a year, maybe two at the most and the community would be moved and the building completed. The future was fragile. And there couldn't be a better time for Ben to be involved.

He could use help but he put his hiring of interns on hold. He needed to interview at the University and not drag each applicant out to Moose Flats before he'd vetted them. It would save money and time in the long run. He'd build a right-to-refuse into their contracts once they had visited and, for whatever reason, found the working conditions not to their liking. He hated the hiring and firing part of his job. It was important to personally oversee that aspect, but it was still a pain in the ass.

With Julie lined up to be in Anchorage for two or three weeks, he'd visit, spend some time with Zac, and get the hiring of interns out of the way, too. He honestly found himself looking forward to a little time in some swanky digs, someplace that was warm, that probably had fluffy towels … well, he had a pang of guilt; if he wanted fluffy towels he should have brought his own. Uki was a great landlady. He shouldn't disparage her in any way.

"You got another. I put him down for two o'clock," Marie called out from her desk. Ben still hadn't gotten used to the human intercom system. He'd barely had time to get back from lunch and confirm his three appointments for the morning, but he wasn't going to turn away someone who wanted to see him.

Ben walked out to Marie's desk. "Any background?"

"This one's a kid. Nineteen. He's Uki Kakee's nephew, Keith. Ahnah and Uki had one brother. He and his wife moved to Oregon in their early twenties and only had the one child. Keith lost both parents while he was quite young and Uki raised him. Keith graduated high school a year ago last spring and has a couple Junior college semesters under his belt—on the playing field, as well as, in the classroom. That's a real success story out here. Brant Thomas had taken an interest in him—groomed him to be scouted by the University of Washington this past fall. I hear he was accepted for next year—caught the coaches' attention as a walk-on, thanks to Brant. Locally the kid excelled in soccer and basketball, but football's his love. Brant was working out with him and teaching him the basics. You know, how to read plays. He really took Brant's death hard. Frankly, I'm glad he's coming in to talk. I think he needs that. His Aunty's been worried sick."

Uki's nephew. That would explain the dirty laundry he'd seen piled on the washer in her utility room. The one thing college-age kids seemed able to produce in abundance. Ben walked back into his office, put two soft drinks on the table, next to yellow pads and pens. "Send him on in when he gets here."

Ben had his back to his office door and was putting finishing touches on the agenda for the next community meeting when he heard a rustle of sound at about the same time Marie's voice rang out, "Keith's here."

"Hi, Doctor Pecos. I didn't mean to interrupt." The kid in the doorway literally filled it up. He had to be six-two or maybe an inch taller, and well over two hundred pounds—with not one ounce of fat anywhere on his body.

"You're not interrupting, I'm expecting you. Come in." Ben walked forward and shook Keith's hand. "Linebacker?"

"Yeah. How'd you know?"

"You've got the size they look for. Have you played much? Weather would discourage having teams out here on the tundra."

"JUCO last year in the NWAC."

"Whoa. You're going to have to help me here. A junior college? Where?"

"Washington State in the North Western Athletic

Conference. I'm going to transfer to UW next year."

"Sounds like you're pretty good."

"Not bad, I guess. Got some recognition anyway—enough for University of Washington to be interested. Actually, they offered me a full ride—all four years on a football scholarship."

"Congratulations. That's terrific." Ben pointed to the conference table. "Let's sit at the table. Soft drink? Or I do have some bottled water in the fridge."

"This is fine." Keith popped the top on a Mountain Dew.

Ben brought his coffee over from his desk and sat down. "You're Uki's nephew?"

"Yes. She's the one who bankrolled me to go to school in the lower forty-eight. I think she's as thrilled about my scholarship as I am."

"I didn't know much about her family other than E.J., and Raven—and, of course, Ahnah."

"I'm their brother's son. He was killed in a snow machine accident when I was five. Then my mom died from cancer when I was nine, and I lived with Aunt Uki during middle school and high school."

"I've really enjoyed living at your aunt's boarding house. I think she could put the Bearpaw to shame if she ever opened a restaurant with her sister."

"Yeah, I agree."

"How can I help you today?" Ben watched the young man bite his lip, look down at the table and trace his finger in the ring of condensation from the cold soda before reaching for a box of Kleenex, taking a tissue and wiping up the moisture.

"I need to tell someone something. I need your opinion.

I heard that because I could be called a patient, you can't tell anyone what I say. Is that right?"

"I think you're thinking of lawyer/client privilege but it works about the same with me. I'll promise I won't say anything that I haven't cleared with you first. Are you comfortable with that? You have my word."

A nod, then, "I killed Brant Thomas—well, that is, I might as well have."

Ben sat forward. Killed Brant? "How? Brant died of a lethal overdose."

"Someone came to me wanting to buy heroin. But then this person wanted to make sure the dealer could make it strong—maybe cut with fentanyl. Said it needed to have more kick. This person was older, hadn't been around here for a while so didn't have any contacts. Doctor Pecos, half the kids I grew up with use—a couple deal. I gave a dealer's name to this person and the next thing I knew Brant was dead. He'd been clean. He was working with me on the field, used his contacts to get me a try-out with the University last fall. He was behind my success. He was like a brother. I didn't know what this person was going to do with the drugs. I was led to believe that it was for a party."

"Why would someone come to you? I'm sure you've never used so why would this person take a chance that you could help?"

"'Cause this person is my cousin. That's why you can't say anything. And I don't believe that Brant would have injected the drug himself. He'd turned his life around. Did you hear that the Hawks were bringing him back as part of their field personnel this spring? He was so happy. Dr. Pecos, he'd help anyone. He only came back to help someone start a business."

"Did you handle the drugs? Buy the heroin and fentanyl and then sell the mix to your cousin?"

"No. I just gave her a name of the local dealer. She did her own buying."

"And you know, for a fact, that she purchased drugs from this individual?"

"He said she did."

"I have a feeling I know your cousin."

"Yeah. Pretty well from what I hear."

Ben ignored that comment; it wasn't meant to be snide, but he couldn't keep from feeling dread as he asked, "Raven?"

Keith nodded.

"But why? Raven was successful. The dogs were her dream."

"Paid for by Brant. She owed him a hundred and forty thousand dollars."

"Aren't you mistaken? I thought Raven sold her business in Anchorage and invested in the dogs."

"She lost her business. When the economy tanked, it killed her business. Nobody's going to afford two to three hundred dollars an hour for a tat—and that was just an average. For high-end, intricate designs, it was more like five hundred. She was good, one of the best in the city, but she didn't have anything to fall back on."

Ben put his pen down and sat back. "I had no idea."

"She'd hit everybody up for money including my Aunt. Raven owed way too much on equipment, and the rent on her store-front in Anchorage was exorbitant. She got behind in the mortgage on her house and basically lost everything. Brant bailed her out."

"You're sure about this? They must have been close."

"He wanted to marry her. It would have worked out great 'cause Zac worshipped him. I know she floated some rumor about Brant hitting her. Another thing that just didn't happen. I knew Brant. That wasn't in his nature." Keith paused and took a deep breath. "I've heard the rumors about your connection to Zac and Raven. I'm sorry. This can't be easy for you to hear, but I thought you'd understand and know how sick I am that I got involved. And you'd know why I have to keep it a secret. Kinda in a way you're involved, too."

The kid was right. Ben's child's mother was being accused of setting up a murder if not actually committing it. What a mess. And what should he do?

Ben pushed back from the table and walked to the window. It was almost too much to process. Raven. And this wasn't the first person with first-hand information of Brant Thomas's overdose. It gave credence to Jimmy Whitehorse's story. He took a breath and turned back.

"Keith, you were right to come here and share this. Yeah, I am involved. And you knew I'd honor your request not to let the name of the person out. It's not a simple problem. And not something that can be proved. No one that we know of saw Raven either buy the drugs or put the needle in Brant's vein. We have circumstances, nothing more. But I want you to forgive yourself. You didn't know and you were approached by, a family member."

"When I came to live with Aunt Uki, Raven had returned from spending the summer with E.J. and you. She'd just found out she was pregnant. Uki and Ahnah thought she got knocked up on purpose. Even E.J. thought so. We expected her to go after you. You know, demand money, make you marry her. But it was weird. She swore everyone to secrecy and declared the baby was hers and she wouldn't share it. Her mom and Uki helped raise Zac when Raven went away to school but even then, she came home for long weekends twice a month. She's done a good job with Zac. He's been her life. She was really pissed that E.J. brought you here."

"Yeah, I know. But why kill Brant? Was it the money?"

"That's my guess. Zac gets everything. And it's no secret Raven wants out of here. She's caught here without the means to leave. I think feeling cornered makes her unpredictable."

Ben didn't really have anything else to say. Keith was wise beyond his years and if he was right about Raven's motive what would he do with the information? What could he do and still honor his promise?

"Zac needs a dad."

"I agree. I'm not going to let him down."

Chapter 26

Ben needed to get out of the office. Once again, he had Uki's Outback and headed toward Ahnah's house and the dog yard. Julie was helping Raven by cleaning and packing harnesses and grooming tools. Flying that many dogs to Anchorage was a big job. The necessary baggage alone was pretty daunting.

Ben stood a moment at the edge of the yard and watched the animals' excited pacing. They knew something was up and the anticipation was being expressed in yelps and a howl here and there.

Folded crates were stacked along the inside of the barn door with food containers holding them upright. Each dog had his own bed and dishes. Nobody shared a crate or eating utensils unless there was no other choice. Even the best of friends could take a nip out of a neighbor for what humans would think wasn't a very good reason. Sometimes it seemed that if one dog sniffed another's rear end uninvited, a fight could start. It helped if the handlers could speak 'dog'. They had to know what would be tolerated and what wouldn't.

"Ben, over here." Julie was untangling a pile of brightly colored waterproof nylon webbing, checking the padding and the reflective strips on each individual harness. Once a harness was checked and either given an okay, put in a pile to be repaired, or simply discarded due to wear, the ones that would be packed for the trip were hung on the wall. The dogs were fairly uniform in size, making worn parts interchangeable with new. Nothing was wasted, thrown away or discarded that might be useful later.

"Are you sure you know what you're doing? No offense intended but that looks confusing." To Ben, the strips of webbing and buckles and rings looked impossible to distinguish from one another. "What are you checking for?"

"All the harnesses are lightweight at twelve-hundred-pound test, waterproof with two ounces of storm coat ripstop on three-eighths inch thick closed-cell foam at the shoulders, breastplate and underarms. Raven's colors are red and black and this type of harness is called the Seavey Harness. Her father used Seavey harnesses when he raced. They've been around for a while." As Julie explained each segment of a harness, she held it up. "Whether the webbing crisscrosses, rides low on the side of the dog or forms a box configuration on the animal's back says whether it's a X-back or an H-back. Then this one is a simple Martin's Ring Collar. And then, of course, there's the traditional X-Back and the Collared X-Back—"

"Enough. I surrender." Ben was laughing. "Where'd you learn all that? Were you afraid of being tested before you got this job?"

"I admit to doing a little reading and looking at a lot of YouTube videos."

"Whatever you did, it worked. You sound like a pro."

"I can't tell you how excited I am. It means so much more to be a real working part of the team and not just a bystander asking questions. Oh, I was going to tell you— we're going into Anchorage a few days early. Pete has everything ready for departure in the morning. They are opening the trail early and we'll be able to walk a portion. This is the forty-eighth annual running of the race and they change the exact course of the race each year so it's always a new challenge. The drawing for starting position will be at the banquet next Thursday. Will you be there for the start? That's on Saturday."

"I'm going to try. There's a pretty good-sized group going from Moose Flats; I'm hoping to catch a ride with the locals. I'll get a schedule from Pete and tell him to count me in."

"Look how big Romo is." Zac walked in from outside. He had the puppy on a leash fastened to a bright red harness. "Puppies need to get used to wearing a harness when they're babies. But he can't pull anything yet."

"Looks like he has his own name tag." A rectangle of shiny brass hung from the center chest-plate ring of the harness.

"Yeah, Mom made that for him. It has my name on it, too. You know if he ran away, people could call when they found him."

"I don't think you have to worry about Romo running

away." Ben watched the puppy snuggle close to Zac's legs as he sat on a camp stool next to Julie and the pile of harnesses.

"He likes me." Zac reached down to stroke the puppy's head and ears. "His fur is really soft. He can't go to the race; he's too small and he's going to be really sad. I know he'll miss me. Could you come and pet him?"

"Sure. I think I could handle that. What does he like for treats?"

"Chicken. He'll do anything for chicken."

"Then chicken it is. When I eat at the Bearpaw, I'll have the cook make me a to-go bag just for Romo. A real doggy-bag." Ben laughed but his humor was lost on Zac.

"He'll like that." Ben was almost knocked off-balance by the impromptu hug Zac hopped up to give him. "Thanks. Oh yeah, he likes the chicken fried."

"Fried, it is, then."

Ben couldn't help but smile as he watched Zac lead Romo back out into the yard and thought once again how very much like his father he was. He didn't even try to quash the pride he felt. And that alone still sounded weird. How quickly his life had changed. And how quickly he'd accepted the new norm.

Julie looked up. "He likes you. And he really reminds me of you—just a little smaller version."

"Yeah, I was thinking the same thing."

"Any plans for what happens when you leave here?"

"I'd like to take him back to the Pueblo. Maybe late summer before school begins but before we get caught up in moving to south Florida. I could take a couple weeks off here before the project is finalized. It's a pretty time of year in New Mexico."

"That would be great. Think how exciting that will be for Zac. He's old enough to appreciate his history."

"I don't know if that will work for me." Raven stepped out of the office. Had she been listening? Must have been. Ben had a feeling that he was about to find out how difficult it was going to be to share a child.

"Other plans?" Ben turned to face Raven. "Nothing's cast in stone. I realize we need to work out the logistics between the two of us—definitely before we talk with Zac. I don't want there to be promises made that will have to be broken."

Raven shrugged. "That depends upon you. I will not have you swooping in and taking over. I mean that. Back off. Three weeks ago you didn't even know you had a child and now you're all lovey planning his future."

"Raven, please—" Julie put down the harness she was checking.

"Not your problem. With due respect, stay out of this. I'm not saying no, I just don't want surprises. Any planning is a group endeavor—Okay?"

"That's fair. I agree to that." Ben looked at Julie who nodded assent.

Raven turned back to Ben. "And another thing. I hear you've been listening to Jimmy Whitehorse and Keith Kakee. Didn't it dawn on you to investigate what part they might have had in Brant's death? Why they felt the need to point a finger at someone else? I think you can do good things in this community; just make sure you also do no harm." With that Raven went back into the office and shut the door—a little too firmly.

"What was that?" Julie whispered, "I feel like I missed something."

"Tell you later," Ben whispered back. "Right now, I need to get Uki's car to her and show up at the office."

+ + +

Ben parked behind the house just as Uki stepped out onto the porch. "I was going to catch your attention before you got out. Go ahead and keep the car till later; I won't be needing it. And it's barbecue tonight—baby-back ribs compliments of Pete who just flew them in from Anchorage. You don't want to miss that." And she was right. Ribs were a favorite.

He parked next to Marie's half-ton pickup in the side lot at the church. Both she and the pastor had reserved spots marked with their names. By default, Ben could have used the Pastor's slot a few spaces closer to the door, but he wasn't really comfortable doing that. He was only borrowing an office and it wasn't going to hurt him to walk the extra feet to reach the front door. As a guest in this community he needed to earn trust and respect, to make sure it didn't look like he was taking advantage of anyone.

"You've had two calls from Dr. Kane. He wants you to get back with him this afternoon if you can." Marie had stopped typing long enough to hand him a slip of paper with Doc Kane's phone number.

She was working on the oldest computer he'd ever seen but younger than the Selectric typewriter she'd used earlier. Now, an oversized monitor took up half her desk space and the Central Processing Unit was sitting on the floor crowding her leg space. It didn't look comfortable.

"I just got my Betty back from the only computer whiz in the village. A couple years at a tech school and he keeps all the Moose Flats' offices in business." She patted the CPU under the desk. "I wouldn't trade her in on a laptop if you paid me double. We've learned each other's quirks together."

"Good to know there's local computer expertise. I'll try Doc Kane now. Oh, before I forget, I'm going to need a flight over to Anchorage Wednesday or Thursday of next week. Do you happen to know Pete's schedule? I think quite a few Moose Flats residents are planning on cheering for Raven at the race's start. I'd like to be there—maybe even attend the dinner Thursday night."

"I'll check. I know Uki and Ahnah are flying over Wednesday morning. Would that flight work if there's room?"

"Perfect, and thanks for making the arrangements. I appreciate your help."

Phone tag. What a waste of time. Ben had tried twice to reach Doc Kane and left messages. Of course, when he steps out to go the restroom he misses the doc's return call. But then Ben's cell phone pings.

"Doc Kane, I was beginning to think we wouldn't make connections this afternoon."

"I'm going to give you an update and then ask for a favor in return."

"Sounds good. I'm hoping you have the results back from the private lab—the autopsy of Chief Pitka."

"That's my update and I'm afraid there's not much to report yet. And that's where my favor comes in. Did you ever know the chief to use eye drops? Either an over-the-counter product or something prescription?"

"No, not that I can remember. I didn't spend a lot of time with him but enough that if he had a dry-eye problem,

I would have noticed him using something. Why do you ask?"

"Well, this is a little premature and I'd rather not say until there's something definitive to report. In the meantime, I'd like you to go dumpster-diving again."

"If it ever becomes an Olympic sport, I'll be in shape."

The doc laughed. "That's the spirit. I was afraid you'd turn me down. And it may not require digging through garbage. Look again in medicine cabinets, night stands, the cruiser, his office desk—anywhere you think he might have kept toiletries or medicines. If you find any prescription eye drops or over the counter drops, preserve the fingerprints that might be on the container, if you can. And, oh yes, try to find out what cooking oil the Bearpaw uses. You can just take a picture of the bottle. I don't think finding peanut oil in use will be of much help. It's the eye drops that may get us closer to the truth."

"I'll do what I can." Ben pressed the off button on the side of his phone then quickly pressed it on again and googled Visine, as one example. It was listed as an Ophthalmic alpha-1-Agonist class drug. It worked in one minute. There were several more brands in the same classification—many of them household standards. Ben quickly jotted down the names of the other products.

One product contained povidone but more than one contained tetrahydrozoline.

That drug had been on the market since the fifties. Highly soluble in water and ethanol.

Lethal if ingested.

Ben stopped and re-read the line. Had he found the basis for Doc Kane's interest in eye drops? Was the chief poisoned? Wikipedia said the product could lead to a slowing down of heartbeats and/or induce seizures. He was amazed to find the number of cases of eyedrop poisonings. He sat back. He was always struck by the number of things he didn't know. And this was one of them.

In order for the drops to kill, they had to be administered over a period of time in food or a beverage. Where did the chief take his meals? Breakfast and lunch were eaten at Uki's. The chief had a room *and* board agreement. His evening meals were almost all at the Bearpaw. They even had an item on the menu named after him: Pitka's Pit-roasted venison loin.

So where to start? He wasn't certain the dumpster would yield anything useful, but he thought he had the advantage of the suspect, whoever that might be, having no idea that a cause of death was even being suspected as something not natural, let alone being investigated. So that broadened the field. Didn't negate checking the dumpsters but meant he needed to be alert to other possibilities. But first he needed to help Julie get ready to leave in the morning.

By the time he got back to their room, Julie had clothing and other items laid out on the bed. She looked frazzled.

"I can take one bag—equivalent to a duffle—and that's all. Three feet by eighteen inches by twelve inches. I'm going crazy. The dinner is semi-formal. At least requires more than snow pants and Muk Luks. Working with the dogs, packing the sled—it's supposed to snow most of the week—but temps are going to be around thirty degrees. Balmy compared to Moose Flats. So how do I take rubber boots, fur-lined boots and dress shoes? Do you know how much room boots take up? And my dress, the little black one with the sequined cape, do I just wad it up under the long underwear and Gore-Tex overalls?"

Ben was fast deciding he was out of his comfort zone and had very limited knowledge when it came to packing women's clothing for travel. Cotton underwear that didn't need special treatment, a pair of jeans, pair of dress slacks, couple dress shirts, one pair of shoes in addition to what he might be wearing … yeah, no comparison. Nothing he owned came close to requiring the kind of care that a sequined cape might.

"I have a plan. I'm coming over Thursday morning— the morning of the dinner. Let me bring the dressy stuff. I'm not traveling with twenty dogs. Pete will have room, and I'm only staying two or three days. I won't be scrubbing out dog's bowls or brushing coats or fitting harnesses."

"Oh my God, I think I just figured out why I married you."

"Should I be worried? I'd thought I maybe attracted you with a couple other virtues?" Her answer was muffled as she threw her arms around his neck and literally jumped into his arms, wrapping her legs around his waist. "Maybe I should clear the bed?"

"And ruin two hours of color-coordinating six flannel shirts with 2 pair of water-proof waders—one in olive green camo? Not on your life but the invite sounds tempting."

He settled for a kiss, well, more than one before putting her down. He wasn't looking forward to having her gone for a couple weeks.

"I'm going to miss you."

"You'll be too busy. Doc Kane will have you diving into dumpsters again."

Ben laughed. "You're actually right. How'd you know I was being sent on another scavenger hunt?"

"Intuition. What's it this time? Someone's lunch? Snack?"

"Eyedrops."

"I don't understand."

"You know, Murine, Visine, or maybe a prescription—something for dry eyes."

"I could save you some time. I know where there's a whole bottle--Ahnah's medicine cabinet. I'm sure that's not unusual. Dry, cold air can literally interrupt the eye's ability to produce and maintain moisture."

"True, but I'd be interested in Ahnah's bottle. That would be a good sample to have. I just have to figure out how to get it." Ben purposefully left out that the product could be used as a poison if introduced to food and even though Doc Kane hadn't said for certain, Ben thought the eye drops were in some way connected to the chief's death. He'd wait until the doc had corroborated his assumption before saying anything to Julie.

"Ben, I think you're inspiring me. I just thought of a great idea. You know that canvas satchel I carry every once in awhile—you always tease me about finding the kitchen sink in there? Well, I think I'll carry that as my purse and not this adorable cross-body leather thing and put all my underwear in it." Julie walked to the closet and came back with the over-sized brown canvas and leather tote. "See? It's perfect."

She turned the tote upside down, shook it and emptied its contents onto the bed. Pens, a pad of paper, lip gloss, packet of Kleenex, coin purse, a couple business cards and the zip-lock bag of Ahnah's brownies. "Oh no, I completely spaced giving these to you the other night. Raven bagged them up, thought you'd enjoy."

"I'm sure they're still good, put them back in your purse for the trip."

"Oh, the last thing I need is more sweets. Uki gave me four cinnamon rolls for the trip."

"Then I'll just be forced to take these to the office—looks like a snack for tomorrow."

+ + +

Five a.m., pitch black other than the lights around the plane and the two spot lights on the roof of the terminal. Even the blinking runway markers were somewhat obscured by the soft snow that was swirling around the plane but not sticking. At least it wasn't bitter cold—probably above zero. The lowered visibility didn't seem to be worrying Pete all that much, Ben noticed. He was reassuring everyone that once they got in the air, instrument flying was easy peasy.

Yeah, right, Ben thought. He couldn't keep Julie from going, but it sure crossed his mind.

The dogs were a handful, each one seeming to try to outdo the others in barking and pulling on their leads. They knew what was going on. They were getting to go somewhere. Julie looked frozen. Thank god they weren't staying in Moose Flats on a permanent basis. His wife was just not a cold-weather enthusiast.

Probably ruled out any more skiing trips to Taos. It might be awhile before he could get Julie into snow country again. But he'd bet he could interest Zac in a ski trip.

He watched his son walk among the dogs, talking to them, patting some on the head, giving a hug to one particularly good-sized Malamute that might be the lead dog. The boy was good with the animals. And Ben would visit Romo while Zac was gone. It was more than just keeping his promise; Ben liked the pup.

Finally, everyone was either seated or crated. Lots of kisses and hugs—Ben even gave Raven a squeeze and she didn't pull away. He stood on the edge of the runway watching Pete taxi the plane. Converted from a commercial commuter plane into a commerce-driven rental, twenty dogs, crates, and four passengers actually fit comfortably with a cargo bay filled with supplies. Pete took the length of the runway before lifting into the cotton-thick whiteness doubling as a sky and was soon swallowed up.

The quiet was suddenly a stark reminder of how alone he was as he walked back to Uki's Outback. But he had enough to keep him busy. He just didn't know where to start his hunt for the eyedrops. He'd keep in mind that he knew where there was a bottle, but he was looking more for something that the chief would have used.

Chapter 27

Once again, he was being sworn to secrecy but Ben understood why. The doc had suspicions but no proof. The autopsy showed the chief's heart had been fine—no clogged arteries. His diabetes was under control so no organs—especially the pancreas or liver—were impacted by ill health. He needed to lose twenty pounds but weight hadn't seemed to contribute to any health issues. He'd lost over fifty pounds after he had the stent put in and changed his eating and exercise habits.

All in all, he was one healthy specimen. But discoloration of the lips and mouth and the report that before death his breathing had slowed dramatically was cause enough to suspect poisoning, and tetrahydrozoline was tough to detect without sophisticated lab tests, yet easy to obtain and administer.

The doc had narrowed cause of death to a possibility of tetrahydrozoline dosing because he'd handled a case that presented almost exactly like this one before. Being so difficult to prove, it was an ideal choice for an area with little or no access to a modern, well-equipped lab. Couple that with a person who had a history of heart problems, and poison would never even be suspected—unless, and the doctor laughed, you had one suspicious SOB as a pathologist coupled with other suspect deaths.

"When do you expect the lab report?"

"I don't think anyone can even imagine how backed up every lab in the state is. I'd like to say within a week to ten days and that's with some friendly pushing on my part. But no promises. When will you be in Anchorage?"

"I'm coming in next Thursday before the start of the race."

"Fingers crossed I'll know something by then. Set aside some time to get together."

Ben put his cell back into his pocket. If Moose Flats did have a killer on the loose, would his not saying anything help the person feel safe enough to try again? That was always a worry. But maybe the person would just mess up, give themselves away.

He had an uneasy feeling and in times like this he could hear the chief's words in his head—*target on your back*. There was something terribly frustrating about not knowing and, of consequence, not being able to do anything.

However, in the meantime, he needed to be retracing his steps to collect any eyedrop meds and maybe check out the peanut oil situation at the Bearpaw and even the Two Sisters Bakery.

"Visitor," Marie's voice rang out. And almost at the same time, E.J. stepped into his office, pulled up his pants leg and declared, "Look Ma, no monitor."

"That's great. How'd you get the charges dismissed?"

"I might want to remind you that I'm a lawyer. The chief was the only one pressing charges and a couple friends of mine in Anchorage agreed that there wasn't enough evidence to hold me—one of those friends just happens to be a judge. So, when circumstantial evidence pointed so strongly to Ed's death being accidental, and the chief wasn't around to say why I should be held, let alone tried, it made sense to dismiss. I swear I think the chief knew the killer and was covering up for somebody. But guess I won't be able to prove that now."

"The important thing is you're out. Just tell me you don't own a deer rifle."

"Not me. Mama's the sharp-shooter in the family—Mama and Raven both share a few trophies. Back in the day, it was Mama who would bag a deer every season."

And at least one of those two, if not both, would have a motive to see Ed Johnson gone, but Ben didn't say anything. He filled E.J. in on the success of his first community workshop and the small but positive follow-up with four individuals. It was a start and forty-nine attendees for a first meeting had to be considered a coup. E.J. was elated. His professional position as community leader was on the line over this.

"Are you going over for the race?" Ben assumed Raven would want his help.

"I should be there, if not helping, at least offering support. Thought I might catch a ride back over that way with Pete late tomorrow. You?"

"I'm tied up here until next week. I'll be there for the dinner and the start of the race. Julie's lending a hand. I'll keep an eye on things here—and pet Romo for Zac."

"I can't tell you how happy I am that you and Julie are being reasonable, maybe supportive is a better word—that you seem to be sharing—helping Raven accept a tough situation and see what's best for Zac."

"Not certain there's been very much acceptance. We still have a lot to work out. But it's a start. I can refer to myself as a father and not flinch."

"Any plans for the next move?"

"Julie and I would like to take Zac to New Mexico. I think it will be important for him to see his roots—other set of roots, that is. Raven isn't thrilled but I'm hoping we can work something out."

"Let me know if I can help. Not that I'm Mr. Popular at the moment but there might be something I could do."

"I'm a bachelor for the next couple weeks, how about lunch later? I've got Uki's car—pick you up?"

"Great. I'll be at Mama's—eleven-thirty?"

"That'll work."

+ + +

Ben was feeling a little guilty. What he really was going to do was pick up E.J. and excuse himself to use their hall bathroom. He hadn't been at all certain that he'd be able to help himself to the bottle of eyedrops that Julie mentioned, but this might be the perfect opportunity.

He walked to the church kitchen and took two zip-lock bags. He'd replace these later—that made him feel better about stealing. Replacing the eyedrops was a little more difficult. It wasn't like there was a Walgreens on every corner.

Most families bought in bulk one or two times a year and traveled to a pharmacy in the nearest large community in between times. Prescriptions were received by mail or picked up at outlying clinics via dog sled during the worst of winter. It wasn't easy to be sick and especially not easy for the elderly.

Ben showed up five minutes early to Ahnah Takanni's house and asked to use the bathroom.

"The church is full of workmen. But not a lot is getting done beside dismantling and packing artwork. One unisex bathroom gets a lot of use. I didn't want to be late by standing in line."

"No problem. First door on your right about halfway down." E.J. pointed to a door that had 'Theirs' painted on it—each letter a different color. "Mama takes the overflow from Uki when she has a busy season. With Raven setting up shop in one guest bedroom, she only has a couple left and that's after my taking up the fourth. She'll grouse about it but I secretly think she's thrilled to have her family around her. She's thinking of adding on another bedroom for Zac."

The salmon-pink tile absolutely sparkled. Not his choice of color, it looked like Home Depot seconds, but someone spent some time cleaning. He was careful to pop the medicine cabinet open during a toilet flush to cover any noise and there it was on the top shelf, the half-empty bottle of eyedrops. He used a square of toilet paper to negate any prints that he might leave and dropped the bottle into the zip-lock bag in his pocket. The snap of closing the cabinet was muted by running water in the sink. Ben had to laugh and congratulate himself. He wasn't quite ready to hire out as a second-story man, but he'd handled this little bit of thievery pretty well.

He stopped to talk with Ahnah on the way out. This was the first one-on-one interaction she'd had with him since the open house to commemorate Ed Johnson's death, and it seemed a little less than cordial. Of course, she would be taking Raven's side over Zac. He was still the bad guy, maybe always would be. He wished things could be different for Zac's sake. Might be a good idea to include Ahnah in the discussion with Raven about sharing responsibility for Zac. At least get her input when it came to scheduling visits.

+ + +

The Bearpaw was packed. When you were the only restaurant in town, you truly had a captive audience. Ben had one more bit of sleuthing—find out if he could what oil might have been used in the dressing for the salad that was served to Andrew Cook.

Another long shot, someone's error more than likely and not intentional. But that hadn't been proved. And more than likely wouldn't be proved one way or the other. Ben had to marvel once again at how the killer, if there was one, had camouflaged his intent so cleverly.

The specials for the day were a choice of fish—fried, poached, grilled or blackened—with a medley of veggies, fresh bread and soup or salad to begin with or moose burgers, choice of cheese. Ben chose the halibut, grilled, and added both New England clam chowder and a tossed salad with house vinaigrette. It looked like there would be a wait so Ben decided to go over the suggestions made at last week's meeting.

"I've got to check on funding but the first thing on the village's wish list is a rehabilitation center—and I think they're right. Getting clean is only ever half of the story. It's a change of life-patterns that will keep people clean. I personally think this is a good time to build in online training. I know there will be a lot of those who are eligible for rehab that didn't graduate high school. So, a basic GED program for starters. Next, the training should have more of a technical and/or industrial slant. There needs to be an appropriately staffed and equipped classroom—let's say, for starters space that can handle twenty-five to thirty students. I know that's small, but I want the first programs to be a success—controlling the numbers can help with that. And success will entice others to get involved."

"I like the plan. Any ideas on staffing or funding?"

"I'll be meeting with University of Alaska personnel when I go into Anchorage for the race next week. There's money for indigenous peoples. State money. And there's support from Indian Health Service. A carefully worded, well-thought-out plan will get us noticed and get us funded. I know I can count on you to put the legal spin on a proposal, right?"

"Sure, count me in. This is exactly the direction that I hoped we'd go in."

"I'm hoping I can add to the plans for a community building at the Annex. Starting from scratch we could design a training center to meet our needs and not be faced with having to gut an already existing building and making do with something second best."

"And equipment? Big stuff?"

"Small engine mechanics training for starters with a bay big enough for a couple racks and individual stations for up to ten snow machines. Eventually, I'd throw in boat motors, and an automotive engine here and there—I'll leave the training needs up to suggestions by the village."

The discussion was interrupted by the waiter serving the two salads and a cup of soup for Ben.

"I'll be back with bread."

"Would it be possible to get a little extra dressing?"

"Yeah, if you don't mind using it right out of the bottle—you may have noticed we're a little busy. Not gonna have the time to get fancy. And this is one thing the cook doesn't mix up himself. Hope that's not too disappointing."

"Not at all." That's even better, Ben thought. He wouldn't have to try to pour dressing into a zip-lock *and* explain to E.J. why on earth he was doing it or have it drip out of the bag and onto his down jacket. How would a person get oil and vinegar out of feathers?

The bottle of vinaigrette was an import from Italy and looked expensive—dark glass, gold embossed label touting the contents as a 'gourmet' mixture. Ben used his phone to snap a photo of the bottle from all sides and almost missed the disclaimer 'may contain peanut oil'. The doc was right. Ben had a feeling that he was holding the killer's implement in his hand.

"What's with the dressing?"

Ben explained the doc's suspicions. But once again finding the culprit didn't mean proving there was any foul play to go along with it, only negligence. "Just helping the doc narrow down the source." That seemed to satisfy E.J. who went back to eating his salad—after taking the bottle and generously pouring more dressing on the crisp Romaine.

"This stuff is good."

Ben nodded and for the hundredth time felt thankful that he didn't suffer from allergies.

"You know, there was one other safeguard suggestion that came out of my meeting the other night. Apparently, something that other villages have done and feel it's really made a difference. Some villages have formed vigilante groups and literally run the drug dealers out of town. Sounds dangerous to me but I'll look at anything that works."

"I think they have the right idea. Getting to the source and keeping drugs from being so readily available makes sense. In fact, Raven decided to get the names of local dealers and do just that—run them out of the village."

"When was this?"

"Fairly recently, maybe a month or so ago. She read an article about how important it was for villages to be proactive and not expect outside help. The article suggested getting the names of the dealers and with or without the help of local law enforcement literally cause these individuals to leave. For one thing, printing their names and addresses in local papers severely cut into their business. I don't think the article suggested foul play, or that any individuals should even carry firearms—that was supposed to be left up to local law. Exposing them and depriving them of customers seemed to be enough. I heard that a clinic a couple villages up the river had to be closed because of illegal opioid distribution. Again, finding the source and cutting it off cleaned up a lot of local problems."

"How did Raven even know where to start?"

"Our cousin, Uki's nephew, a kid about nineteen, is fairly representative of that age-group. Like all kids, he knows what goes on. Not that he's a user; he's too smart for that and he's already got his ticket out. But he knows who does use and where to buy whatever you want."

"That's who Raven talked to?"

"Yeah, him and his pal, Jimmy Whitehorse. Apparently, she made it sound like a deal—like she was buying. I told her that was dangerous but she felt it was the only way to get legitimate information."

"Was she able to get names?"

"Yeah, but it wasn't information that she wanted."

"I'm not following."

"One of the local suppliers was Brant Thomas."

"Seriously? I thought he was clean and had been for a while."

"Not using doesn't mean you walk away from a lucrative business altogether. He apparently kept his contacts and made use of that list out here. I know Raven had no idea. I think she was in shock."

"What'd she do—once she found out?"

"Basically, turned him in. She was working with Chief Pitka. That's why his suicide made sense."

"You think Brant committed suicide?"

"Yeah, no way I'd ever believe it was an accidental overdose. He had a lot to lose and thanks to the chief, he was on the edge of disaster."

Ben sat back. Interesting information and supported in part what Keith and Jimmie had told him. And thanks to the chief's untimely death, there were more questions that only he could have answered.

"Was the chief well-liked?"

"As much as any hard-nose member of law enforcement could be. A love/hate relationship for the most part. People applauded his strictness unless it hit too close to home. Some thought he overstepped his authority, that he should have given more breaks to felons. For example, poaching should have enjoyed a blind eye and the perps not detained and had their game confiscated. The chief was also known to report illegal fishing—boats over limit, for example. Yet, he made villagers feel safe. If they were on the right side of the law, he had their backs."

The plate of grilled Halibut placed in front of Ben stopped conversation for the moment. And E.J.'s moose burger was quickly disappearing.

"How long had Chief Pitka lived in Moose Flats?"

"Off and on pretty much his whole life. He was engaged to my Aunt but it didn't work out."

"To Uki?"

E.J. nodded. "Uh Huh. She's around ten years younger than Mama but never married. Her brother's kid lived with her when his parents died. So, there were reasons for her to stay close to family and not move. But I bet if the truth were known, she's had regrets."

"Have you decided to go into Anchorage before the race?"

"I'm going over with Pete in the morning, why?"

"I'm going to have one more meeting before I join Julie. I was hoping you could be there. I want to discuss what rehab at the Annex might look like and get an idea of what's wanted, even tolerated. I'm hoping to have some sketches of a possible facility for technical vocational classes."

"Sorry I'll miss out. Keep me posted. I'm hearing good things around the village about your plans. You're doing exactly what I'd hoped you would do. And I want you to know how much I appreciate that."

+ + +

Another thorough scouring of the dumpster outside the Village offices, the chief's office, file cabinets. and cruiser turned up no new evidence—at least nothing that called attention to itself. It looked like Ben had only the one bottle of eyedrops to send to Doc Kane and that had no direct tie to the chief. Probably only proved that Ahnah Takanni suffered from dry eyes.

If that was the poison used to kill the chief, it only underscored how diabolically perfect the killer was in covering their tracks.

He'd texted the photos of the Italian vinaigrette bottle last night and slipped the eyedrop bottle still in its zip-lock bag into a courier's pouch and handed it off to Pete that morning. It wasn't much. He could feel Doc Kane's frustration over the phone when he shared what to expect. So, he was back at Chief Pitka's office to double check that he hadn't overlooked anything.

His office had been cleaned as had the cruiser which was now being used by the new, temporary chief, Daniel Deniki. No time had been wasted in replacing Chief Pitka. But there was already gossip in the community that a man in his late thirties from another village wasn't a good fit. The fact that he'd been educated—a degree in criminal law—in the lower forty-eight made him outright suspect to some.

But the mayor and what passed as a board of directors for the village interviewed three applicants and chose the outsider. The other two local men both had drug possession records and in keeping with trying to clean up Moose Flat's reputation in order to get federal money, the right decision had probably been made, Ben thought.

Plus, Ben liked the man. Chief Deniki had stopped by Ben's office to offer his time. He wanted to show support for Ben's plans by speaking for ten to fifteen minutes at Ben's meeting that evening. Ben was thrilled and included his name on the flyers that he planned to post that morning.

It might be a little challenging to keep the meeting focused on Ben's issues and not let it turn into some kind of forum on possible new approaches to local law enforcement. But a case could be made for law enforcement needing to be a part of any community plan to eliminate crime associated with drugs. It would be Chief Deniki's first general address to the village. The worst it could do was attract new faces.

Chief Deniki also wanted to share a short video shot in Alaska that addressed the opioid problem as one that was state-wide. He felt, and Ben agreed, that it was important for people to know they weren't alone. The struggle was, in fact, one also being addressed in the lower forty-eight. Moose Flats could learn from others' experience—dont's, as well as, do's. Ben previewed the film and thought it would be a great opener—a good lead into discussion.

This time the RSVP numbers were staggering—seventy-four members of Moose Flats would attend Ben's workshop called, 'Looking Ahead—Let's Plan Together'. The minute he had a read on numbers, Ben asked the mayor if he could hold the meeting in the high school gym. For once, there wasn't a conflict with a basketball game and Ben went over early in the afternoon to help set up chairs.

Uki and Ahnah provided bakery goods with some killer muffins purported to be healthy just because they were called apple spice. Ben wasn't sure about any health benefits but doubted they would last long.

Chief Deniki helped him welcome participants at six-thirty and they were pretty much on schedule to begin at ten after seven. Ideas tossed around included using a comic book format to educate elementary aged school children about drugs; forming family-based vigilante groups to police neighborhoods, especially to routinely check any buildings that might be vacant like storage units; establish a hot-line; have a physician or nurse practitioner speak regularly to groups of adults, as well as high school students, on topics of safe practices; publish when milestones were met, including building goals such as a gym for the Annex; guarantee anonymity to anyone reporting an infraction; and finally, hire personnel such as exercise instructors locally.

Ben was impressed. These were people who had given their needs some thought. He'd make certain that E.J. and the mayor got a copy of the list.

In addition to a gym as part of the physical clinic, Ben's idea of a classroom area for retraining that would offer a two-year technical/vocational or AA degree that was free to local students seemed at the top of everyone's list. The enthusiasm for continued education led to the suggestion that loans for additional schooling be made available through a contributing government agency and maybe an exchange program established with a university in Washington state. Ben was thrilled—these were concrete, doable, well thought out ideas.

Ben could not have asked for a more productive meeting. It was everything he'd hoped for. He'd remembered to hand around a sign-up sheet for volunteers and marveled at the twenty-eight people who had put their names down. This was success and then some. A follow-up meeting date was chosen and they adjourned. Ben stayed to put up the chairs with the help of the new chief, washed the now-empty plates the treats had been on, and even gave the floor a once-over sweep. He could not get over the feeling of absolute euphoria. There wasn't one thing mentioned by the audience that wasn't doable. It was more than a wish list; it was a place to get started before ground was even broken for the clinic itself.

He started up the Outback and just sat there reliving a couple highlights of the night. He wouldn't soon forget the eagerness of the audience to problem-solve or their willingness to get involved. He put the car in gear, then reached for his phone. He'd missed a call from Doc Kane but there was a message.

"I hope you're sitting down. I think we've got something. The eyedrops bottle you sent this morning had minute traces of cocoa powder on the tip and under the cap. I'm sure you didn't even notice but it made me remember those half-eaten brownies you'd collected from the chief's desk. Yeah, you guessed it. The brownies tested positive for tetrahydrozoline. I lifted a pretty clear set of prints from the bottle. I'll get them checked out. But I knew you'd want to know—the chief was poisoned by treats from the Two Sisters Bakery. Call me when you get a chance."

Chapter 28

He couldn't even think straight. Ahnah, Uki, Raven? Murderers? Just one, or two of them, or all three?

Once the prints were matched, that person, or maybe even persons, could be arrested on suspicion of murder. At this time only he and Doc Kane knew—not the who, but the how. Which left the why and that might lead to the who. Damn. It was beginning to sound like a bad comedy routine.

He was going in circles. The chief had arrested E.J. on murder charges. Circumstantial evidence was a little flimsy, but the chief didn't back down and insisted he had the right man. Who would be most upset? A mother? Or a sister? Definitely not the person who really did kill Ed Johnson.

Had E.J. unconsciously put himself in a position to get someone else off the hook? Hadn't the chief been a little too adamant about E.J.'s guilt and keeping him locked up maybe to keep an eye on him? And then someone felt it was safest to just get rid of the real murderer? Was that why the chief had been killed?

Frustrated and confused—that described himself, Ben thought as he backed out of the parking space and turned toward the main street. The street was slick with a frozen coating of powdery snow. He was careful and drove slowly finally pulling in behind Uki's and sat a moment before he turned off the car.

Not even ten p.m. and the house was dark. Uki was probably at her sister's. He picked up his phone from the console and checked again for messages but nothing from Julie. Of course, she knew he had another workshop so was probably waiting for him to call her. But Ben's attempt went to voicemail. He left a message to call him, that he was excited to share his evening with her. He tried E.J. but again, voicemail. The crew must still be at dinner or working with the dogs.

A little early but he was tired. And he missed Julie. It was tough to shut his mind down. He couldn't help but run through some of the points made that evening, and realize how excited he was to put some of the plans discussed into action. He had two people offering to head up a group to patrol some of the rough areas, especially out along the river, where there were empty houses that acted like magnets for users.

He wasn't fooling himself. He was churning through the evening's events because he didn't want to dwell on the fact that he had sent the murder weapon to Doc Kane. The weapon and the method of delivery—a bag of half eaten brownies. He had an almost identical bag sitting on his desk.

Should he have those tested? Might not be a bad idea. Raven had sent them with Julie but hadn't they been for him? Or had they been meant for Julie? But did it matter who was supposed to eat them if they were positive for tetrahydrozoline?

Could he face the fact that someone wanted him or Julie out of the way? And was that someone Raven? Had she faked all the chumminess with Julie as a way to win their trust? And what kind of ramifications would that have? What would he tell Zac? Sorry, son, your mother tried to kill me or your stepmother, and she's in prison. Too farfetched?

Maybe not. What would he do? What *could* he do?

Ridiculous. He had to shut his mind down. He needed sleep. He was letting fantasy override reason. He draped shirt and jeans over a chairback, turned the electric mattress pad on low and climbed into bed. He'd be with Julie next week and be able to spend time with Zac.

In the meantime, he had lots of work to do. The kind of planning and implementing he'd been looking forward to. The Iditarod would provide a nice break from what he knew would be an intense couple weeks.

He'd choose team leaders first and begin their training. In turn, they would train the volunteers who had signed up to help. He would put the finishing touches on a questionnaire designed to determine level and type of support that might be needed by members of the community and that would help him divide tasks. Everything was falling into place. And he really had the willingness of the village to thank— they wanted action and weren't shy about stepping up.

Ben had to hand it to E.J.; his timing was perfect. He'd known not only interest level, but simply when the community had had enough and needed to take action.

This was also when Ben needed two interns probably both working in the field, which would free him up to work on the physical design of the clinic itself. And that would mean spending a part of each week at the Annex. He'd contacted the psych department at the University of Alaska, Anchorage, and had three interviews set up, one per day, for the three days when he'd be in the city for the start of the race. It was tight time-wise to get everything done before his six months loan-time was up. He could stretch his loan past the end of summer but had to be out of there by the first of October. It was doable. That's where good ground-up organizational planning was going to come in handy. And he had a head start.

A couple deep breaths and he stretched out pulling an extra comforter up over his feet. The bed was a little soft for his liking but tonight he didn't care. He bunched a pillow up under his head and cleared his mind of any residual thoughts concerning the program.

That was better. He concentrated on the complete silence of the night. Snow always seemed to deaden sound. The curtains were tightly shut. If he were lucky, he might be able to get an extra half-hour's rest in the morning. Sleep, at last.

Two-forty-five by the bed-side clock and his phone was ringing. He'd left the thing on his desk which meant leaving the warm cocoon of his bed to face the bracing cold just to answer.

"Ben?"

"E.J.—you know what time it is?"

"Just listen. I'm not going to tell you not to panic; I need to tell you what's happening. Julie's in the hospital—Alaska Regional. We brought her to Emergency about twenty minutes ago and she's been admitted. She'd felt faint earlier in the evening after dinner and wasn't feeling well. Raven decided to check on her about two and couldn't wake her. That's about all I know. The doctors are with her now"

Ben sat back on the bed and had to hold the phone with two hands to stop it from shaking. "What's being done? Is she awake?"

"I don't know. I've called Pete and he'll be in Moose Flats to pick you up in an hour. Pack a few things and get to the airport. I'll meet you at the private, small plane airfield outside Anchorage at six a.m."

"E.J. I want you to get a doctor on the phone—now!"

"Ben, I don't think—"

"NOW."

Ben took a deep breath. When the on-duty doctor picked up the phone, Ben was ready. He explained that his wife could have been poisoned. He gave the particulars of the poison and how it might have been administered. He didn't know how many doses or over what period of time, but he was guessing it was recent and possibly only offered in food one time per day.

The doctor thanked him and hung up assuring him that he would mobilize the lethal substances team. Ben was left holding a silent phone.

He had to think positively; he couldn't give in to panic. If the amount was miniscule and she was having more of an allergic reaction than a terminal one, there was hope things could be turned around. He had to believe that.

If ingestion was recent, activated charcoal was an approach along with establishing an intravenous fluid line to literally speed up flushing her system. Barbiturates would be used with care, if at all. They were tricky. Obviously, they would be monitoring cardiac function and blood pressure. There were so many what-if's. And he'd just about reached the end of his poison control knowledge.

He hurriedly dressed, threw an extra pair of jeans in an overnight suitcase, toiletries in a shaving kit, his laptop in a shoulder bag, grabbed his parka, and he was out the door, but not before leaving a note for Uki. He'd leave her car at the terminal with the keys inside.

If Pete left Anchorage at three, he'd be in Moose Flats at four fifteen, turn around and be back in Anchorage by a quarter to six. The waiting and not knowing was deadly. But Pete was on time. He set down, picked Ben up and was in the air again in record time.

After a couple words of condolence, Pete turned his attention to the plane and seemed to sense Ben's need for silence. Still, an hour and fifteen-minute flight might as well have been twenty-four. True to his word, E.J. was standing beside an Uber SUV at the edge of the private landing strip. A brief hug instead of a handshake, and E.J. insisted on taking Ben's bag and putting it in the back.

"Any changes?"

"No, but that's not all bad. After you talked to that doctor, the poison control unit got involved. Any reason you thought it might be poison?"

"Long story."

"And now's not the time to tell me, right?"

Ben nodded. He was reluctant to tell anyone that the chief had been murdered and possibly a couple others. Besides how did you tell a friend that his mother, aunt and possibly sister were suspects in those murders. "Trust me on this. I don't have any facts, just supposition. It would be way premature."

E.J. looked at him, waiting, then realized that Ben wasn't going to add anything and turned away.

Ben wished he could say something—anything. But E.J. would be the last person to share with. Would anything keep E.J. from confronting his mother, or aunt? Or sister? Family aside, wasn't the element of surprise always preferable? Murderers weren't exactly predictable unless they were cornered and then preserving their own skin came first.

And if his guess concerning Julie's possible poisoning was right, the murderer had already broadened his or her list of victims. Who else had been slated to die?

Ben felt certain that the person was still clueless to Doc Kane's discovery of the tainted brownies and assumed everyone still believed the heart attack scenario. And there was safety in that.

But at some point, and probably before he left Anchorage, he and Doc Kane would have to meet with State law enforcement. Moose Flats with a temporary Chief of Police wasn't set up to detain, incarcerate and try a murderer. And there was always the possibility that there were two people involved. There was no discussing any of this with E.J. Not until things were a lot more certain.

+ + +

Alaska Regional Medical Center oozed new technology and know-how. Ben was met at the door by two doctors who ushered him into an office off the main waiting room.

"Let me start by telling you what we know. Thanks to your suspicions, we were able to isolate the probable cause and aggressively begin to treat it and not just the symptoms.

We'll have definitive answers in twenty-four hours."

"Which means her condition is—?"

"She's stable, but I would have to say guarded. Preliminary lab work turned up tetrahydrozoline. First time I've run into it but it's not that uncommon—just really difficult to detect. I'd be interested to know why that was your assumption, but not now. We have a pretty sick girl to get back on her feet. Oh yes, I almost forgot. I assumed you would want to stay with your wife so I've had a cot made up in her room. I'm sure you're exhausted. And one more thing. I don't want you to be in any hurry to take her back to Moose Flats, she's going to need special care for a while. Rest and quiet. Her system's been put through a wringer. I would suggest alerting relatives but there should be no reason to panic and unduly raise fears of her passing. If you can put off such a call, I think you should wait twenty-four hours. I'd rather have you passing on facts and not scaring a mother and a father before we have sound knowledge of just what's going on. Are you comfortable with that?"

Ben nodded. The last thing he needed was Julie's parents here. Arizona was a ways away. It wasn't a quick flight over. And he was toying with the idea of sending Julie to them. Rehab in Phoenix away from snow and cold might have an appeal. It made sense that to keep her out of danger, he needed to remove her from Alaska. Not just change her headquarters to Fairbanks, but send her home.

Overkill? Maybe. Peace of mind came first. He didn't want a separation, but he also didn't want to be worrying about her wellbeing while she was working in Anchorage and he was trying to put his community plan into effect a couple hundred miles away. The possibility of sending her to the lower forty-eight totally depended on whether the killer or killers were apprehended. Another unknown.

Still, he'd rather have the two of them decide on the best plan and not involve her parents at this time.

He couldn't forget that further adding to the confusion, there was Zac. He didn't need to be explaining a ten-year-old son in the middle of everything else. When the time was right, Zac would be added to the family equation and explanations made—but now wasn't the time.

Would her parents be angry that he hadn't called them immediately? Probably, but he'd risk it. One complication at a time for now.

Chapter 29

There's never any way to prepare to see someone you love intubated, on a ventilator with two IVs.

Ben pulled a chair up next to the bed and took Julie's hand. She was cool to the touch but the noise of the ventilator seemed to vibrate through her body. He never thought of Julie as frail or vulnerable until now. She looked lost in the tangle of tubes and wheezing of a machine that was actually breathing for her—forcing air into her lungs while maintaining the correct levels of oxygen in her blood, then allowing the air to come out as the machine mimicked the lung's natural function.

He'd caused this. He had almost gotten her killed. Whether it was Raven, Ahnah, or Uki who poisoned the food, it was clearly his fault. Someone wanted either Ben or Julie out of the way. She was targeted only because of association. He was certain of that.

She hadn't done anything on her own—just marry him. Would he have been next? And could they stop the killings now? Prove who was to blame and move forward?

He was afraid to move her hand but very gingerly stroked the back and each finger, and he honestly thought he could feel tension escaping through her finger tips. Her hand relaxed; he could feel it. But maybe he was imagining it. He wanted so badly to see a positive sign. He didn't even know if she could hear him, but there were things he needed to say.

He leaned close and whispered, "We'll get through this. And we'll find out who did it. I love you. I won't let anyone hurt you—not again, not ever. Come back to me. Our life is ahead of us—you are my life. I don't want to live without you."

He kissed her on the forehead before sitting back in the chair and closing his eyes; his hand never leaving hers.

"I thought you could use this." Ben startled awake. E.J. was standing in the doorway with a tall Styrofoam cup of what was probably coffee. "I can disappear if you need to be alone."

"No, I'm okay. I'm hoping that's coffee."

"Coffee, two creams. And here's your bag. Thought you might need it."

"Thanks. I thought I'd go over to Julie's apartment later to clean up—unless I'm needed here."

"Good idea. I can pick you up. How about a couple hours rest and I'll be back at nine. Will that work?"

"Sounds perfect."

"Then ignore the coffee and make use of that cot. I'll see you later."

Ben stayed sitting next to the bed. He was reluctant to

leave Julie even to go to the other side of the room. He wadded a pillow under his head and uncomfortable as it was, he dozed and then would jolt awake, check on Julie and try to go back to sleep. There was no change.

Each time he woke, he wanted to see her eyes open, feel her hand move against his. But the ventilator continued to whoosh air into her lungs, expel it, and repeat—and she didn't move. By eight he gave up trying to get any rest, got dressed, grabbed his overnight case, and met E.J. in the lobby after first making certain two floor nurses and the attending doctor had his cell number.

+ + +

The landlord of Julie's apartment house lived in a downstairs, two-room efficiency in the same building. He was sorry to hear of her illness and provided a key for Ben to stay in Julie's unit as long as he needed to. E.J. left to help Raven with the dogs and apologized for needing to get back and making Ben rely on Uber.

Ben unlocked the apartment door, stepped in, and simply looked around. The living room had a sofa which obviously was also a bed, and two chairs, a dining room table with four chairs. The kitchen was separated from the living area by a bar with four stools. Beyond the bar was a counter with sink, stove with microwave above and a fridge to the right. Counters matched the bar and were a cheap, wannabe granite. Track lighting held eight small crystal shaded bulbs in a curving line that gave light to every square inch of the food preparation area.

The bathroom was a closet. Well, maybe a bit larger, but not by much. It was two winter parkas wide with one-foot deep and one-foot wide shelving, floor to ceiling on the right side. There was a shower that had to have been modeled from something found in an RV, no tub, a narrow pedestal sink with a medicine cabinet above. The apartment was the absolute definition of efficiency.

He should have known that there would be nothing out of place. Julie was anti-clutter. Even Julie's work clothes—jeans and a couple crewneck wool blend sweaters—were hung in the closet. The same with her cosmetics—foundation, eyeliner, a couple pencils—all aligned beside the sink. And nothing was left out in the kitchen. Counters sparkled.

Ben sighed. Had he just taken for granted that he'd find whatever the purveyor had used to poison Julie? That it would just be sitting there waiting to be discovered? Nothing stood out. There were three trash cans—one in the bathroom, the living room and the kitchen. He carried all three to the kitchen sink. She hadn't been there long enough to amass more than a couple burger wrappers, a soft drink cup, a wadded-up napkin and some really stale fries. The bathroom trash contained Kleenex and wood shavings from sharpening a lip-liner pencil. That left one to go—the kitchen trash can. Two empty plastic water bottles and two plastic caps. That was it.

He felt defeated. A lot depended on being able to prove his suspicions. Julie was poisoned by tetrahydrozoline and he needed to find evidence of the actual culprit. It would get them closer to who was behind this, the third probably food-related poisoning. And it could very well save other lives.

He pulled up a bar stool and sat down. If she had brought food from Moose Flats, the remains would be in evidence, but the trash held no clues. Think. What was he overlooking?

For one thing he was thirsty. He hoped the two empty water bottles weren't her last ones. But there might be something else to drink in the fridge. He pulled the fridge door open and found an unopened bottle of water tucked behind a jar of mayonnaise on the door's second shelf.

Then, as he turned to close the door, he saw it. Two cinnamon rolls—one whole, one half eaten—in a zip-lock bag. And he knew. This was it; the missing link to the killer. Brazen? Would the murderer be so open about using poison in this way? Handing it out without worrying about detection? Yes, because he or she knew nothing about the lab results. And the person who gave these to Julie knew she would probably eat them all and not share.

Ben carefully removed the bag from the fridge, called Doc Kane and filled him in. It would be pushing it but the doctor thought he could get lab results back by the end of the following day if he pulled some strings. He told Ben to sit tight; he was on his way. Waiting was never easy for Ben and now there was an urgency to the situation—putting a murderer behind bars before there might be another attempt on someone's life.

He forced himself to take a shower and put on clean clothes. He felt better, marginally, but better. He pulled out the zip-lock of brownies that had been meant for him and put it next to the bag of cinnamon rolls. Might as well get them checked at the same time. What was the next step if one or both tested positive? He didn't even want to go there yet. One step at a time. That was what was helping him stay sane.

Chapter 30

Ben locked up the apartment and met Doc Kane out front. He'd hand off the suspect food-stuffs and have the doc drop him off at the hospital. Just in case he'd be spending the night there again, he'd brought his suitcase. The laboratory that Doc Kane used was on the University campus and it wouldn't be too far out of his way.

The doc did have good news—once he explained the urgency to lab personnel, room was made in the queue for testing the brownies and cinnamon rolls within twenty-four hours.

"You know if our suspicions are correct, the worst is yet to come. Or maybe I should just say the most difficult part—when we need to confront a suspect." Doc Kane was maneuvering his Ford Escape through traffic.

"I agree. That's going to be rough."

"If we have a positive, I suggest we meet and plan what's next."

Ben had a distinct feeling of foreboding, of knowing that very shortly his life would change forever.

+ + +

Doc Kane let Ben off at the hospital's front steps, wishing him well and promising to call the minute he had any news, but reiterated not to expect anything before tomorrow. Ben nodded to the nurse on duty at the nurses' station and continued down the hall to Julie's room. The doctor on floor-duty met Ben at the door to Julie's room and motioned for him to step back out into the hallway.

"Is something wrong?"

"No, no, exactly the opposite. Your wife's breathing is improving to the point that we're backing off of sedation and tentatively plan to take her off the ventilator by tomorrow morning. Things could change and we're monitoring her condition carefully, but I'm guardedly optimistic that we'll be able to move forward. There's a lot to be said about being young and healthy." The doctor, who had to be in his sixties, smiled and shrugged, "I'm afraid those days are behind me."

"I'm relieved; best news I've had in a while."

"I should add that we're restricting all visitors. You'll be the only one we'll allow unless, of course, her parents or other family members will be here?"

"No, I'm taking your advice and letting them know when there's some positive news."

"Good. But just to let you know, we had to turn away an E.J. Takanni and his sister earlier. I'm sorry but I'm sure you understand our protocol? They may be very close friends but Ms. Pecos is in a precarious position—I don't want her unduly exposed to any illnesses that might be in the community. The influx of tourists for the race just means we have to be doubly vigilant."

"Yes, of course, not a problem." He could appreciate their visit, but with Raven as a possible suspect, thank God, someone was guarding the door. The results of the lab test could not come soon enough.

"I also wanted to mention that you're welcome to use the desk in the office next to mine. My colleague is on leave—elderly parents in Montana—he's grappling with everything from setting up assisted living to selling a ranch. He won't be back until the end of the summer. You'll have privacy and Wi-Fi for however long you need it."

"Thank you. I'll take you up on the offer." Ben was relieved. He'd been wondering how he would be able to spend time with Julie and monitor his work in the village. He'd gotten a text from Chief Deniki, who offered to start organizing the community work force, patrol the deserted areas, set up the planned phone bank and mail campaign for donations, and organize a potluck with raffle. Ben should be in on all that, but there was no way he was leaving Julie's side until she was completely out of danger. He needed help.

Ben was impressed and forever grateful. He couldn't ask for better village involvement. He owed the new chief bigtime.

He set up his laptop and brought up the resumes of two grad students who had sent inquiries about the internship. He was forcing himself to work. He couldn't make Julie heal any faster and he needed something to occupy his time. In some ways, he was thankful he had a diversion and depending on the speed of Julie's recovery, he planned on being in Anchorage for at least a week or two.

There were things that had to be done. He needed to establish connections for the clinic—guest practitioners, instructors—contacts that would be supportive once he had gone. He tentatively set up intern interviews for the following Monday. Just knowing Julie was responding to treatment felt like the weight of the world had been lifted. And thank God he could be close by.

He checked on Julie hourly. Ten minutes of assuring her that he was close by, holding her hand, stroking her cheek, kissing her forehead. There was no response but he thought her color looked better. She wasn't pasty white any longer. But, once again, he didn't trust himself not to be seeing what wasn't really there, only seeing what he wanted to. The mind could play tricks—wasn't that his field, after all?

He'd called E.J. and apologized for hospital protocol keeping him from visiting and asked how the preparation for the race was going. It sounded like they could use his help. He promised to continue to update them on Julie's condition but stopped short of sharing the doctor's upbeat prognosis—that sedation was being withdrawn as they spoke; possibly by late afternoon tomorrow or even sooner, she would be breathing entirely on her own.

And then felt guilty. Was he just being extremely cautious or had he already blamed Raven? Blamed her and was afraid to incite what might be another attempt on Julie's life? He was going to go with his gut this time. The less information leaked, the better.

The loan of an office was a godsend. Private and quiet,

it was exactly what he needed. By four he was just getting ready to check in with Julie's doctor when his cell beeped.

"I'm at the lab and just picked up the report. The brownies were negative but you were right to suspect the cinnamon rolls—there was enough tetrahydrozoline in the frosting to deliver a wallop. Not eating them all saved her life."

"What's the next move?"

"I've got to report my findings. I'm looking at murder and attempted murder without even mentioning the PETA kid. I need to have you meet me at police headquarters downtown. I'm sure they'll assign a detective to the case. Julie became ill within the jurisdiction of Anchorage law enforcement. I imagine they'll want to bring Raven in for questioning."

"I'll grab an Uber and meet you there within an hour." With a small bout of nerves over leaving Julie alone, Ben shut down his laptop and stuffed his phone in the pocket of his parka, then took it out.

It was decidedly warmer in Anchorage by plus thirty-five degrees. Balmy, and way too warm for the heavy parka this time of day. He was glad he'd packed something lighter and opened his suitcase. Not a lot to choose from; he'd kinda thrown things in a bag and hadn't made sound choices, but then he was also hoping he wouldn't be in Anchorage for more than a few days before being able to return to Moose Flats. He found the insulated ski pants and a fleece-lined hoody which he pulled on over a wool-blend Henley. He could strip a layer or two off and be comfortable inside an office, or go for a short walk and not freeze to death.

Julie's doctor gave him a thumbs up when he stepped

into the hall, motioned him to wait and then hurriedly caught up with Ben at the front door.

"I'm optimistic. I think we're on schedule to start removing equipment in the morning. She's made a solid turnaround. I don't promise she'll be ready to talk right away but it won't be too long. Tomorrow will be a good day."

Chapter 31

Interrogation rooms weren't pretty. They were tiny—on an average, little more than ten by ten or one hundred square feet. They were stark, usually underheated, only decorated with functional metal furniture and nothing else. There were never extra chairs only enough for the persons involved and always arranged with the person or persons being interrogated facing their interrogator.

Tables were standard in design, as small as three feet by four feet, and sometimes fixed to the floor. Lighting was recessed, cameras were in the ceiling and there were usually four—one per corner. Windows to the outside were non-existent and only the expanse of a two-way, internal, viewing window broke up the monotony of four usually off-white walls. Sometimes there would be a map of the area, no frame, no glass, just taped up. No pens, pencils, pads or paper of any sort. Whatever was brought into the room was done so by a detective.

Any outsider entering was frisked, pockets emptied, purses left in trays, and cell phones confiscated to be returned when leaving.

Grim. Could he put Raven through an interrogation?

If she were innocent, it would tear apart any good will that had been built up—any future with Zac would be settled in a court of law, not between the two of them over coffee. Maybe it never would have been entirely amiable, but if he announced to the world that he suspected the mother of his child was a murderer, there would be hell to pay.

And if she were guilty? Prison? Maybe worse?

He had to shut down that way of thinking. Because one way or the other, he knew what he had to do. Confront Raven himself. Talk confidentially and enlist her help. Innocent or guilty, Raven needed to be a part of determining her own fate. He owed her that. And he had to prove to her that he wasn't making a judgement.

He wanted to believe in her. He wanted her to be innocent. But if he wasn't incriminating her, he was directly pointing a finger at her mother or aunt—maybe both of them. And should he forget, he reminded himself that Ahnah Takanni was his son's grandmother.

"We need to talk. Before we meet with a detective." Ben was sitting next to Doc Kane in the reception area of the county building that housed the Anchorage police department and jail. The doctor was filling out paperwork to be attached to the lab report.

"I think I know where this is going. It's not a secret that you are the father of Zac Allen. By the way, cute kid and smart as they come. Let me say, he'll benefit from having you as a father. But I understand the parameters here. What's your plan?"

"I want to meet with Raven first—before law enforcement shows up to bring her in for questioning. If she's to come in, I want it to be on her own terms. Either as the perpetrator or a witness."

"And you don't think she'd be a flight risk?"

"Not with twenty dogs here and her son."

"You've got a point."

"I'd like you to go with me—the two of us meet with her together. You'd be able to present solid evidence— irrefutable. She'd know you were telling the truth."

"It sounds like you think she's innocent."

"I do; and not just because I want it so badly for Zac's sake. Personality is pretty much in place by the age of six. I don't remember observing any abnormalities or what I might view as personality disorders at eighteen. She pretty much had it together especially for someone her age. Proof of that is the good job she's done raising Zac. I never saw her as vindictive or malicious with an intent to do harm. Would she want to get rid of Julie? The question would be, why? Raven was appreciative of Julie's offer to help with race preparations and write an article on the dogs and the Iditarod. I would have picked up on some underlying anger if it existed. And I assure you, it doesn't."

"I trust you; I'm there for you. But pointing a finger at her mother or aunt won't be easy either."

Ben nodded. This was going to be a long afternoon.

+ + +

The Uber driver knew exactly where Hatcher Pass Kennels was located. Apparently, it was a major tourist attraction offering half-day to day-long dog sled rides through alpine country. Availability was limited to April but some tourists would come for the race and stay over to experience a like-adventure of their own.

Summer dog cart tours began in May and didn't end until November. But next month with snow still on the ground, participants could even attend a mushing school and learn how to harness a team and handle a sled—graduation being a six-mile solo sled drive through moderately challenging terrain. The school even provided snow gear free of charge.

The Uber driver let them off close to a barn that had a wide wraparound porch with a large sign signifying 'information/registration'. A man came out from what looked like an office and offered to page Raven. He thought that her dogs were being exercised but didn't think she'd gone out with them.

Ben paid their driver and had barely turned around when E.J. and Raven came out of the barn.

"Ben, how's Julie? I guess you heard they wouldn't let us visit her yesterday. I've been worried." Raven's concern was evident and real. This wasn't an acting job, Ben reassured himself. He filled her in on the doctor's latest report. "Oh, that sounds so promising. Call me tomorrow and let me know how things are going. Zac's out with the dogs. He's going to be sorry he's missed you. I didn't know you were coming out today. I haven't checked my phone; did you leave a message?"

"No. This was truly a spur of the moment decision." Ben introduced Doc Kane and then asked if there was somewhere where they could talk—hopefully uninterrupted.

E.J. led them back through the barn to a conference room behind the office. "This will work."

Ben helped himself to a cup of coffee before sitting down.

"It's difficult to know where to start; so, I'm just going to throw it out there—and then let Doc Kane tell you what he knows." Ben paused, took a breath before simply saying, "Julie was poisoned."

"Poisoned?" Raven leaned forward, "I remember distinctly that the three of us ate the same thing at dinner— Coho salmon, mixed vegetables and a salad. We shared dessert—bread pudding. In fact, two of the guys who are helping with the dogs ate with us. No one else got sick."

Doctor Kane quickly explained, "We're not talking about food poisoning. Julie ingested tetrahydrozoline. It's a major ingredient in most brand-name eyedrops. If added to food stuffs, it's lethal and very difficult to detect. In Julie's case the poison was administered in the frosting on the cinnamon rolls that she was given to bring with her on this trip."

"I know where she got them. I gave them to her. The rolls were from the Two Sisters." There was the slightest quiver in Raven's voice. "Oh my God." She clutched the edge of the table as if to hold herself upright.

Doc Kane continued, "We might not have guessed what was behind Julie's collapse if we hadn't had a recent ... murder ... by the same means. Chief Pitka ate brownies saturated with tetrahydrozoline."

"But his heart, wasn't it a heart attack?" E.J. asked. "He'd had some major operation fairly recently—didn't they put a stent in year before last?"

"Yes, he had a history of heart trouble, but this time he was poisoned. I have the lab reports here." Doc Kane opened a manila envelope and pulled out two sheets of paper.

No one reached for the reports and no one moved. Ben felt like all the air in the room had been sucked out, and Raven looked like she was going to be sick.

"Please tell me you didn't think that I had anything to do with this?" She looked directly at Ben. "Things have not been easy having you here—back in my life and Zac's. But I've ended up liking Julie. I've convinced myself it would be to Zac's benefit to have a father and stepmother in his life. I would never cheat him out of opportunities that I can't give him."

"I believe you. That's why we're here sharing what we know and not letting our findings blindside you. I couldn't face having you brought in for questioning. The last three weeks have been traumatic, but I have faith that we'll arrive at the right answers—for all of us."

"Thank you." Raven reached across the table and lightly touched Ben's arm. "I appreciate that."

The doc cleared his throat. "Let me just add that there is reason to believe that the young man from PETA was also murdered—being highly allergic to nuts in any form, this time someone, possibly purposefully, used peanut oil in his salad dressing. It would have been difficult to miss the warning of toxins listed on his medical bracelet. And Brant. It's been reported that the dose of heroin with fentanyl was administered after he had passed out from drinking."

Doc Kane clasped his hands in front of him and

leaned on the table. "Which brings us to the question that we may never find the answer to—was Ed Johnson mistaken for game and accidentally shot? Or was that, too, a planned elimination? By the way, Mr. Takanni, I believe tentative findings by the State's forensic lab suggest that Mr. Johnson's death predates your return to Moose Flats."

"Good to know I've been exonerated." E.J. didn't try to keep the sarcasm out of his voice. "But the rest of this? It's unbelievable. Serial killings? And you're directly pointing a finger at my mother and her sister. Is that correct?"

Doc Kane nodded and glanced at Ben. "We both want you to know that we're presenting facts here. We're not making a judgement. At this time about all we know is that the tainted foodstuffs came from the bakery. A bottle of eyedrops found in Ahnah Takanni's home proved to have cocoa powder on the applicator. The brownies taken from Chief Pitka's office contained tetrahydrozoline. As I mentioned earlier, peanut oil was used in the salad dressing given to a young man highly allergic to nuts, the frosting on the—"

"Circumstantial," E.J. interjected. "I'm lacking motive here."

"You're the lawyer but I think a good prosecutor could prove otherwise." Doc Kane added, "I want to say there's no finger-pointing going on. Facts are simply that. And as my granddaughter would say, I don't mean to be 'throwing shade'. I want the severity of what's happened to sink in. And then, quite frankly, we'll need your help in knowing the best way to proceed. I have a report that needs to be filed. We don't have the luxury of time."

"It isn't like our family doesn't have secrets." Raven was looking directly at E.J.

"Don't. Not now."

"And why not now? Ben and Doc Kane have been fair to us." She waited for E.J. to comment but he simply shrugged.

"Do what you have to do."

"Even you would admit it's been a long time to keep the truth buried." Raven paused but E.J. didn't comment. "Bear with me. I'm sharing this story because it might hold some answers to things that have happened." Raven paused, folded her hands in her lap and then looked up. "When I was ten, I found my father dead in his office. I had been playing with a litter of puppies in a room we called the nursery. When I had walked into the barn earlier that evening, I had seen an ATV with police insignia parked by the double doors, and I had heard shouting coming from the office. I continued to the back to play with the puppies and didn't pay attention to what was being said.

"The sound of a gunshot startled me—it was only a single shot. I waited but didn't hear anything else—not even the shouting. I quietly walked to the nursery door and opened it a crack in time to see a man hurriedly leaving the building. It was only a moment later that I heard the ATV fire up and head back up the road toward the house. I ran to the office. The door was open and I could see my father in his favorite chair. He was completely still. I called his name and tip-toed to his side. He was holding a gun in his lap, the handgun he kept in the office. His finger was on the trigger. But there was something wrong.

"He was holding the gun in his right hand. Only my father was left-handed. I was ten and I knew that he had not pulled the trigger with his right hand. Yet, I could see the blood and entry path of the bullet—on the right side of his head, his temple. He did not do this. This was not a suicide. He had been shot by someone else. I knew I should call the police but hadn't the police already been there? I had seen the police insignia on the ATV, I knew the man I saw leaving the building was a policeman. I came to believe later that the man was Chief Pitka."

"Why is that?" Doc Kane asked.

"Here's where the family's dirt comes out. Chief Pitka had been engaged to Aunt Uki but she had broken up with him—because she had fallen in love with someone else. In this case, my father. The summer before this happened, I had walked into the barn and saw them kissing. Aunt Uki tried to make me think there was just something in her eye that my dad was trying to help her get out. I was ten, not blind. I knew exactly what was going on. I'd seen Dad even pinch Uki on the butt and the two of them laugh when she pushed him away.

"There's no doubt in my mind that Ronnie Pitka killed my father because of Uki. But the villagers thought it was suicide and rallied to support my mother. My mother put on a stoic façade. Uki was inconsolable. I found her sobbing in the office more than once. She was too upset to even go to my dad's funeral, but I think that Mama kept Uki from going to the funeral. She was probably afraid that Uki would embarrass her and give away her feelings for my father in public. I was always certain that my mother knew of the affair but just chose to look the other way. She never mourned my father, not like Uki did. I always resented the fact that she sold his dogs—she even burned his sleds. She tried to erase everything from her life that would remind her of him. I always thought she hated him and I hated her for it. You want to know why this race next week means everything to me? It's redemption. My father will be racing with me in spirit. All these long years later. I owe this to him."

"Why would your mother be so kind to Uki? She could have easily blamed both of them for the affair," Ben said.

"Mama thought my father had taken unfair advantage of someone younger. She has always taken care of her younger sister. And I think she thought he did it just to get at her—hurt her, force her to turn on a sibling she had almost singlehandedly raised. Actually, I don't think she ever blamed Uki. I've often thought that Mama might have been in on the chief's plan to kill my father. Maybe, even a partner. A suicide made her the grieving widow and a worthwhile catch for Ed Johnson. And it was the ultimate hurtful thing she could have done to her sister, her competition—if I can't have him, neither can you.

"But she had to present a united front—and protect her sibling. So, right after the funeral to quiet any gossip, Mama announced the formation of the Two Sisters Bakery. A family supportive of one another in sorrow. So, when Uki disappeared a couple months after Dad died, no one was surprised. Especially since the word was that she was in the lower forty-eight getting a degree in nursing. My mother had everything covered. Uki was preparing for this new career and Mama had a new boyfriend, Ed Johnson.

"Uki was, in fact, living with my uncle, their older brother, in Bellingham. He and his wife were older, settled, with no children. So, imagine everyone's surprise when my uncle's wife gave birth later that year—a much cherished, late-in-life, first child. And when I tell you his name, you'll put the pieces together. Yes, baby Keith, Ben, the one who wanted to point a finger at me over Brant's death. The baby who lost both of his adoptive parents at an early age and returned to live with his rightful mother in Moose Flats. He may not, even today, know his true relationship to Aunt Uki."

Doc Kane shifted in his seat. "I realize I'm a little behind here. But Ben can fill me in on who this Keith person is later. I think you've made a convincing case for Chief Pitka killing your father but who would have wanted the chief killed? And what about the more recent deaths?"

"I don't think I have any more information that could help you," Raven said.

"C'mon, Sis, finish what you've started. You're not going to save Mama. And do I have to remind you, you're going to be interrogated. There'll be those who think you have a pretty good reason to kill Julie Pecos. Get rid of the competition for Zac's love, maybe even reunite with Ben. I know Mama wanted you to rethink that possibility. She was disappointed to hear that Ben had recently married. Even killing the PETA guy—people could make a case for you being angry that he was trying to shut you down. When you talk about the race and what it means to you, people could think you'd stop at nothing to make sure you get a chance to race."

"Then I would have killed him that night I found him in the office. I felt threatened and rightfully so. There wouldn't have been any questions—I was well within my right."

"True. But that still leaves you incriminated because you handed off the cinnamon rolls. You're in this up to your neck. Now's not the time to hold back. Tell the rest of what you know and I'll be able to know how to proceed. I just never thought I was getting a degree in law so that I could represent my own family."

"Mama hasn't done anything that wasn't out of love for her family, and hatred for our father and the wrongs, perceived or otherwise, that he did to her family."

"And that's an excuse for murder? No one has the right to take the life of another—not without due process of law, anyway. You've lived here all your life. I haven't; I got away. Tell what you know and save your own skin. Don't you owe that to Zac? Mama made her choices. She's an adult. She knew the possible consequences. Don't try to save her at the expense of your son and your future."

For a minute or two, Ben was afraid that Raven was going to refuse. She had pushed back from the table, and Ben half expected her to leave the room; but she took a breath and continued.

"I think the chief can be tied to the murder of Ed Johnson. It wasn't a secret that Ed beat Mama and was primed to take his anger out on Zac. I'd kept Zac in boarding schools when I wasn't here but as he got older, vacations were becoming a problem." Raven turned to E.J. "You even had a run-in with Ed over disciplining Zac. Ed had a temper and a heavy hand. You know what that was like. I just had to lock my bedroom door at night."

"Yeah, the reason I ran away. You think it was the threat to Zac that prompted Mama to take action? To set up the chief to take Ed out?"

"I do." Raven paused, "It was a tipping point. I wasn't quiet about the danger to Zac. I threatened to kill him myself. I think Mama was afraid I'd follow through. So, Mama and the chief had a number of late-night meetings—too many not to be planning something. And it was the chief who knew where the body was buried. E.J. was just a convenient cover-up, a stand-in that exonerated the chief. I'm certain that he was the one who followed you, photographed you. You were a gift. It was just that no one knew, when they were planning Ed's death, that you would visit the body."

"That makes sense but why would the chief want to get rid of Brant?" Ben asked. "I don't see him as Brant's murderer; it's not logical."

"I think he did it for Mama. She was upset that Brant was into domestic violence, too. I know she didn't want me hurt—not like she'd been. I don't think either one of them thought he was really going to remain clean and not add to the community's drug problems. There was talk that he was a dealer. She never liked Brant, thought he was too into himself, too good for the village. And I think she thought he'd take her daughter and grandson away from her—move us permanently to the lower forty-eight. That would have been a blow."

Ben nodded, "I can see that he posed a threat. And it makes sense that the chief could have told her about the PETA kid's nut allergies, and she made up the lunches. So, now we're left with the chief himself. Any theories? Did Ahnah kill the chief?"

"I'd say the toxin in the brownies narrows it down," Doc Kane said. "I'm leaving you out of the equation, Raven. So, only two people would have had access to the Two Sisters' kitchen. And the eyedrops were found in Ahnah's house. But why would she want to get rid of him? Her partner in crime, so to speak."

"Because of just that, I think. My theory is that the chief knew too much. He covered his own tracks by jailing me and he wasn't going to release me. But he overstepped his bounds or didn't plan on the depth of a mother's love.

Mama couldn't stand to see her only son incarcerated. She couldn't take a chance that allegations might stick—even I admit, thanks to the photos, things didn't look too good for me," E.J. added.

Raven sat back. "I still can't believe that I'm doing this—my own mother."

"It's the right thing, you're doing. Parents are not infallible. Ahnah knew what she was doing. She's an adult and needs to face the consequences of her actions. What if Julie Pecos had died? Tell yourself that in all likelihood you've saved a life or lives. And don't stop thinking of Zac. He's your responsibility. He depends on you to do right by him and your community," Doc Kane said.

Ben didn't think that Raven looked convinced but she nodded. "So, what is next?" Ben asked.

"I suppose my mother and probably her sister will have to be brought in. Because a member of law enforcement was killed, I'm assuming they will be brought to Anchorage." Raven looked at E.J., who nodded.

"For starters, I have some paper work to file. There are some pretty strict guidelines for reporting foul play discovered during an autopsy. My findings will be turned over to a detective assigned to the case and the local department will take it from there."

"It would appear that the murder of the chief and the attempted murder of Julie are the only two episodes that have strong circumstantial evidence indicating one person. It would be very difficult to prove the other three deaths."

"Maybe, yes, and maybe, no. I was going to mention earlier that I was informed this morning that the PETA organization on behalf of the parents of Andrew Cook have filed a wrongful death suit against the village. Because the young man was incarcerated in the Moose Flats jail, he was under the care of local authority," E.J. said. "The village has retained me to represent them."

"I'm not sure what that entails," Ben said.

"Wrongful death is a type of civil suit, not a criminal one. There's a lower standard of proof in civil cases. Negligence is usually fairly easily proved even if something more sinister is suspected as it is in this case. However, as we've discussed, murder would be impossible to prove beyond doubt. Murder charges even in two unrelated cases could change the outcome of the wrongful death suit. Muddies the waters so to speak."

"Do you think Mama has been told about the civil suit citing negligence on her part? I talked to her this morning but she didn't mention it," Raven said.

"I'm pretty certain that the new temporary Chief— Deniki, I think is his name—has contacted her, but she didn't say anything to me either. At this point, it's not something she would be locked up for," E.J. added.

"Well, I don't know how fast things move around here but after I turn the paperwork in, I'd imagine they'll be pretty quick in sending an officer or two to the village. And then your mother will be brought in. Whether Uki will be included—as a possible accomplice—I have no idea."

"I'll contact Pete. I want to be there when Mama's served with a warrant for her arrest. Ben, how about you? If Mama couldn't use a little moral support, I know I could," E.J. said.

"I don't want to promise anything until I have definitive news about Julie. I'm assuming we'll be joining Pete on his red-eye flight?" Ben's phone suddenly began to vibrate and jiggle across the polished surface of the conference table.

He barely had time to see 'hospital' before grabbing it and standing.

"Excuse me, I need to take this." Ben went out into the hallway. "Ben Pecos, here."

"Dr. Pecos, this is your wife's doctor at the Center. Can you hold for just a minute?" Ben was suddenly treated to elevator music. Hold? How could he be put on hold? His imagination was going crazy. What was going on? Was Julie all right?

"Hello."

Ben almost dropped the phone. The voice was muffled, thick sounding and guttural. But he would know that voice anywhere.

"Julie?"

"Ben. I'm going to be okay. I love you so much."

"I love you, too. I'll be there in fifteen minutes. Oh, baby, this is the happiest day of my life."

Chapter 32

The group at the airport all looked a little blurry-eyed—
Ben, mostly from lack of sleep. He'd spent the night
beside Julie at the hospital. It was amazing how much
better she looked. Not one hundred percent by a long way,
but night and day better than yesterday morning. She still
wasn't strong enough to sit up and take solids and talk was
limited, but he held her hand and filled her in on what had
happened and what the next step was. He sort of indicated
she'd been the victim of food poisoning without being too
specific—something from the Two Sisters kitchen. And
that wasn't too big of a lie. The exact details could come
later. He did mention the wrongful death suit brought
against the village by the PETA kid's parents. Ahnah
Takanni was being singled out as the defendant. He thought
it made sense to accompany E.J. back to Moose Flats in

the morning and be there when Ahnah was served. But he promised to be back by the following day. The doctor had frowned on too many details and stressed the need for Julie to rest, and she didn't seem to be aware of the holes in his narrative. There were no questions, just Julie begging him to come back quickly. One of the most difficult things he had to do was leave her that morning.

+ + +

Moose Flats, six a.m., Thursday morning.

The pale gray, pre-dawn light made the scavenging hulks of fur appear menacing.

There were six of them roaming between dog huts, rattling empty food bowls, fighting over what must have been leftovers or just the scent of food from the night before. Wolves drawn in from the tundra by the scent? He put his hand on the holster attached to his police-issue belt and slowly unsnapped the narrow strap snuggly anchoring his revolver in place. Slowly he drew his gun.

Then he laughed out loud. If the boys in the office could have seen him, they'd never let him live it down—these were Malamutes or Husky mixes, sled dogs that had gotten loose. Two of the larger dogs stopped their tussle over a food bucket and ran toward him, tails wagging. The question was *how* had they gotten loose? What was more perplexing, every single dog was dragging remnants of harness behind him. Some just the padded collar, others had side pieces trailing along in the snow.

Had there been an accident? Had the dogs been on an exercise run when something had happened? But as the dogs came closer, he could see that the strips of colorful nylon across their chests and back had been cut or on some, unbuckled—there was no doubt that they had been released from pulling something. And they were hungry. Wherever they had been and whatever happened, nothing could stand in the way of breakfast.

But where were their handlers? He knew this was the week Raven was racing, but he also knew she had help—young men from the village. And as if he had conjured them, two snow machines rounded the corner of the barn and slid to a stop.

"Sorry we're late. Couldn't get this thing started." The young man on the first machine pointed over his shoulder. "Why'd you let the dogs loose?"

Chief Deniki explained that he'd just driven up and found the dogs in the yard.

"I'm not sure I know why they would be wearing sled gear or bits and pieces of it."

"Oh shit. I don't like the looks of this." The kid who the other one called Paul had already been taking off the harnesses, putting on collars and fastening each dog to its hut.

"Ms. Takanni had me harness up a sled last night. Six of the older dogs now in retirement. She and her sister were going out for a short run. I didn't think anything of it—nice night, clear, not too cold. They've done this before. But from the looks of the dogs, they ran into trouble. She cut the dogs loose because they'd come home. Like she sent these guys for help. This is better than sending up a flare."

"Know where she was going?"

"Not a clue. If you'll excuse me here, I better get these guys fed. Then I can take the snow machines and cover

some of the area close to the house." With that, both
handlers went into the barn.

Chief Deniki checked his watch. He was supposed
to meet Dr. Pecos and E.J. at the Takanni residence, but
the plane must be late. He should probably just drive to
the airport because he had a plan. There would be no way
to find the women without using a plane. He was pretty
sure he could talk Pete into gassing up and doing an aerial
search. He couldn't help but feel a sense of urgency. Two
women alone all night in minus twenty degree temps? Not
pretty.

+ + +

They had all opted to go up—Chief Deniki, E.J., Ben
and Pilot Pete. There wasn't any talking. Ben thought each
of them knew what they would find. So, when the plane
dipped low over a depression in a bank of snow, no one was
surprised to see the two bodies stretched out side by side
each holding the other in one last familial embrace. The
sled discarded to the side. There hadn't been an accident.
An autopsy would probably prove some kind of drug to
blunt the inevitability of death. No struggle, no pain, just
a peaceful passing from the earth—together. Pete marked
the location on his GPS so that Chief Deniki's search and
rescue team would be able to easily find the bodies.

Back at the airport they all climbed into Pete's truck
and went to E.J.'s mother's house. Ben made coffee and
was tempted to put out a plate of brownies but couldn't
bring himself to do it. He wasn't real sure he'd ever be able
to eat another brownie in his lifetime. He knew cinnamon
rolls were out. He carried cups, sugar and cream to the

table, put the carafe of coffee on the sideboard, pulled out a chair and sat down.

"I was wondering who had tipped her off about the law suit. Look at this." E.J. held up an envelope from the Mayor's office with a copy of the legal filing of the wrongful death suit. "I guess I was hoping that she had left a note, but maybe she didn't have to. I think Raven summed things up fairly well yesterday. We're not going to have answers in writing but I think we know the truth."

Ben turned to Pete. "If you can give me half an hour, I'll throw my stuff together and fly back with you tonight."

Pete nodded, "I'll be glad for the company."

+ + +

This time Ben carefully packed one little black dress with sequined cape. There was no doubt in his mind that Julie would be able to attend the dinner one week from today. They'd all have time to pitch in and make Raven's dream a reality—winning the race wasn't as important as knowing she'd replicated her father's dream and had given dogs from his breeding a chance. Yes, he believed Tom Takanni was with his daughter.

And with Chief Deniki's help, the village clinic would be well on its way to serving the community of Moose Flats by early summer. So, in three months' time, in the month of June, when the Jemez River would be flowing full after spring runoff, behind the New Mexico Pueblo he called home; he could see himself standing on the bank with his son, Zachary Allen Pecos, by his side and telling him all the stories that he'd grown up with.

Thank you for taking the time to read *The Thaw*. If you enjoyed it, please consider telling your friends or posting a short review. Word of mouth is an author's best friend and is much appreciated.

Thank you,

Susan Slater

What's next for Ben and Julie?

Ben Pecos is back in Florida and heading to the Everglades, where the threat of fracking for oil is a huge issue. But is it huge enough to kill for? You won't want to miss *Paper Arrows*, coming next from award-winning author Susan Slater.

Books by Susan Slater
THE BEN PECOS MYSTERY SERIES
The Pumpkin Seed Massacre
Yellow Lies
Thunderbird
Firedancer
Under a Mulberry Moon
The Thaw
A Way to the Manger (a Christmas novella)

THE DAN MAHONEY MYSTERY SERIES
Flash Flood
Rollover
Hair of the Dog
Epiphany

STANDALONE NOVELS
0-60
Five O'Clock Shadow

+ + +

Visit Susan's website at susansslater.com where you can sign up for her free mystery newsletter and a chance to win some very cool stuff.

Contact Susan: susan@susansslater.com
Follow Susan on Facebook